Zoë Marriott is twenty-five years old and works as a civil servant. In her spare time, she likes to paint, hike and read. She lives in north-east Lincolnshire and has two cats, Echo and Hero, and a dog called Finn. *Daughter of the Flames* is her second novel.

Books by the same author

The Swan Kingdom

Daughter of the Flames

ZOË MARRIOTT

**WALKER
BOOKS**

First published 2008 by Walker Books Ltd
87 Vauxhall Walk, London SE11 5HJ

2 4 6 8 10 9 7 5 3 1

Text © 2008 Zoë Marriott
Cover illustration © 2008 Steve Rawlings

This book has been typeset in Golden Cockerel

Printed in Great Britain by Cox & Wyman Ltd, Reading, Berkshire

British Library Cataloguing in Publication Data:
a catalogue record for this book
is available from the British Library

ISBN 978-1-4063-0861-7

www.walkerbooks.co.uk

*This book is dedicated to my
editor, Emil Fortune,
and my agent, Yasmin Standen,
with the deepest gratitude*

PROLOGUE

The screaming woke Surya. Her eyes flicked open and she was out of bed, flinging back the furs and reaching for her robes, before her mind had even registered the noise. She had become used to the sound of screaming that winter, and her body knew what it had to do.

It would be the Sedorne again. Whoever they had caught would need her help.

Ignoring creaking joints that had aged forty winters in the chill of the mountains, she wrapped herself in a practical, dun-coloured habit, with only the golden band at the waist to show her rank, and shoved her feet into fur-lined boots. Before she could catch up her long braid of crinkly, greying hair and hide it under the noirin's gold headdress, there was an urgent clapping outside the curtain of her room.

"Come," she called, already stepping forward to pull back the heavy fabric.

"Noirin Surya." The young woman outside was a novice namoa, barely sixteen, the dark skin of her face greyed with fear. She sketched a hasty bow. "They're attacking Aroha."

Surya felt a cold trickle of fear that lifted the small hairs all over her body. Aroha was the seat of Ruan's government. "Then – they've invaded?"

"Yes! There are survivors coming up through the hills. They say … they say the palace is burning."

Surya swallowed. "The rei? His family?"

"I don't know." The young holy woman wrung her hands. "There's a woman from their household and she's demanding to see you. She's badly burned, but she won't let anyone near her – she just keeps saying we have to fetch you."

"I'll come at once." Surya stepped over the threshold, paused, then turned back and quickly caught up the short, curved sword hanging from the wall. Her fingers closed into their familiar places on the hilt and she found herself relaxing, her breaths slowing as battle-ready calmness settled over her. The worn leather grip was cool against her calloused palm, and she realized she was sweating.

She turned back to the novice namoa, and they ran together along the corridor and down the steep, slanting steps into the octagon room. The sound of panicked shouting, hoarse voices lifted in pain and children crying made Surya wince as she entered.

Dozens of smoke-stained, bleeding people sat in forlorn clusters on the floor. The doors were flung open on to the courtyard and the room was flooded with the tarnished, flickering light of the great tapers burning outside. The inner gates beyond were open and a steady trickle of survivors filtered in, guided – in some cases almost carried – by some of the red-robed namoa from the outer walls.

Surya shook her head. "So many…"

The novice heard her. "This is only the beginning, Noirin. The hills are swarming with people."

More namoa weaved efficiently through the refugees, bringing food and water, blankets, and treatment for their injuries. The everyday odours of herbal remedies and spiced chickpeas wafted through the air, mixing oddly with the smells of burning and blood and fear. Rubbing the chill from the back of her neck with her free hand, Surya ran a practised eye over the arrangements, returned the hasty greetings of the supervising namoa, and then nodded, satisfied.

"Where is the woman?"

"In the courtyard, Noirin. She wouldn't come in."

They picked their way swiftly along the outer edges of the room to the inner courtyard of the temple complex. The air was sharp. Surya's breath turned to frost in her mouth as they crossed the flagstones, their shadows warping and jumping strangely under the capricious candlelight. Never in her life had she seen so many tapers lit in one night. She glanced up and saw the great arc of the sky turned dusty grey against the flames.

In the darkest corner of the courtyard a woman huddled, a swathe of cloth wrapped around her body, covering her head and trailing on the floor. She looked up at their approach and Surya sucked in a sharp breath as she saw the blistering burns covering the left side of the woman's face. The undamaged side of her face was the pale toasted almond brown of a lowlander, her smooth skin marking her as a young woman, perhaps not yet into her thirties.

"Let me see," Surya said briskly, stepping forward. The woman cringed back and Surya stopped in bewilderment. "What's wrong with you?" she demanded, pity making her voice rough. "Why come to the House of God if you want no healing?"

"I didn't come for me." The woman's voice crackled like dry leaves. "Are you the head of the Order? The noirin?" Her eyes dropped to the gold belt at Surya's waist and returned to her face in sudden hope.

"I'm Noirin Surya, yes. Why did you ask for me, then, if not for yourself?"

"Send her away." The woman looked at the novice namoa, and Surya, with a sigh, gestured at the girl to leave them. The novice shook her head and walked reluctantly away.

—

The woman shuffled further into the shadows. Frowning, Surya moved closer until her body shielded the woman from the view of the rest of the courtyard. The woman reached up with one blistered hand and pulled back the bulky fabric from her chest.

"I came for her."

The cloth fell away to reveal an unconscious child draped limply over the woman's shoulder, dressed in the charred remains of a nightgown. The small, delicately featured face was obviously female and might once have been beautiful. It would never be beautiful again. A horrific burn ruined the left side of the girl's face, turning the skin of her eyelid into a twisted, purpling mess.

"She's the last one," the woman was muttering frantically. "The others were dead, all dead. There was nothing I could do. I could only get her out – only get her here."

"In God's name, woman! You should have brought the child to our attention the moment you arrived."

Surya began to turn away, her hand lifting to signal to the others; but before she could finish the gesture, the woman's hand had clamped over her wrist, the shaking, blistered fingers exerting amazing strength as she pulled Surya's arm down.

"No!" she whispered. "No one else must know! They're hunting for her – if they find her she'll be dead too."

"Hunting for…" Surya stiffened. "The Sedorne are hunting her?"

"She's the last one. The only one. Little Zahira. I saved her."

Surya looked at the woman's desperate face, and then again at the child.

Zahira.

At that moment, the girl's good eyelid flickered, revealing a cornflower-blue eye, vivid against the honey gold of her skin. Surya took a sharp breath. The rei's wife was a golden-haired Sedorne, married in happier times, when the two nations were friends. It was said her eyes were blue as cornflowers – and that her children had inherited them.

"You're telling me this is the rei's youngest daughter?"

"The others are all dead. And the rei. In their beds, in the night." The words tumbled over one another in their eagerness to be heard. "Little Zahira had a nightmare so she slept with me, in my room. I woke when the fire started. I tried to get out, but the soldiers were there so I had to go the other way. Through the fire. A beam fell on us; it hit her head. Please help her. She's the last one. She's the reia now."

Surya nodded, dazed. The child must be taken somewhere safe, quiet, hidden… She looked around, saw that no other survivors or namoa were near. "Come – now, while no one's looking. Follow me."

Still clutching the sword, she picked up her heavy robes and ran, the woman a shadow in her wake as they raced out of the courtyard, past the octagon room, along the inner wall of the temple.

"Where ... where...?" the woman panted.

"Somewhere no one will look."

Surya led the woman round the curve of the wall to an alcove, and pressed an almost invisible indentation in the stone. There was a hollow click, and a panel, made of wood but cunningly faced with stone that acted both as camouflage and armour, slid back with a faint grating noise from the runners. They moved through the opening, out of the orange light and the noise into the darkness and quiet of a hidden passageway.

"What happened? What happened at the palace?" Surya demanded as she led the woman along the narrow corridor, her feet finding the faint depressions in the stone that told her which direction to take. "Treachery?"

"Yes." The woman's voice was almost noiseless as she struggled for breath. "The Sedorne ... their rei. He came to talk – to negotiate, he said. Claimed that the raiders attacked us ... without his knowledge. Wanted to ... stop ... the fighting. Wanted to make a treaty. Stayed in the palace – as a guest. Then ... in the night ... the fire." The woman made a small sound, half sob, half gasp. "No warning."

Surya swallowed and shook her head. "Say no more

now. Come this way."

They pattered quickly up a narrow flight of stairs, took another turn, and then climbed another, narrower run of stairs. Surya was horribly aware of the laboured, rasping breaths behind her. The woman needed medical help, probably just as much as the child she carried. The child ... dear God.

They reached the top of the stairway, and Surya pulled back a thick brocade curtain. A gust of cool air blew into her face. She breathed it in gratefully.

"What is this?" The woman inched forward.

"It's the shrine. The shrine of the Holy Mother of Flames."

"Am I ... am I allowed?"

"I would not have brought you, else. There's nothing to fear from God, child – She is your mother, just as She is mine. Come on."

The woman following hesitantly behind her, Surya ducked under the heavy wooden lintel of the entrance. The moss underfoot was springy and thick, crushing with a faint astringent odour. There was no trace of snow anywhere. Snow did not fall in the shrine.

Light shone here day and night, a warm glow that glinted, starlike, through the boughs of the ancient lir trees. The circle of trees was over four hundred years old, their roots trained up into giant curlicues that snaked and twisted around the papery silver trunks and almost blocked the centre of the shrine from view.

Surya led the woman forward through the gap between two of the curved trunks.

This was the heart of the House of God. It lay at the very core of the complex, hidden and protected by the lives of every namoa, Surya most of all.

Cut deeply into the smooth, round belly of earth at the centre of the tree circle was a stone-lined pit. It was the source of the light. Flames the colour of a peacock's feathers pulsed lazily in the pit. The air above the fire rippled gently, like a heat haze, and yet the fire shed no heat. Surya heard a soft exhalation from the woman – a sigh not of awe but of contentment.

"Give her to me," Surya said, dropping the sword and reaching for the girl. The woman did as instructed without question, her eyes filled with the light of the flames. "There now. Rest. Lean against the tree."

As Surya took the warm weight of the child into her arms, the woman sank down and settled against one of the lirs. Her burned face was peaceful as she watched the fire. Surya spared a moment to look at her, and what she saw was worrying. But the reia must be her first concern now.

Surya went down on her knees and carefully laid the little girl on the moss, then turned and reached into the shadows under a bulging section of roots in the nearest tree to pull out a wooden case. All new healing equipment – from bandages to ointments to sharp needles – was placed in this circle for one turn of the moon before it was used, so that God might bless it. The cavernous spaces under the tree roots served as storage places. Surya opened the case she had retrieved and sighed in relief at the contents. It held all that she needed.

She turned her attention back to the little girl. She had not stirred. Something in the way the child lay, so limp and still, reminded Surya dreadfully of the dead rabbits she used to remove from her father's traps when she had been a child herself. This wasn't a natural sleep; it wasn't even the shocked, unconscious state some injured people entered. But the fire seemed to have left her unscathed, except for the awful burn on her face. Surya knew that would require attention soon, but there was probably no hope of saving the child's eye, so she put it aside for the moment.

Swiftly she cut away the rags of the nightgown from the girl's body. There was nothing more than a bruise or two on her, and those probably from the nursemaid's desperate grip. Lifting the lid of the good eye, Surya saw that the pupil was huge, massively dilated against the blue iris. It did not react when she shaded it with her hand. She lifted the little head, propped it against her knee and began probing the scalp for injuries.

Almost immediately her fingers found the source of the child's unnatural stillness. It was a dent – as long as Surya's thumb – in the back of her skull. The area was thick with clotted blood, pulpy and soft to the touch.

Despair filled Surya as she realized how massive the

blow must have been. Even a grown man could not take such an injury and survive. She sat back on her heels, pushing a stray wisp of hair out of her face with a shaking hand. This child … this poor, tiny child. If what the woman said was true – if the whole Elfenesh family was dead – this child was Ruan's last hope. And she was dying. What would become of them now?

"What is it?" The woman had managed to tear her eyes from the sacred flames and was examining Surya's expression. "What's wrong?"

"I cannot save her," Surya said roughly. "There's nothing to be done."

"No!" The woman lurched to her knees and began to crawl towards them. "No – please. *Please*. She has to live! I've given my life to save her. It can't be for nothing. She can't die!"

Surya shook her head, unable to answer for the tears that choked her throat. Oh God.

The flickering of the flames in the pit stilled as if they were listening.

"Do something!" the woman pleaded, raising her blistered hands. "Anything!"

My daughter.

The voice was deafening, painful, ringing in Surya's head with the joyful roar of wildfire and the terrible, triumphant scream of hunting birds. She had never heard it before – had never hoped to hear it – yet it was so familiar to her that it might have been the echo of her own voice. Without realizing she had moved, Surya was flat on the ground, her face pressed into the earth, her heart jumping into a shocked, irregular rhythm. There was a soft thud behind her as the other woman copied her movement.

"My ... my Mother?" Surya whispered hesitantly.

You cry, daughter. What would you ask of me?

"I – I am sorry. I never meant…"

Daughter.

Warmth and comfort settled over Surya's her trembling body, as if God's hand had touched her. In the midst of her turmoil she felt a smile curving her lips, tears of joy welling in her eyes and soaking into the moss. She took a deep breath, easing herself up from her prone position to look down at the fragile, dying shell of the child reia.

"Holy Mother. Please. I do not want the little girl to die. Can she be saved, Mother? Can you save her life?"

If you ask the gift of me, my faithful one, I will grant it.

There was a gentle warning in the voice.

Surya hesitated. She knew the laws of balance as well as any living woman. Life and death must always be even. If the Holy Mother intervened, then the equilibrium of the world would be disturbed. What life was given ... must also be taken. A shiver went down Surya's spine.

"What – what are the consequences?"

Zahira was born for this death. If instead she lives, many other lives will also be changed, now and for ever.

"Can you tell me what her fate may be?"

I cannot.

Surya winced at the finality of the answer. "No. I'm sorry. Mother, can you tell me – should I ask this?"

I can only tell you what you already know. There must be balance. If Zahira is to live, my daughter, there will be a price.

The beautiful, terrible voice of God paused. Then it named a price that made the noirin's heart bump wildly in her chest. She slowly lifted her gaze from where it rested on the reia's pallid face, and stared into the sacred fire. The flames were so still now that the green and blue ripples looked like the surface of a calm pool of water. A myriad of thoughts burst into her head in that one instant, even as her lips were opening to frame the reply.

"Great Mother, I ask you to save her life."

There was a sigh, a sound of sorrow that stirred the dry leaves of the lir trees.

Then the voice came again.

Bring her to me.

PART ONE

CHAPTER ONE

I never knew my mother's name.

I knew she was a hero. The first story Surya ever told me was of my mother and her death. How, gravely injured herself, she dragged me from the fire that consumed our home, and carried me all the way from Aroha to the House of God in the mountains. How she refused any treatment for herself, and died of her injuries, peacefully, only when she knew that I would live.

But she never told anyone her name. Only mine.

Zira.

The story was all I had of my family. After the Sedorne came, slaughtering and burning their way across Ruan, so many families were scattered, so many homes destroyed, so many people murdered and abandoned to rot by the roadside, that Surya said there was no way to trace my identity. I was alone in the world from that day: the day my mother died to save me.

I was lucky. Incredibly lucky. I always knew that. I could have been one of the poor orphan children, dying of starvation or disease on the streets of Aroha. I could have been dead myself. Or I could have been living as a slave – in all but name – under some bloated Sedorne lord.

My childhood was not perfect – whose is? But I had a precious gift, one denied to so many children in our troubled country. A home. I cherished it and thanked God for it – until the day it was taken from me.

Sunlight sparked from the curved blade as it slashed downwards. I shut my eyes hastily and twisted away, the soft hiss by my cheek telling me that the sword had almost found its target.

Half blinded by sun shadows, I spun past my opponent and brought the flat of my sword down hard where instinct told me his hand would be. I was rewarded with a snarl and a juddering clash of metal as the blade skittered off his padded gauntlet; then I was turning again, the movement sweeping my short hair across my face.

Keep moving … keep moving… I saw the dim shadow of his bulk to my right and feinted left, then snapped towards him, bringing the sword up in the half-crescent move. Metal screeched as our weapons slid together. I threw all my weight into my sword arm with a grunt of effort and wrenched upwards. I felt the sudden release as the sword popped from his hand and I leaped back, eyes clearing just in time to see his blade flick up in a jagged arch against the sky, then plunge back into shadow as it landed in the dirt of the practice ring, raising a small puff of dust.

He gaped at his empty hand, then burst out laughing. "Excellent, Zira!"

I lowered my sword and bowed, tugging my rumpled robe back into place. "Thank you, Deo."

"It was well done. Though I hope you realize that move was a dangerous one. It could just as easily have ended in you losing your own sword."

I shrugged, trying to keep my voice even as I replied, "But if it had been a real fight and you had blinded me, I would have been desperate enough to take the chance."

Deo loved it when I lost my temper. He grinned approvingly. The tattoo that curved over the ridge of his left eye and cheek – a stylized leaping wolf for his warrior status, surrounded by stars that symbolized his commitment to God – gleamed blue against his dark skin.

"It was a dirty trick, yes," he admitted. "Yet you coped, as always. We'll make a fighting namoa of you yet." He turned away to address the small huddle of young people gathered at the edge of the practice circle. "Did you all see that? Yes? Would anyone like to try it themselves?"

Most shook their heads vehemently. My irritation disappeared and I had to cover my mouth to hide my smile. I didn't blame them.

He continued. "Well, perhaps something simpler then. Don't worry – I won't let her gut you."

As if that's what's worrying them, I thought.

Deo beckoned the children forward and reluctantly they filed into the circle, arranging themselves in a ragged line before him. He clasped his hands behind his back and rocked on his heels as he addressed them. "Now, I know many of you have never held a sword or a weapon before. But all of you would like to learn to fight. Yes?"

The children – ranging in age from nine to about my own age of fifteen – looked at one another and shuffled uneasily but stayed silent. They were the latest ragged group to arrive in the temple complex. None of them had been here longer than a month. I examined them closely, though I had seen children like them all my life. They were bony, and quiet, and frightened. But they were proud too – still proud enough to be disdainful of the baggy hand-me-down clothes they wore, of the kindness that the temple people offered, and the lessons the namoa tried to teach.

If they have pride, I can teach them strength. The thought rippled up like a memory and I frowned. Who had said that? I couldn't remember. Surya perhaps. With a small shake of my head, I stepped forward to talk to the refugees.

"Most of you are here because the Sedorne stole your homes, hurt your families, and drove you out. Is that not right?"

Several of the children nodded hesitantly, avoiding my eyes. Others only stared at their feet. They knew that Deo was a namoa and therefore a servant of God, to be respected. But I was not even a novice namoa yet – I wasn't tattooed – so despite what they had seen of my skill with the sword, they knew I was only a little older than them. And then there was my face. The afternoon light was bright and golden and reflected off the stark white of my scar, making it uncomfortable to look at me. So they didn't.

Yes, I had a good idea what they were thinking. I crossed my arms and waited, drawing out the silence until they began to shuffle again, nervously, and each of them had braved a swift look at me out of curiosity. Deo smiled, but said nothing.

"Is that not right?" I repeated finally.

They were so relieved the silence had ended that this time almost all of them had an answer for me.

"They burned our farm."

"The lord accused our pa of stealing."

"They said we were helping the resistance."

"They hanged my uncle."

"They killed my mama."

I looked at the child who had spoken last and felt a little lurch of recognition. The girl, perhaps nine or ten if she was small for her age, had raggedly chopped hair – even shorter than mine – which stood out in black spikes around her thin face. To the Sedorne, long hair on men or women was a sign of status and pride, and they often shaved the heads of their Rua prisoners, thinking to humiliate them. It was another example of how little they understood the people they professed to rule.

I dropped to one knee before the girl. Her amber eyes were defiant, as if daring me to raise a hand to her. Holy Mother, she was so young... I had to swallow before I could speak.

"They killed my mama too," I said.

The little girl blinked. I blinked too, and looked away. The attention of the group was now fixed on me. I looked back at them, forcing each one to meet my gaze.

"When the Sedorne soldiers – the gourdin – came to your homes, what did you do?"

A chorus of defiant voices answered.

"Ran. Ran away."

"We hid from them. We had to."

"They would have killed us."

"We had to run."

"You'd have run too."

"We had to."

I asked them, "What did you *want* to do?"

They were silent again. Outside the practice circle the temple people and namoa went about their business with cheerful noisiness; but within, the stillness was absolute.

"I think you wanted to stay. Didn't you? To defend your homes and your families. I think you wanted to stay so much, it must have almost killed you to run. You didn't know how to fight and you had no weapons. You were afraid. You had no choice." I heaved myself to my feet and looked them over. "You have a choice now. If you want to learn to fight, we'll teach you. If you want to walk out of this circle and never come back again, we'll let you go. It's up to you. I'll promise you this, though: make the right choice and the next time the Sedorne come, *they'll* be afraid of *you*." I waited for a beat. "Is that what you want?"

Every head nodded, hard enough to send braids whipping across faces and caps flying away. Some of them were even brave enough to step forward.

This time I didn't try to hide my smile.

Forty minutes later, the air was filled with the sharp crack of the light softwood practice staffs meeting, grunts of effort and the occasional yelp of pain as someone forgot to get his or her glove-padded fingers out of the way quickly enough.

Deo rubbed a giant hand over his curly hair as he inspected the pair of children I had been supervising.

"Remember – watch those fingers!" he said, then nodded in satisfaction and stepped outside the circle to lean against the wall next to me.

When he spoke, his voice was pitched low. "That's a real gift you have there, girl."

"Thank you, namoa." I bowed my head to hide my pleasure and embarrassment. I was relieved when Deo turned his gaze back to the practice ring.

I knew that out of the dozen we had begun training this afternoon, probably less than half would take the oath and stay in the House of God when they came of age. Of that handful, there might be one or two who had the talent or inclination to be a warrior namoa. That wasn't the point of the training sessions. When we taught the children to defend themselves, we taught them courage. It was amazing how quickly they could recover from the fear which had dogged them all their lives when they had a sword in their hands. They would not cower from the Sedorne any more. They would have pride.

If they have pride, I can teach them strength. The Rua needed all the strength they could get.

Deo cleared his throat, breaking into my thoughts. "Is Surya sure you don't come of age until after Green Equinox? I could do with you teaching here full-time, instead of only alternate afternoons."

I shrugged, embarrassed again. "She's not sure of anything, including whether I'm even sixteen this year or not, but that's the date she's set and she'll be true to it. Besides..." I shifted position on the wall. "Even once I take the oath, I might not get a placement in the fighters."

"You'll get the placement, girl. It'd be a waste of God's gifts if you didn't come to us, and Surya knows it. Mark me – in two months you'll be a novice fighter." He rubbed his hands together gleefully, whether at the prospect of adding me to his fighting unit or of having more time to torment me, I didn't know.

I won't mind him tormenting me, I said to God. Only please let me be a fighter. Please don't set me to minding the goats like Rashna... I noticed a loose thread on my much-mended hose and pulled hard on it, then stared at the hole I'd made. "Burn it!"

"Mind your language," Deo admonished. "Stop worrying. You're almost a fighter now. It's your destiny, girl." He pushed himself away from the wall and strode ahead into the circle, clapping his hands for attention. Most of the trainees were panting and sweat-soaked, all too ready to let their weapons fall.

"Excellent. A very good first lesson. Now, for your entertainment, Zira and I will stage a little demonstration of how the long staff can be used in the hands of experts."

My heart sank, though I tried to keep my expression

blank. I should have known. Deo was well aware that I disliked the staff, so he made me use it every time he got the chance.

"If you continue to work as hard as you've worked this afternoon," he continued, "one day you may be able to do this. Clear those staffs away and give those gloves back – all of them!"

He waited until the trainees had handed their weapons in and regrouped outside the ring, then reached into the barrel and pulled out, from among the short greenwood staffs, a long polished one, bound at both ends in plain brass. He tossed it to me and then picked out his own staff, lavishly carved with designs that echoed the wolf and stars of his tattoo, and capped with silver.

"Ready?" he asked me, twirling the wooden staff idly in one hand. Show-off.

I rolled my shoulders to loosen the tension I could feel contracting my muscles. I was tall for a Rua, a head taller than most women and an inch taller than Deo, but he had several inches on me in reach and the long staff was his favourite weapon. He was a demon with it. Resigned to the bruises I knew were coming, I took up the fighting stance, legs braced, staff held diagonally across the body, and nodded.

The familiar grin split his face, and he struck, his staff moving in a dark blur of speed towards my chin. I threw myself forward under his strike, which passed narrowly over my head, and jabbed towards his stomach. He turned at the last instant and I missed, sliding past his belly. I allowed the momentum to carry me past him, but he brought the staff around in a one-handed whirl and it glanced off my collarbone. I sucked in a sharp, painful breath as I dropped.

I rolled across the dirt and came back to standing with a pump of my legs, turning and kicking out sideways with my right foot in one movement, aiming for his knee. He deflected the kick, his staff hitting the sole of my boot and forcing me to drop back. As he blocked, his left side was open for a second and I brought the staff around in a horizontal two-handed strike. The brass cap thudded soundly against his side. The watching trainees gasped.

Deo responded with a savage overhand sweep of his staff. I panicked, dropping again. My shoulder hit the ground badly this time and I hissed as I tumbled forward, flattened and dived between his legs. A faint titter of laughter rose from the children. Scorch it! The staff was not my favourite weapon.

Deo's weapon thudded into the ground by my head, ripping a few stray hairs out as I rolled and popped up. I slid left to avoid the powerful kick he aimed at my torso, blocked a high strike at my face and a low one at the hip, caught a sideways blow to my stomach that almost made me double over as the air whooshed from my lungs, and managed to get in a light hit on his right forearm.

We could be at this all day, I thought. Time to try something different.

I slammed my staff point into the dust and, still holding the other end with both hands, flung myself up and sideways in a two-footed flying kick. He brought his staff up but it was too late – my weight thudded into his shoulder and knocked him literally off his feet. I fell as he did.

He hit the ground with a shout and rolled, hoping to knock me over as he went, but I'd already backflipped off him and out of range. He snapped to his feet at the same moment that I came upright. For a split second, we faced each other, breathing hard as the sweat made flesh-coloured runnels over our dusty skin. Then Deo lunged. I twisted left, but the turn was too slow and I recognized his manoeuvre too late. His staff hit my bad shoulder with enough force to numb my arm, and before I could adjust my grip, the second strike came, hitting the staff at the exact right point to scoop it from my fingers. My staff flew from my hands, rapping me sharply on the head as it turned in the air. It rolled off my shoulder and landed behind me.

"Ow." I rubbed my bruised head and heard the children giggling at me. Wonderful.

"An excellent bout!" Deo planted his staff in the dirt and leaned on it. I saw with a mixture of irritation and admiration that his breathing was barely disturbed and already slowing. "Your two-footed kick is improving, though your aim is bad. You know you should go for stomach, not shoulder. If you'd hit me right I wouldn't have got back up again."

"I will practise, namoa," I said through gritted teeth. I winced at the pull on my shoulder as I bowed.

Deo waited for me to straighten and then returned the bow neatly, but I noted with some satisfaction that his spare hand had risen to surreptitiously massage the shoulder I had kicked. My aim was bad, was it? Ha!

He turned to look at the children. "Do you see how the movements we have taught you today can be used in a fight?"

There were some dubious nods. I couldn't help laughing. Deo was a wonderful teacher, but sometimes his love of showing off was counterproductive.

"Come on! It's easy!" I called.

"Easy for the teacher's little pet," a mocking voice said.

Everyone turned to look up at the steps along the inner wall. I felt the laughter wilt and die away as I saw the woman with a stylized wave tattoo on both cheeks, leaning against one of the stone pillars. There, as if my earlier thoughts had called her up, was Rashna.

Rashna was a year older than me and had taken her vows to God the year before, but despite all her promises of humility and compassion, her nature was as prickly as a porcupine's back. I was just grateful that, for the most part, her new duties as a novice kept her busy and out of my way. Hopefully by the time I took the oath and became a novice myself, she might have advanced again and be too busy to bother with me.

"I assure you, novice, that I do not have pets of any kind," Deo said sharply. "If you would care to spar with me yourself, you'd have the bruises to prove it."

I looked at him in surprise. It wasn't like him to snap.

Rashna raised an eyebrow. "I certainly meant no disrespect to you, namoa. Or, of course, to your favoured pupil." She nodded to him, then turned and swiftly mounted the stairs.

"That girl..." Deo muttered between his teeth.

I stooped to collect my staff from the dust. "She has a wicked tongue," I agreed, hoping my tone did not give away my rampant curiosity.

Deo's scowl suddenly turned into a grin. "I hear Surya put her on duty with the goats. Not precisely what Rashna expected, eh?"

I hesitated for a moment, then asked, "Did she request a placement as a fighting namoa, then?"

"Demanded it, more like. It never crossed her mind she wouldn't get it."

"Then why didn't she? We all know she was the best fighter in her age group. I thought she must have decided not to take the placement, for some reason."

"Oh, she has a definite talent. Especially with the long staff." He grinned again.

"Then why isn't she in your unit?" I repeated.

"I have a shrewd idea that her temper's got her into trouble one too many times. Hopefully goat duty'll cool her down, and then Surya can reassign her somewhere more to her taste." He shook his head and glanced at me. The smile turned to a look of concern as he saw me massaging my shoulder. "I'll take care of this lot. You should go to the herb room and get Mira to mix up some ointment for your shoulder."

Mira was Deo's wife, a gifted herbalist and fellow namoa. She was two months pregnant with their first child.

"Would you like me to request some extra for you?" I asked, straight-faced.

He narrowed his eyes. "No, thank you. Go on – before I change my mind and have you scrub the rust off my battle plate."

"Yes, namoa." I bowed primly, handed him my staff and walked out of the ring. Only when I was out of sight did I allow myself to laugh.

CHAPTER
TWO

By the time I had finished all my chores and got back to my cell, it was almost dark. The shoulder bruise had been numbed with a judicious application of Mira's salve, but my head was pounding. I pulled the thick curtain of blue fabric across the doorway, blocking out both sound and draughts, and sat down cross-legged on my thick pallet of blankets and furs with a quiet whimper of relief.

Closing my eyes, I concentrated, counting each breath until my mind was focused and I had fallen into a light trance. Gradually the bass thudding behind my eyes began to smooth out.

By the time I stirred again, the silvery light at the window had been submerged in darkness. My head still felt a little tender and my hands trembled, but I knew that would pass soon. I'd been getting the headaches all my life and I was used to them. At least this one hadn't been too bad. Sometimes the pain was so intense that I saw flashes of light, strange faces, and thought I heard voices. It was like going mad. When I was younger, Surya had nursed me through the fits. Now I tried to keep them to myself as much as possible. Surya had enough to worry about.

With an effort I uncrossed my legs and kneeled up. I sat for a moment in the darkness, adjusting, then reached out for my candle and tinderbox. I lit the candle very carefully and placed the thick glass shield over the flame as soon as it caught, then set it on the windowsill.

There was an earthenware jug of water and a basin on the little wooden table by the bed. I stretched out absently for the jug and poured the basin full, then realized what I was doing and set the jug down so abruptly that I slopped water onto the floor. I stared at the basin with something close to loathing, struggling against the urge to complete the ritual.

It was a stupid habit. Stupid and childish. Most of the time, I didn't even remember. But it was dark and I was alone and – as if the headache had stirred up emotions that at other times lay dormant – I couldn't resist.

The rich yellow light created strong reflections in the water as I bent over it. I raised my hand, cupped the trembling fingers over the left side of my face and looked down.

I saw waving black hair, cropped at chin length. The movement of the water made it seem to drift around my face like a shadow. Skin the colour of toasted almonds, a right eyebrow that was thick but naturally arched, lashes a glossy frame to the slanting, amber eye. The nose was thin and hawkish, but balanced by the wideness of the mouth.

I met my own eye, and saw the wariness there. Why do I do this to myself? My reflection had no answer. Sighing, I took my hand away.

The scar began as a puckered white line cutting through the deep widow's peak on my forehead, but it thickened as it curved, and was an inch wide by the time it trailed down over the top of the nose. It slashed across my eye and upper cheek, ending at the left ear, where it had seared away the bottom of the lobe. There were no lashes on the scarred lid of the left eye, only a ridge of pinkish tissue that made an S shape and created a lopsided, hooded effect over the eye that, by some miracle, had been spared.

I brushed a finger over the scaly, uneven skin. In some places the scar tissue was so thick that I felt nothing; in others, so fine and delicate that even a faint breeze seemed to rasp against it. I stretched my mouth into a smile, and watched the way the normal skin around the scar wrinkled.

Every time I looked into the water, or a mirror, I saw the same thing. The same old face, the same old scar. And yet, every time, I somehow expected it to be different. I didn't understand myself. What did I really want to see? It wasn't as if I could ever remember looking any different. In exasperation, I plunged my hands into the water, shattering the reflection into a thousand drifting black-gold fragments.

Enough, now. Enough.

The octagon room – where the temple's population gathered to eat – was almost deserted that evening. When I entered, fresh from the bathhouse with my hair still curling damply, there were only a handful of people seated at the long, low tables that filled the large space. Surya was one of them.

The noirin was seated on a square cushion at the corner table, her legs tucked neatly under her and her hair – almost entirely grey now – falling down her back in a dozen thin braids. She had a book balanced on one knee, and her free hand, holding a ring of sesame seed bread, was frozen halfway to her mouth as she read.

I smiled at the characteristic scene. The only thing that could make Surya sit still for more than five minutes was a book. I did not share her fascination with written words because, like most people, I couldn't read. The only book that interested me was the Book of the Holy Mother, and Surya would read aloud from that to anyone who asked.

I collected a wooden tray and went through the archway into the kitchen, where the sleepy namoa on duty doled out sticky stew made with diced lamb, chickpeas and olives, a bowl of rice, and some of the sweet sesame seed bread rings, along with sour black cherry jam to spread on them. I added a cup of mint tea to the tray, and then carried it back out and sat down opposite Surya. While I'd been gone she had managed to eat her bread, but had paused again, this time with a cup of pomegranate juice in her hand. She didn't look up, so I applied myself to the fragrant stew, knowing that she would notice me in her own time. The rice was fresh, fried in butter with almonds and dates, and I hummed in appreciation as I spooned it up, taking the opportunity to scrutinize Surya's appearance.

I was relieved to see her looking better than the last time we talked – what? Three days ago? Four? The fine lines around her eyes and mouth were not so pro- nounced, there was good colour in her dark skin, and the tattoo of tiny stylized birds – a motif common to namoa – around her left eye looked nice and crisp, which meant she'd finally found time to have it redone.

Surya had been frantic lately, dealing with an influx of new refugees sent to us by the Rua resistance and covertly organizing for food and other essentials to reach the fighters who had been forced back into the foothills by the gourdin. She also had to fend off the Sedorne lords who always wanted to come up and perform a "friendly" inspection of the House of God. Surya walked a careful line with the Sedorne who had divided Ruan up after the invasion. She needed to keep them convinced that the temple complex was neutral, just an archaic institution of worship and not a worthwhile target of Sedorne aggression – but at the same time she had to make them respect the Order and her, so that they would not try to steal the Order's land or interfere with its running.

As the fighting in the region worsened, Surya's task had been made considerably more difficult, and my time with her had been restricted to the odd five minutes here and there. I missed her. When I was younger we'd enjoyed much more time together. In fact, before I was deemed responsible enough for a cell of my own I had lived with Surya in her generous quarters. Somehow she had always kept the evenings free for me, whether we practised our sword work, played games of chance, read from the Holy Book or just talked.

Looking at her, I had a sudden flash of memory of a time many years before, when I had asked Surya if I could call her mother. She had pulled me onto her lap and embraced me, imparting that familiar sense of love and safety. Her voice, when she spoke, had wobbled, and I had been astonished to think that she could cry, just like me.

"I'm honoured that you should ask me," she had said, stroking my hair. "But you had a mother, my dear, and though she may be gone you must never forget her. She was a great woman, a hero. So was your father. They died for this country and for the people of Ruan."

"But..." I had whispered. "But I don't even know their names. Or who they were."

"One day you will, little *agni*, I promise. One day."

I sighed, coming back to the present as I tucked my hair behind my ear. I was still waiting for one day.

By the time Surya closed her book, looked up and saw me, I had begun spreading sour cherry jam on my sesame bread.

"How long have you been sitting there?" she asked, smiling as she stretched her arms. "You should have spoken, dearest."

I shook my head. "You looked too peaceful. What were you reading?"

"Oh..." Surya picked up her pomegranate juice again, sipped, then stared down into the cup. "It's a book about the reis."

"Is it interesting?" I offered her one of my bread rings, since she had eaten all hers. She almost snatched it from my fingers. Her sweet tooth is her greatest weakness, I thought with a grin. Thank the Holy Mother the Sedorne haven't found that out.

"More sad than interesting. The bloodline was unbroken for eight hundred years – and undone by the

Sedorne in a few short hours. I don't believe the Rua will ever be at peace until we have a rei back in Aroha."

"That will never happen," I said. "So we'll have to find a way to get rid of the Sedorne without a rei."

"Rei Toril and his wife had four children. Only five bodies were recovered from their apartments – two adults and three children." Surya repeated the facts calmly. It was a familiar debate, one we'd had before.

"There were dozens of bodies found in the ruins of the rei's palace. The missing child could have been one of them," I pointed out.

Surya rolled her eyes. "I do not believe that is the case."

I decided to try a new argument. "Then let's say you're right, Surya. Let's say there is a missing heir somewhere, waiting to be discovered. What difference could he or she actually make to our situation? Just because they come from a family of rulers, does that make them a ruler? They cannot magically unite the Rua and banish the Sedorne. So if the missing heir appeared tomorrow, what would really change?"

Surya stopped rolling her eyes and looked at me with sudden intensity. "When the reia is found, everything will change, Zira. Everything."

I blinked in surprise, but before I could ask her what she meant, she shook her head. "Zira, listen. I have been meaning to talk to you but I've been so busy. I have a task I need your help with. I'm going to have to go down to the settlement at Mesgao, and I'd like you to come with me."

I forgot our debate and leaned forward intently. Mesgao was a region at the base of the great river, a day's journey into the foothills. The town there had been taken by the Sedorne in the first wave of the invasion. Although many Rua still resided there – and fairly peacefully under the rule of the current lord – it was most definitely enemy territory.

"There is an important member of the resistance who's been trying to get through to us." Surya reached across and helped herself to my pot of cherry jam. I was too fascinated by what she was saying to stop her. "There are so many gourdin patrolling the foothills, he doesn't think he can make it without being caught. He's managed to get as far as Mesgao and he's hiding there with a merchant."

"Is he so sure the gourdin would catch him?" I interrupted. "Why doesn't he disguise himself as a namoa?"

In general, the Sedorne tended to treat namoa with a certain gruff respect, the same way they treated their own wandering *depote*. Unless they were massacring indiscriminately in a given area – which had been known to happen – they left the holy people alone. I thought this might be because they mistook the Holy Mother for an aspect of the fire element they worshipped, but I didn't know enough about their heathen religion to be sure.

"Because he was a lord. Though he was stripped of lands and title in the invasion, he does still have the rank mark in his tattoo. He refuses to have it altered to something less conspicuous. Thinks it would be cowardice."

I felt my eyebrows go up. Surya sighed again. "Yes, I know. In any case, I do have to talk to him. There's a monthly bazaar in the town and I shall ostensibly be taking samples of our wool to the merchant who is sheltering him. I'll be travelling as a normal namoa in order to avoid notice. You can be my assistant."

I bowed from the waist, trying to hide my grin of delight. Surya had never asked me to do anything like this before. Usually she was reluctant even to let me off temple grounds. Unlike most of the other novice elects I had only been to Aroha once, and my travels to other areas could be counted on the fingers of one hand. It had annoyed me in the past, but I knew that Surya was only trying to protect me – and I had to admit that the reactions I'd received to my scar away from the House of God had made me less eager to meet strangers. Perhaps this new trust meant she was beginning to see me as a potential fighter.

"I would be honoured. Thank you," I said.

"Excellent. I'll speak to your teachers about re-assigning your duties, and we'll set off tomorrow."

CHAPTER THREE

The house where we found the merchant was in the older part of Mesgao town. The building was small, built on one level from planed wood panels, with peeling red and yellow flame designs painted under the double-peaked straw roof. The front was open to the public, with wooden doors folded back to reveal piled bolts of cloth to passers-by, and a tattered orange canopy extended out over the packed dirt path to provide shade and an extra area to display the wares. Cheap tin and cloth God charms tinkled cheerfully from the canopy posts as we brushed underneath into the cool dimness of the shop.

A girl in a pink tunic and a colourfully patched headscarf looked up from the threads she was sorting, then went back to her work as the merchant rushed forward to greet us. He was a portly man of average height with thinning hair and a deceptively young face. The tattoo around his left eye depicted a pair of running foxes surrounded by cotton flowers. The flowers were a reference to his trade as a cloth merchant, and the foxes were probably a pun on his name, Zebhan Dhindir – a zebhan being a black fox found in the lowlands. But I thought the design had been well chosen for other reasons. Despite his innocent face, the man's eyes were sharp and constantly moving as he spoke to us, and it wasn't hard to believe he was as cunning as his namesake.

After an exchange of pleasantries – effusive from the merchant and guarded from Surya – the man began what was obviously a prepared speech.

"Oh, these crowds, these crowds!" he lamented over the clamour of the marketplace outside. "I hate them, you know. A man can't do any business with all this noise!" He held one hand to his head in a convincing impression of a sensitive, beleaguered soul. The girl looked up from her thread again in bewilderment, but glanced away when the merchant glared at her.

I shot Surya an amused look. It was the first time I'd ever heard a trader complain about the number of potential customers being too high. Surya's lips curved in an answering smile, but her eyes were shadowed beneath the hood of her red robe and I could not see their expression. When she pushed the hood back, her face was blank. She had been in an odd mood since we'd set off yesterday morning and I had left her to it, thinking she would sleep it off. Unfortunately she hadn't. If anything it had worsened when we left our cart on the outskirts and began the walk into town.

"Let us go into my sitting room where it is quiet," he said. "My manservant can bring us tea."

Dhindir pulled back the curtain that concealed the back room and obsequiously gestured us through, following on our heels. This little room was brighter than the one we had just left, with shards of light tumbling through the bamboo screens on the high windows, but it was equally stuffed with multicoloured bolts of cloth. Only a small area at the centre was clear, with some threadbare cushions tossed onto a greying carpet and a low table. Dhindir whistled softly, and a moment later a man pushed his way out from behind a pile of yellowing linen. He was the same height as the merchant – shorter than me by a few inches – and I guessed he was in his early fifties, his hair an unusual silvery grey. The stylized curlicues of rank decorated the cheekbones.

"Zebhan, must you whistle at me as if I were an errant dog?" he said shortly, his cultured lowland voice, with its rounded vowels, contrasting with the flatter, softer mountain accent I was used to. Before Dhindir could answer, the other man had turned to bow to Surya, gesturing her to a cushion every bit as smoothly as if he were in his own home rather than the shabby back room of a less than prosperous cloth shop.

I raised an eyebrow, knowing my face was shadowed by the deep cowl of my hood. Who was he trying to impress?

The merchant, rolling his eyes good-naturedly, disappeared back through the curtain. The man continued. "I am Casador Fareed. You must be Noirin Surya. It is an honour to meet you, my lady. And this…" He suddenly looked at me, narrowing his eyes to try to make out my face under the hood. "This must be—"

"Zira, a novice elect from the temple," Surya interrupted sharply. "Push back your hood, Zira."

I started, and stared at her in surprise. Why?

She nodded reassuringly. "Go on."

Hesitantly I reached up and pushed the hood away, feeling the warmth of the light fall onto my skin.

The man jerked with shock as he saw my face properly for the first time. I stood tensely under his shocked eyes, waiting for him to remember himself and look away. It usually took a moment for people to realize how rude they were being. This was why I always kept the light hood of my robe up when I left the House of God.

But he continued to gape at me, his gaze tracing the path of the scar with agonizing slowness. My shoulders hunched and my hands balled into fists as the appalled silence stretched on. I twitched my head round and flicked a glance at Surya, but she avoided my eyes. Finally I reached up and jerked the hood forward again.

"Looked your fill?" I asked. I heard the jaggedness of my voice and hated it.

"I..." The casador wet his lips. "My apologies. I was not warned—"

"Enough," Surya said, meeting my enraged look with an apologetic grimace. "I'm sorry, *agni*. I think Casador Fareed and I should talk in private now. Go out and buy yourself something to eat – enjoy the bazaar. Here, take my purse. I won't expect you back before noon."

Pressing my lips tightly together, I took the purse from Surya's hand and walked from the stifling room without even bowing, forging through the clutter in the shop and out into the street. The throng of people on the path bumped and buffeted me until I reached the other side and ducked down the narrow gap between two buildings. The God charms that hung from the eaves above danced happily over my head as I leaned against the mud-brick wall and gulped the slightly frosty morning air.

I realized I was cradling the left side of my face in my hand, as if it were a fresh wound that caused me pain. I whipped my fingers away angrily and pressed my forehead against the rough wall.

Why had Fareed reacted like that? It couldn't have been the first time he'd seen a scar, not if he worked in the resistance. Yet a look at me had been enough to make him go white. And Surya had done it to him – to me – deliberately. She'd known he would react like that. Why?

This was awful. I should have stayed in the House of God, where I belonged. It was always this way. I hated the curious looks, the faces of strangers as they turned away. I had days when I cursed the scar myself, and others when I never even thought about it. Either way, how I felt about my face was my own decision. Why did other people have to impose their pity and revulsion on me?

I heaved a sigh and pushed away from the wall. The purse in my hand clunked dully. I looked at it blankly for a moment and then untied the drawstrings. Surya had given me a handful of copper pinch tokens, and another of silver half-moon coins. A small fortune. I retied the drawstrings hurriedly, pulled up the hem of my short red over-robe – a novice's that I had borrowed to look the part – and tucked the purse into the pouch of my belt. The belt also held my long knife, its scabbard arranged cunningly to the front of my thigh so that it did not produce the telltale bulge.

Rua were not supposed to carry weapons of any kind without specific permission from a Sedorne lord; but no Rua in their right mind would ever leave their home unarmed. Not with the gourdin wandering around just looking for an excuse to beat them.

I tugged the over-robe down again, made sure my hood was in place, and emerged from the shelter of the alley, resolved. Surya owed me for what she had done back there. This was my first free day for months, I had a purse full of money and there was a market to explore. I intended to enjoy myself.

I was immediately caught in the stream of bodies heading uphill towards the richer part of town. I allowed them to sweep me along. I had never visited Mesgao before so I wasn't sure of direction; besides, this way I avoided the bumps and collisions I had suffered earlier, moving against the flow.

The road broadened as it climbed steeply. I passed outcrops of dun rock where tiny houses built of white stones and straw clung to the hillside, their roofs jutting between the spiny trees. I managed a quick glance back and saw lower Mesgao spread out below, the long curves of the terraced fields edged with brightly painted houses and flowering vines. Below that was the base of the valley, with the River Mesgao rushing through a golden channel of stones.

The hills were so green here – it was like another world. The House of God was only a day's travel further into the mountains, but it was surrounded by a landscape of blue and copper rock, deep gorges, icy tumbling water and distant white peaks. Vegetation was sparse, and more often beige or purple than true green. They couldn't have been more different, yet I found both landscapes beautiful.

The noise and crowds increased as the road widened. I dodged out of the path of a bellowing ox and its cart – and bumped into a gourdin. The man had inches on me in height and breadth, and I almost bounced off the wall of his red and black lacquered chest. To my astonishment he grabbed me before I could fall, his fingers hard but not painful round my upper arm. I looked up at the face under the spiked helmet and long, intricately braided copper hair, bracing myself for anger – and telling myself to act the part of a cowed Rua subject.

"Watch out there," he said as he steadied me on my feet, his words flattened by the queer Sedorne accent. He released my arm, nodded politely – Sedorne didn't bow, so a nod was the best you could expect – and stepped past me without another word.

I blinked incredulously as he strode away. The gourdin I had come across in Aroha last year would have spent ten minutes yelling at me for the affront of touching them, if I was lucky. I looked down at my red over-robe. He must have thought I was a namoa, I decided. I just hoped he didn't take his temper out on someone else later on.

"You all right?" The man driving the ox had stopped it – forcing the other pedestrians to make their way round the cart as best they could, with much muttering – and was leaning over, his face creased with concern.

"Um … yes," I mumbled, pulling my hood further forward. "I – he…"

He nodded, his face smoothing out so I could see the rearing horse design on his left cheek. "You were expecting a beating? Never been to Mesgao before then, sister?"

I realized he thought I was a namoa too. I saw no point in correcting him, so only shrugged. "No. Why?"

"Ah, the gourdin be all right around here," he told me comfortably. "None of that rough stuff they get away with in other places. Lord Mesgao don't let 'em."

"Lord Mesgao?" Now I was thoroughly confused. "I thought the lord here was called Sorin?"

"Aye – Sorin Mesgao. He took our name for his own," the man said, nodding proudly. "He's not bad, as Sedorne go. He lets us alone and we let him alone. Could be a measure worse. Good day to you, sister." He bowed, slightly awkwardly because of his position, and I returned the courtesy before he cracked the switch over the ox's ears and set it on again.

As the corridor of space opened by the ox and cart closed, I was pushed forward again by the people behind me, and I carried on blindly. I was remembering the little girl I had taught the day before yesterday, with her shorn-off hair and frightened eyes. Where had she come from… That was right, Madha, not Mesgao. In fact, I didn't think we'd had any refugees from Mesgao. Interesting.

A breeze washed over my face and my attention was caught by the sweet, smoky scent of cooking. I hadn't broken my fast that morning, and I was more than ready to spend some of Surya's coins. I followed my nose, leaving the main track for a smaller, paved one. The way was less crowded here, but there were still multitudes of brightly coloured stalls and customers heaving around them.

Many of the people were familiar to me, though I did not know them – fellow Rua, with their dark skin and short, muscular bodies. They dressed in colourful, functional robes and trousers and their hair was cut short more often than not. There were a few travellers here from Thessalie in the south, buying and selling exotic goods. They were taller and darker skinned than the Rua, with beautiful pointed faces and slender bones.

Then there were the Sedorne, tallest of all, with skin ranging from pinkish white to olive, and hair of every colour from white to coppery red. Their faces tended to be long, with high cheekbones, their noses thin and blade-like, and their eyes were pale. They walked proudly through the crowds, wearing dark embroidered leather and fine linen. The women in particular were fascinating. They tottered along in tight slippers and wide multilayered skirts, their hair all knotted up under lacy transparent veils. And they were always in twos or threes, since their men did not trust them to go out on their own. I knew that if any man tried to make me wear such things – or told me I could not leave my house alone – I would hit him. Hard.

I passed an open-fronted tent loaded with fine glass jars, each one containing something different – jams, preserves, olives, anchovies, vine leaves stuffed with meat, artichokes and aubergines in oil. Another stall was selling huge bunches of dried flowers, their fragrance making me sneeze as I passed. There were pyramids of creamy jasmine and propolis soap, pumice stones, and yellow sponges from the sea.

I was tempted momentarily by a pastry seller, offering me bubbly golden honey cake or bird's-nest-shaped delicacies filled with cream, pistachios and saffron. But the price was exorbitant and I resisted, moving on again, past candied dates, lemon peel and cherries and glowing green angelica with hordes of wasps buzzing around them. The iridescent plumes of peacock feathers appealed to me powerfully, but again the price was scandalous – and what would I do with feathers anyway?

I stopped abruptly at the next stall when I saw it offered soapstone sculptures in the shape of the heathen gods that the Sedorne worshipped. The things had been well carved, showing fire and earth as beautiful women with flowing hair, and water and air as well-muscled men. The statues even had tiny gems for eyes. They were very pretty. But for a Rua to be selling them... I glared at the woman behind the counter. She looked at my red robe, blushed, and turned away.

Shaking my head, I walked on. A glint of light caught my eye, and I noticed a stall that sold silver wind chimes. The delicately wrought chimes sang gently in the breeze, each voice unique, some high and laughing, others deeper and more mysterious. One had tiny leaping fish made of bone and mother-of-pearl; another was decorated with flames shaped from slices of carnelian and garnet. They were so beautiful that my fingers were reaching for Surya's purse before I realized what I was doing.

Then I noticed something else and slid past a giggling pair of Sedorne girls to the wide, stone-paved road that continued up the hill. I had walked across the edge of the town and was now at the opposite end. Fifty feet above me, built into the hillside, was the place where the road ended. The fort of the lord who ruled Mesgao.

The building loomed against the emptiness of the sky, a square pile of cloud-coloured rock that must certainly have been imported from Thessalie. It was three storeys tall, dotted with ugly little slit windows, and each corner had a squat, square tower with a pointed wooden roof. Long green pennants snapped from the top of the towers, and I knew what was on them, though I was not close enough to see. The image of a golden hawk, claws outstretched to strike, its beak already tipped with gore. The emblem of the Sedorne.

How very appropriate.

My eyes, used to graceful, asymmetrical Rua architecture, found the whole structure odd. Deo had told me that all Sedorne buildings were constructed with one thing in mind: warfare. He'd added that this particular fort had taken six years to build. Looking at it, I could believe him on both counts.

I turned away from the oddly disturbing sight of the foreign structure imposed on a familiar landscape, and found at last the source of the savoury aroma that had been teasing me. It was a hut, built of the same sort of painted wooden slats as the merchant's house. There was no wall at the front; instead a large blue canopy was extended over raised wooden decking where grass mats, low tables and cushions had been scattered. At the back of the building I could see a Rua man and two women enveloped in clouds of steam as they cooked, while another woman served the people already seated within. My stomach rumbled loudly. I licked my lips and stepped up onto the decking.

Then chaos broke out behind me.

CHAPTER
FOUR

The noises of collision, the shriek and clash of metal and screaming voices, seemed to explode behind me. I spun so quickly that I lost my bearings for a moment. Then another scream – the high-pitched whinny of a horse in pain – pierced the other sounds, and I took off, instinctively heading towards the commotion. I had to push through clots of people blocking my path before I reached the verge of the road again and had a clear view of what was happening.

A Sedorne-style two-horse carriage had crashed into a stall, sending barrels and crates of fruit flying everywhere. The carriage lay half on its side in the middle of the road, surrounded by debris. No one appeared to be injured. The more serious problem was why the coach had crashed in the first place.

It was under attack.

Three Sedorne men had managed to put a rod through one of the wheels as it passed. The axle at the front of the vehicle had buckled and was obviously ruined. Two of the Sedorne were trying to reach the door of the carriage, but were being forced back by the plunging hooves of the panicked horses, rearing and bucking amid the wreckage. One of the men was tall and athletic-looking, with a handsome young face. The other was older, darker and running to fat, but with massively muscled arms. Both had the ragged short hair and mismatched armour that identified them as outlaws. The third man – with better armour, but a badly pockmarked face and longish greasy hair – was attempting to cut away the horses, hindered by the coach's driver. The driver was Rua, standing precariously on the edge of his seat and laying about him with a horsewhip.

The youngest Sedorne, ducking away from the lash of the whip, managed to cut free one of the horses. The terrified animal bolted towards us, forcing the people in front of me to leap out of its path. I was swept back in the ensuing confusion and briefly lost sight of what was happening. When I managed to push my way forward again, the fat outlaw had climbed over the remains of the stall to the other side of the coach – out of range of the Rua driver – and swiftly freed the second horse. The animal, its heaving sides streaked with blood and foam, crashed through the debris and followed its companion, galloping up towards the stone fort. I stepped back just in time, and it narrowly missed me.

Without the horses in the way, the outlaws converged on the carriage, the young and fat pair making for the door again. Instead of trying to force it open as I'd expected, one pulled a mallet from his belt and began whacking the hinges, while the other heaped heavy pieces of wreckage over it.

They weren't trying to get in at all. They were trying to keep whoever was inside from getting out.

The occupant of the carriage obviously realized this at the same time as I did. There was a hollow booming from inside as whoever was in there banged hard on the door, but the makeshift barricade held. The young Sedorne tossed the hammer aside and took a leather canteen from his belt; the fat man produced a clay bottle. They leaped up onto the coach and started pouring a liquid on and around the carriage. It was oil.

With a sick lurch of my stomach, I understood. They were going to burn the coach – and whoever was inside. Horror froze me in place as if solid ice had encased my limbs.

Then there was a shout and my gaze went to the third Sedorne. Without the horses for protection, the Rua driver's whip was little use. As I watched, the pockmarked outlaw caught the driver's whip hand and pulled him down. The driver landed on the road with a heavy thud and lay motionless, dazed. The outlaw raised his sword.

I didn't even realize I was moving until I hurdled a pile of spilled oranges and heard the gasp go up from the spectators. Oh God, what am I doing... I must be insane... It was too late to change my mind. I sped up, jumped, and went into a two-footed kick.

My full weight hit the Sedorne directly in his fleshy midsection and we went down together, me scrabbling under my tunic for my knife. I hit the ground, rolled and came up on one knee, the blade ready in my hand. The man was curled into a ball on the ground, vomiting violently. Ha! Deo was right about aiming for the stomach.

I looked up to find the other two Sedorne staring at their fallen friend. Their expressions were not happy. As the pounding from inside the carriage intensified, the fat one turned towards me, reaching for the straight sword that hung at his waist as he jumped down. I scrambled hurriedly to my feet.

There was an almighty crash from the carriage and the barricaded door exploded open, sending the outlaw who had been stood on it flying. A man vaulted out and landed lightly on the paving on front of me.

He was tall even for a Sedorne, probably in his mid twenties, and dressed in a blue linen shirt and breeches tucked into battered leather boots. Long silver-blond hair was pulled back from his forehead, displaying a nasty bruise, presumably gained when the carriage had hit the stall. His eyes – the same golden blue as the peacock feathers I had admired earlier – fixed on me. He took in the fallen Sedorne groaning at my feet, the injured coachman, the dagger in my hand.

Then his eyes widened at something over my shoulder. I ducked just in time and the lethal slice of the sword passed over my head. I twisted and dodged away, my body falling smoothly into the familiar rhythm. The fat outlaw lunged at me again. I waited a split second, until his greasy, unwashed scent filled my nostrils, and then I slid sideways and brought my dagger down into his sword arm.

Blood sprayed up, glittering horribly in the sun as I wrenched the knife free. The outlaw screamed, his sword clattering to the ground as he clutched at his wounded arm. I brought the bony point of my elbow around hard into the back of his neck. He folded with an incongruously gentle sigh, joining his friend at my feet.

I looked round to see the blue-eyed survivor of the carriage wreck engaging the third outlaw. He had a sword and the blue-eyed man held only a long chunk of wood – more debris from the stall – but it was obvious that this was no real fight. Even as I watched, the club connected solidly with the outlaw's head and he went down.

The blue-eyed man turned away before his opponent even hit the ground, his gaze seeking me out. The chunk of wood dropped from his hand as our eyes met. He stepped forward. I found myself doing the same. There was something about his face – the high cheekbones, the shape of his eyes, the way the sun reflected off the paleness of his hair. Almost as if … as if I recognized him.

Then the outlaw whom I had left vomiting on the ground lurched to his knees. I saw the knife in his hand an instant before he lashed out, slashing the blue-eyed man across the back of the thigh. He cursed foully as his leg gave way and he crashed to the paving stones.

I reached the outlaw a second later and stamped on his knife hand. I cut off his cry of pain with a hard smack to the temple using the hilt of my dagger, followed by a kick to the jaw. I retrieved his knife and flung it into the open door of the carriage, shoving my own dagger back into its sheath.

I turned back to the blue-eyed man, who was trying to rip off the sleeve of his shirt with one hand while clutching the wound on his leg with the other. His face had gone white with pain. Kneeling beside him, I grabbed the stubborn fabric of the sleeve and yanked, shredding the seams.

"Let me see," I said curtly, prising his hands away from the cut. The wound was long and bleeding profusely, but it seemed superficial. "Can you move your foot? Wiggle your toes," I instructed, turning my head to watch his foot move. "Good. He didn't hit anything vital. Stay still."

I wrapped the long piece of material from his sleeve around the wound twice and pulled tight, relieved when he responded with no more than an audible teeth grinding. I hated it when people screamed. It was one of the reasons I was no good helping Mira in the herb room.

As I went to work knotting the ends of the rough bandage, he spoke to me for the first time. "I don't know what I've done to deserve such a rescue, but you have my thanks."

The distinctive flattened vowels of the Sedorne accent jolted me. My fingers stilled for a second. When I forced them back into action, they were shaking. Was I insane? This man was Sedorne, and here I was patching him up as if he was a friend or ... a Rua. What would Deo say?

Before I could even begin to formulate an answer, a shadow fell over us. I jerked my head up, then relaxed when I recognized the Rua coachman on whose behalf I had first intervened.

"My lord..." he whispered, appalled, as his gaze took in the bruised and bloodied state of the blue-eyed man.

My lord? This time my hands fell away from the knot of material completely. "Lord?" I echoed softly.

He didn't hear me. "Are you all right, Abha?" he asked the driver.

"Yes, yes – I am so sorry, my lord!" the Rua babbled.

"Never mind that," he interrupted hastily. "Do you think you can get up to the fort and bring some help down? I'll need a litter to get back up there with this leg. And I'll have to compensate the stallholders and anyone else who might have been injured in this. Get Costin and Sergiv to take names and details."

"Yes, my lord. I – yes." The driver hesitated for a moment, then turned and trotted off up the road. As I watched him go I noticed the crowds of people, Rua and Sedorne, who were gathered around the wreckage of the coach, watching with wide eyes.

"I think we may have caused a scene, sister," the blue-eyed man – no, his name was Sorin, Lord Sorin Mesgao – muttered to me.

Again, I couldn't think of a reply.

He raised his voice, addressing the crowds. "I'd like to get these outlaws safely trussed up before they come round and start causing more trouble. Would anyone be interested in tying them up for me, and then watching over them, while someone else fetches the gourdin? You'll be rewarded for your trouble."

There was a small rush of people, who eagerly grabbed the unconscious outlaws and began securing them with any handy bits of rope or cloth they could find. The outlaws were soon bound hand and foot and surrounded by watchful eyes. A couple of others – both Sedorne, I noticed – went to find the gourdin. Typical that the Sedorne soldiers had managed to be absent when they were actually needed, I thought with some bitterness. They were always around to help in the persecution and murder of innocent Rua.

The man – Lord Sorin – nodded, satisfied. "Excellent. My men should be here soon, and you'll get your payment then. In the meantime…" He looked at me. "I don't suppose you could help me up, could you?"

I found my voice enough to reply, "Ah – of course."

"She speaks," he said teasingly as I slid my arm round his back and braced myself to take his weight. I blinked at him, momentarily distracted by the heat of his arm as it settled over my shoulder, then realized he was laughing at me. I set my teeth grimly. Insane, I told myself. Completely insane.

He saw my carefully blank expression and smiled wryly. "Never mind."

He grabbed the side of the carriage and, with my help, pulled himself upright. Both of us were still breathing hard from the effort when he spoke again.

"I'm famished. You?"

I stared at him. "Eh?"

"I can smell something wonderful. I think it's coming from over there." He nodded in the direction of the food hut I had been about to enter before all this began. "Help me across, would you?"

"You want to eat? Now?" I asked incredulously. I let him lean on me as he limped towards the blue canopy.

"Why not?"

"Because ... *because* – you're mad," I finished in a mutter.

"Just hungry."

He managed the step up onto the decking with a grunt of effort, leaning heavily on me. The cooks, who had been clustered at the front of the hut with their patrons, watching the uproar, rushed back to their steaming cooking plates. The customers eyed us warily as they returned to their cushions.

"We'll sit here on the deck," the lord said to the flustered serving girl.

"We?" I questioned, helping him lower himself onto the plump cushion before a low table. He folded his good leg neatly under him and stretched the bandaged one out comfortably.

"You'll join me, won't you?" he said as I straightened and stepped away from him. "I need someone to keep me company until my men arrive, and I think you and I have lots to talk about."

Now that his body was no longer in contact with mine, I found myself reluctantly amused by his arrogance. Lots to talk about, indeed. Egotistical man! Of course, he wasn't just any man, was he? No doubt he was well accustomed to getting his own way.

And I'd just saved his life...

The fleeting amusement died. What had I done? He was Sedorne, and ruled over stolen lands at the behest of a despot. The Holy Mother only knew what awful things he had done to gain his position of power. The resistance probably wanted him dead anyway. Perhaps I shouldn't have intervened. Then I felt a surge of guilt. Sedorne or not, he was a living being. No living being deserved to die like that – in the choking smoke and the flames. No living being, not even a Sedorne.

"Please." The laughter was gone from his voice now, and I saw that he was completely serious. His eyes were almost pleading. "Sit down at least."

I looked away and sighed. "Very well."

I kneeled on the cushion across from him. The serving girl hovered over us, wiping her hands nervously down the front of her brown tunic. I tried a reassuring smile, but she winced away rather than meet my eyes. I twitched my hood into place and stared down at my knees.

"Aniseed tea, please," I mumbled.

"Do you have any river prawns?" the Sedorne – I must remember that – asked. "Are they fresh?"

"Oh yes, my lord," the girl answered anxiously. "Fresh this morning."

"How are they prepared?"

"Stir-fried with onion and garlic. There's cold

sesame sauce and butter rice. Or we can do them on spits…"

"No, the fried ones will do. Two bowls of those, please, and aniseed tea for two."

"Yes, my lord. Right away."

I heard the girl's swift footsteps as she scurried away. "I'm not hungry," I said flatly to my knees.

"Well, you will be when the food arrives; and if not, I can always eat yours. I'm hungry enough."

A large calloused hand laid itself on my folded ones. I jolted, pulling back instinctively. The hand withdrew. I resisted the urge to wipe my fingers on my breeches.

"What's wrong?"

What isn't wrong? What am I doing here? "I shouldn't be involved in this," I blurted out.

"I quite agree. But you'll forgive me if I'm glad you are. I'm almost completely uninjured, thanks to you."

"It's my fault your leg was hurt," I felt bound to point out. "I didn't check the outlaw for weapons and once he was down I forgot about him, until he attacked you."

"Your fault?" he asked coolly. "Strange. I rather thought my injury was the fault of the man with the knife. Don't try to change the subject. I owe you a great debt for this. What would you like as payment?"

"I see!" My confusion and guilt vanished and I looked up angrily. "You want to pay me off! Well, I won't take anything from you, do you hear? Honour is not measured in gold!"

He looked surprised, holding his hands up in a gesture of peace. "I know it isn't. I'm sorry if I've offended you, sister. I was only offering because I thought you might have a good cause that needed ... or ... something," he finished feebly.

"I'm not a sister," I corrected sharply. "I'm ... I'm—" Abruptly I remembered that I was supposed to be a novice. "I'm a novice. And the House of God can take care of its own, thank you. We don't need blood money." The last words slipped out before I could stop them, and I stiffened, waiting for his reaction.

"Ah. I see." He nodded slowly. "Well, that settles that."

Silence fell between us. Somewhere behind me I could hear the sweet singing of the wind chimes I had admired earlier. I tilted my head to hear them better. After a moment, I sighed and turned back to find him examining my face with narrowed eyes.

"How did you get that scar?" he asked quietly.

I was surprised – especially after the stares I had been forced to endure this morning – to find that I didn't resent the blunt question. There was no pity in it. I answered evenly, "In the fire that killed my family."

"The Great Fire?"

"If you mean the Invasion Fire, then yes, it was."

"I'm sorry."

"Are you?" I met his eyes, expecting them to fall. He

looked back steadily and it was me who had to look away.

There was another moment of quiet. Then the serving girl arrived, plates piled on her arms. She laid out two bowls of giant river prawns, two of rice and one of sesame sauce, and returned a few seconds later with the pot of aniseed tea and cups. The smell of the hot food reached my nose and my stomach let out an embarrassing rumble. I was reaching for the nearest bowl and a spoon before I realized what I was doing. I picked up a prawn, pinched off the head – I disliked eating things that looked at me – and took a bite. It was delicious. I hummed with pleasure, and saw the Sedorne cover his mouth to hide a smile. I didn't care; I was too hungry. The food seemed to soothe the hollow feeling under my breastbone, and I relaxed a little.

"What's your name?" he asked, spooning up some rice.

I hesitated, then said, "Zahira." It was close enough.

Before he could ask me anything more awkward, I asked him the question that had been bothering me since I realized what had happened to the coach.

"Why did those outlaws ambush you like that? You're the lord; even if they'd succeeded, the gourdin would have hunted them down and killed them. It was madness."

"Ah, well." He sipped his tea, not bothered by the question. "Those men serve a rather powerful master, and he doesn't worry about things like that."

I frowned. Lords held absolute power in the lands they ruled. The only person more powerful than a Sedorne lord was ... *the* Sedorne lord. Their king, Abheron. I looked at Sorin Mesgao. Was he implying that his own king had ordered him killed? Why?

"They had very expensive swords for penniless outlaws," I ventured, dipping my spoon into the sesame sauce and drizzling it over the rice. "And it seems odd that they intended to set fire to your carriage. A very indirect method of murdering someone."

He shrugged. "Perhaps. Who knows?"

You do, I thought. You know all right. You just don't intend to tell me.

I shrugged and concentrated on my meal, listening to the wind chimes again. I had just scraped up the last of my rice when the lord's men arrived. There were five of them, all Sedorne, and dressed in much finer clothes than the lord himself. They rode down the hill on tall slender Sedorne horses – very different from the stout furry ponies the Rua favoured – looking around in appalled silence at the devastation on the road, the tied-up outlaws and the crowds of people patiently waiting for the next act of this entertaining play. Finally their horrified eyes found Sorin and me, seated together on the decking under the blue canopy. They dismounted in a hurried clattering of stirrups and bridles and rushed over to their injured master, bombarding him with concern.

"Ioana, my lord! What happened?"

"Your leg? How bad is it? Do you need a healer?"

"Are these the men who attacked you? They're Sedorne!"

I tensed in anticipation of the interrogation I was sure would be coming my way – I was singularly out of place in the midst of these pale foreigners. But the men didn't address a single word to me, and after a moment I realized gratefully that I was being ignored. The lord gave a highly abbreviated account of events to his men before instructing them in what to do next. I noticed with some amusement that despite his fulsome thanks to me, I was not referred to as a rescuer, only as a kind bystander who had bandaged his leg.

Strange, I thought as he muttered to one of his men in the guttural Sedorne tongue. He couldn't be a particularly vain man – his servants wore nicer hair ornaments and clothes than he did. Still, what did I know of men? Especially Sedorne men...

The servants hurried off to their different tasks, leaving Sorin and me alone.

"Well," I began, "I don't think you need my company any more. I'll just—" I started to rise but he caught my arm. This time, despite my instinctive recoil, he held on.

"Don't leave yet," he said gravely. "There are three more things to be dealt with."

I frowned, looking down at his hand; the contrast of

pale gold fingers gripping my brown forearm gave me a funny feeling in my stomach. I didn't resist as he pulled me back down onto the cushion. He promptly released me and I sighed in relief.

"Three more things?" I asked warily.

"Yes. The first is a warning. Many people saw what happened here today, and I'm sure the story will travel quickly, but if anyone asks you about it I pray you will deny all involvement. I told you that those men serve a powerful master; I don't wish you to suffer because you have foiled his plans. Hopefully the stories will die down in a few days, if you do not confirm them."

"You need not worry," I assured him drily. "I'm hardly likely to boast about it."

"I didn't think so. The second thing is this. You gave me aid here today, risking your own life to save mine. I owe you. No." He gestured sharply when I opened my mouth to disagree. "This is not about gold. It is, as you said, about honour. Believe it or not, we Sedorne value our honour. I owe you my life and I will not forget it. If ever you need anything from me, no matter what it is, or why, you will come to me, understand? I want no arguments. Promise me."

I remained silent. I didn't want to make any vows to this man. It seemed to me that he was an opportunist, and that he would find a way to turn any bond between us to his advantage.

"I won't let you go until you promise," he said with

a touch of grimness. "I mean it, Zahira."

I believed him. I sighed. "Then I promise. But I doubt I'll ever need anything enough to come to you."

"Perhaps not. I hope not." He relaxed, the intensity replaced with an easy smile.

"The third thing?"

"Costin is returning with it now," he said looking over my shoulder.

I turned to see one of his men coming towards us, carrying a small wooden box with some ceremony. He reached us and gave it to Sorin.

Sorin held the box out to me.

"Please accept this as a token of my gratitude."

After a moment's hesitation, I gave in to curiosity and took it. After all, I could always return it once I'd looked. I lifted the lid and saw, lying on a silk bed and held in place with fine wires, a silver wind chime. The chimes themselves were shaped into graceful curls like the ripples on the surface of a river, with tiny mother-of-pearl fish leaping between them. I gaped at it, speechless, and then looked back up at Sorin.

He was grinning at my surprise, as gleeful as a child.

"How – how did you…?"

"I noticed you listening to them while we ate. Your face changed, as if the sound made you happy. Do you like it?"

"It's beautiful. Thank you," I whispered. I felt awkward. It was as if he had discovered some private thing about me that no one else knew. We stared at each other. I opened my mouth, then closed it again. Finally I attempted a smile. He smiled back.

The man who had brought the wind chime cleared his throat noisily. "My lord? I think Sergiv has the litter ready."

Sorin sighed. "Thank you." He leaned forward, braced himself on the table, straightened his good leg, and pushed himself to his feet. While he favoured the wounded leg, it was clear that it could bear his weight.

I glared at him indignantly. "You didn't need my help to walk at all!" I exclaimed.

"Well, no." He grinned. "I just wanted to put my arm round you."

While I was still gasping, he grabbed his servant's shoulder and stepped down carefully from the decking.

"Don't forget your promise, Zahira," he called.

Then he was surrounded by the group of servants, and hustled out of my sight.

CHAPTER FIVE

"You're very quiet," Surya said.

I looked up to see that her eyes were fixed on the shoulders of the ponies pulling our little cart, not on me. Her hands on the reins were as relaxed and easy as always.

I shrugged. It was true. We hadn't had much to say to each other since we left lower Mesgao yesterday afternoon. I'd just been trying to get Surya out of there as quickly as I could, before the tale of the attack on the Sedorne lord spread that far. I had been stopped three times on my way out of the upper town by people asking if I was the namoa who had saved Sorin Mesgao, and, when I denied it, if I knew her or who she was. I did not want the same thing to happen to Surya.

"Are you still angry with me?"

"What?" I shook off my thoughts and turned to her again. It took me a moment to work out what she meant. "Oh. No. Anyway, I was more shocked than angry."

"You were more hurt than angry, you mean. And you were angry enough. I'm sorry."

I shrugged again, uncomfortable. "I expect you had a good reason."

"A very good reason." There was a pause. "I can't tell you."

I found a smile from somewhere. "You do surprise me."

We fell silent again as Surya carefully guided the ponies through a narrow rocky gorge overhung with twisted silver-grey trees. We had left the lush greenness of the terraced farmlands behind early this morning. The tumbled rocks on either side of us were almost bare, home only to scrubby, dusty plants that looked half dead. To our left, over the brown shoulder of the hill we were climbing, I could see the highest peak of the Subira range, Emany, its violet and black slopes crowned with drifting clouds.

"*Agni...*" Surya began. "It was important that Fareed see your face. He will remember you now, and if you ever need to call on the resistance, he'll help you."

I frowned, bothered by her tone. "Why would I need

his help? Is there something wrong, Surya?"

"Oh, there are a million and one things wrong." She smiled, her mood lightening suddenly. "There are always a million and one things wrong. Really, life is only a series of interconnected disasters. Each one pushes us forward to the next."

I wasn't reassured. "Is there a particular disaster that's worrying you?"

She sighed. "Only that I cannot live for ever, dearest. Ignore my moods; I'm getting old and cranky."

"You're not old," I disagreed automatically.

"Old enough, *agni*. Very nearly old enough."

She didn't say anything else, and I let the silence be.

The rest of the journey home passed in a blur for me. I went over my memories of the attack and the conversation with Sorin, trying to fit them together in some way that made sense. They seemed almost like events that had happened to someone else – but at the same time, they were more clear and vivid than any other memory I had. The sounds of the crash, the attack, my own actions... I wasn't sure if I was trying to forget, or fix it all in my head for ever. The weight of the box hidden under my robe was the only thing that convinced me I wasn't imagining it all.

When we arrived back at the temple, Surya tried to talk to me again. For the first time in my life I avoided her, heading to my cell instead. The tiny room, with its three-day coating of dust and neatly made pallet, seemed so utterly normal that I felt as if I were waking from a strange dream. I took the box from the inside pocket of my robe and opened it. The room was dim, but the wind chime seemed to have a silver and pearl glow all its own.

Not a dream.

I removed the amber God charm that dangled in my window and hung the chime in its place, my fingers wrapped around the metal curls so that they would not ring. When the little loop was placed on the hook, I stepped back, opening my fingers.

The chimes rippled gently, sending out a spray of silvery notes like a sigh; the fish bobbed among their shining waves. I sat down on my pallet and watched the tiny ocean dance.

It was night-time in the palace when Lord Tiede received the message, and went to find the king in his indoor garden.

The glass roof should have flooded the room with frosty starlight, but the light had to trickle down through layers of foliage before it reached the path, and the way was swathed in shadows. The darkness whispered mysteriously as Tiede passed, making him start, and walk quickly.

He was relieved when he located the king at the centre of the garden, despite the tidings he had to impart. King

Abheron was seated at his work table in the clearing, repotting a large spiny plant by candlelight. His hair glowed red gold, but his face was hidden in shadow.

Lord Tiede stood nervously among the trees for a moment, examining the king for signs of mood. Abheron's hands, hidden in leather gardening gloves, moved with slow competence as he gently patted the soil down around the roots of the plant and added water. The adviser took the calmness with which his king performed these actions as a good omen. He knew from experience that on the rare occasions when the king lost his temper, he moved very quickly indeed.

"Yes, Tiede?"

The lord jumped, then hurried forward. "I didn't want to disturb you, Your Highness."

"I'm surprised you came then," the king said, reaching for a rag to wipe the dirt from his gloves.

Not sure how to take the comment, Tiede risked a small chuckle. "Indeed. But I … ah … have some news from Mesgao, Your Highness."

"I take it the news is not good?"

"Well. Apparently Mesgao was injured. We're not sure how badly."

"He is alive?"

"Yes."

"How disappointing. You hand-picked those men, Tiede. You assured me they could easily complete the task. What happened?"

"I – I can only apologize, sire. I assure you the men will be suffering most unpleasantly in Mesgao's dungeons, for they know nothing that could appease his torturers—"

"Sorin doesn't keep torturers, Tiede. Just tell me what happened."

"Well. It seems there was ... interference."

"Intriguing. From whom?"

"We're not entirely sure. But," he rushed on as the king stirred restlessly, "most agree that it was a Rua woman. One of those holy people – what do they call them?"

"Namoa."

"Yes, one of those. She was highly skilled, apparently. She dispatched two of my – er – of the men herself, and then saw to Mesgao's wounds."

"She was travelling with him?"

"Well. I'm not sure. The reports are sketchy."

"Are they? How distressing for them."

Tiede hesitated. "Indeed, Your Highness."

The king sighed. "Never mind. Tiede, that resistance worker we've been keeping an eye on – he is in Mesgao, is he not?"

"Hiding with a cloth merchant, yes." Tiede paused, thoughtful. "Actually, there was a report that two of these namoa people visited a cloth merchant a few hours before the attack was foiled."

"And later a namoa saved Sorin's life. Wheels within

wheels, Tiede. Could it be that the Order of the Holy Mother and the Rua resistance are connected to our troublesome cousin Sorin in some way? I had no idea such a link existed. This interests me. I'd like some more information. Bend your mind to the task of getting a spy into his household, Tiede. You've let that matter slide for too long. And..." The king's voice trailed off into silence. After a moment, he picked up a tiny pair of shears and carefully began pruning the twisted branches of the plant.

Tiede shuffled anxiously. "Your Highness?"

Without looking up, the king gave Tiede a series of instructions, his voice confident and crisp. Tiede hesitated, torn between shock and admiration, then nodded, deciding to be admiring. It was safer.

"Yes, Your Highness."

"Tiede – have your men do things cleanly. If there are children..."

"Let them go, sire?" Tiede said doubtfully.

"If at all possible. I like children, you know. I don't like them to suffer."

Tiede raised his eyebrows at the king's back, but said, "Of course, Your Highness." He moved away, relieved that things had gone so well.

Abheron waited until Tiede's footsteps had grown distant, and then sat back to inspect his plant. He had lavished a great deal of attention on it, but the shape was still too round, and it had barely produced any flowers this year. Even the new pot he had commissioned did not make it look right.

Involuntarily, his eyes went to the candles burning beside him on the table. He struggled with himself for a moment, then gave in and lifted one. He held the flame to the plant.

The dry branches caught immediately, flames curling and coiling along the delicate spines of the leaves. Tiny white flowers turned black in the heat and crumbled into ash as Abheron removed his gloves.

The fire swallowed the plant with greedy crackles of delight. He held his fingers close to the flames, feeling the heat thrum against his skin, breathing in the charred hot scent, watching the plant twist and writhe at the centre of the blaze. His face, dappled with shadow by the undulating flames, was clenched in what might have been pain or ecstasy.

He did not look away until there was nothing left.

CHAPTER SIX

It was a normal evening, cool and calm, the sky fading from blue to silver to grey. The day had been warm and sunny, and the gardens needed a second watering now they were in shade. Joachim, the garden master, had sent me out to turn on the irrigation lines, so that the rainwater stored in barrels throughout the garden would run down and moisten the soil.

I moved from one barrel to another in the deepening shade, barely seeing the familiar rows of miniature fruit trees, vegetables and herbs. My mind was occupied with the next day. It would be my sixteenth birthday. Well, we would treat it as my birthday, since we had no way of knowing when I had really been born, but the result was the same.

Tomorrow I would take the oath to God and

become part of the Order. A novice namoa. Surya would decide my fate – whether I would join Deo's fighting unit or be relegated to the goats.

To be a fighter was what I had always wanted, from the first time I had picked up a sword. The sword was Surya's, taken down from its rack on the wall to be cleaned, and left on the cushions when she was called away. My fingers weren't long enough to close on the hilt properly, and it was so heavy that my wrist ached trying to hold it up, but I had known then that to be a warrior was my fate. My place, my purpose in life. With a sword in my hand, I knew who I was.

There was a rustle behind me, and I looked round to see Surya making her way through rows of beans, wearing her noirin's gold habit and headdress. Since we had returned from our trip to Mesgao she had been making an effort to spend as much time with me as her business allowed. I thought at first that she still felt guilty, despite my assurances that the incident with Casador Fareed was forgotten, but lately I had begun to wonder if there wasn't more to it – or if it was all part of the same thing. There was a niggling sensation whenever she was around now, a sort of *waiting*. I felt she wanted something from me but I didn't know what it was, and the sense of expectation grated on my nerves.

"Hello, dearest," she said, sitting down on a nearby barrel.

I tried a smile. "How was your meeting with the traders?"

"As well as could be expected. They're suffering under that Sedorne pig's tithe, and they have little to spare. But that is no excuse for providing inedible, rotted produce, or for trying to cheat us, and I've made that clear. They're humbled enough to mend their ways now – at least until the next tax increase."

I snorted, imagining the group of shrewd, dignified Rua merchants shuffling shamefacedly from Surya's room. There was a moment of companionable quiet, which I savoured.

Then Surya sighed. "I came out here for a reason, Zira. I need to tell you something."

I had crouched to pull up a weed, but sat back on my heels as I heard her tone. "What is it?"

She bit her lip. "Oh, this is difficult." She stopped, bowing her head and kicking her heels against the base of the barrel. "I've started to tell you so many times. But I could never – you see, I told myself that God had taken your memories for a reason. I thought it was wrong of me to… But perhaps that was only cowardice."

Alarmed now, I stared at her. "Surya, what's the matter?"

She looked at my anxious face and immediately jumped up from her seat to come and kneel before me.

"Don't look like that, please. I've done this all

wrong, I know. I'm sorry. It's nothing terrible, not really."

"Then why are you so upset?" I asked softly. I reached up to her cheek, where a tear had traced a shining path, and wiped the moisture away. I had never actually seen her cry before. "Don't cry, Surya," I whispered. "Please don't."

She laughed suddenly. "Zira, this is all backwards. Let me start again."

I nodded, schooling myself to patience. I knew something was troubling her, and now she was finally ready to tell me, I had to be strong for her.

"Go on," I said.

She took a deep breath. "You will be sixteen tomorrow, *agni*. I've always told you that we didn't know your real birth date, but I'm afraid that wasn't true. I *do* know it, and it *is* tomorrow. It's the day I've dreaded and looked forward to for ten years.

"I've … I've kept a secret from you, *agni*. Partly because I wanted to protect you, and partly because I didn't know how or when to tell you the truth."

I swallowed nervously, licking dry lips. I felt suddenly that I didn't want to know whatever it was she was about to tell me. But she was already speaking.

"Your name is not Zira. Your name – your real name – is Zahira. Zahira Elfenesh."

My breath left me in a hard huff of shock. It was like falling back into icy water that engulfed my body.

A black whirlpool edged my vision as I looked at Surya, and there was rushing and pounding in my ears.

I heard my own voice distantly through the swirling cold. "Elfenesh... My name is Zahira Elfenesh? That's – that's a royal name."

"Yes." Her answer seemed to come from miles away. "It is."

There was a shout somewhere to the left of us, on the other side of the garden wall. Neither of us took any notice. I was gasping for air now, clawing my way back up from the darkness and the rushing in my head.

"Who am I?" I whispered. "Tell me. Please."

Surya squeezed my fingers and opened her mouth—

On the other side of the wall, there was a jarring, clattering crash of metal and a scream, abruptly cut off. I shook my head dazedly and looked away from Surya.

"What—?"

A rising tide of sound spilled over the wall, gathering momentum: voices yelling, confusion. I heard a voice shouting, but didn't understand the words. Then I realized: it was speaking Sedorne.

Sedorne – *inside* the walls.

"*Attack!*" Deo's voice, raised in the training bellow he used to drill his fighters. I was on my feet instantly.

Surya scrambled up beside me. "No. It can't be," she whispered. Her face had gone the colour of ashes. "Not now. Not like this. *Not like this!*"

Another voice – I recognized it as Rashna's – joined Deo's. "Get the children out! Get them back!"

"*Fighting units!*" Deo bawled. "*Close the gates! We're under attack!*"

PART TWO

CHAPTER
SEVEN

I ran, leaving Surya behind without a thought, pulling my voluminous robe over my head as I went and flinging it away as I reached the garden archway. Clad only in linen tunic and leather breeches, I paused to snatch up the rake leaning against the wall and then raced for the stairs on the outer wall of the House, taking the steps two at a time.

I was breathing hard as I hit the top of the wall and looked down into the inner courtyard. Terror and disbelief at what I saw almost doubled me over.

Dear God. How can this be?

The Great Gate was open and Sedorne – outlaw Sedorne, armed to the teeth – had penetrated the Great Wall. Anyone who had been going about their business between the Great Wall and the inner wall must have either fled or been killed. The outlaws swarmed like hornets in that broad semicircle of ground between the outer wall and the inner; more poured through the open gate as I watched. There were dozens – no, hundreds – of them. At least two hundred Sedorne. Inside the Great Wall. Temple people were fleeing the inner courtyard, streaming through the doors below me; some carried children, others were wounded.

Oh God. Oh my God.

A few Sedorne were trying to scale the inner wall, but without success. The wall had been built from perfectly matched blocks of stone, fitted so well that barely a join could be found. Most of them had realized this, and were gathered around the two entrances in the inner wall, which would allow them access to the courtyard and to the House of God itself. South Gate, the furthest from me at the top end of the semicircle of the inner wall, had been barred in time. A group of namoa and temple people were piling heavy objects up against the door, while the Sedorne on the other side beat at it.

But North Gate had been only half closed. Deo and four other namoa, including his wife – dear God, Mira was four months pregnant! – were behind the gate, trying frantically to push it shut. But there were more Sedorne on the other side pushing back, and they were succeeding in keeping it open.

Joachim the gardener and a group of other temple

people were wielding spears, rakes and long wooden stakes to good effect, jabbing at those who tried to set foot in the courtyard, but several Sedorne had managed to get through. A crowd of namoa and temple people had formed a defensive wall around the entrance to fight them back.

Rashna, a meat cleaver in her right hand and a wooden club in the other, was ducking and jabbing like fury at a pair of Sedorne who had evaded Joachim's group but been caught inside the ring of defenders. She slashed one across the chest, cleaving him open. He fell and was still, blood pooling around his body. His companion backed away, and was tripped by another namoa. Rashna clubbed him while he was down and kicked him for good measure.

The press of people pushing the door on both sides made the gap too narrow for many attackers to squeeze through, preventing the superior Sedorne numbers from sweeping in and overwhelming the defenders. But there were too many Sedorne – far too many – and the gate was slowly, steadily being forced wider.

We had to close North Gate. It was our only hope. How… How? I looked around frantically, as if the answer might present itself from nowhere. Glancing below me, I saw a small pile of casks against the House wall. They hadn't been there this morning. The merchants must have brought some goods with them. The merchants – of course. Pitch – the pitch we'd asked for and been cheated of last time. My eyes went to the corner of the courtyard where one of the great tapers had been lit and was burning steadily.

I was halfway down the stairs before my brain had even caught up. As I reached the courtyard I heard Surya's voice. She had left the garden and was shouting orders to the temple people on the other side of the wall. "Get the children into the shrine! Find a namoa to show you one of the doorways!"

I nodded. The shrine was well hidden and could only be found by way of a handful of concealed entrances. Once inside it, the children and any non-fighters would be safe. There were too many people down there now; it would only take one or two Sedorne to get past the defenders and there would be a slaughter.

We had to get the gate shut.

I dropped the rake and reached for a cask of pitch. Before I could lift one, there was a scream of warning behind me. I turned to see a red-haired Sedorne break through the wall of defenders around North Gate. He headed straight for me – for the entrance to the House behind me – sword in hand. I sucked in a deep breath and quickly bent to pick up the rake, grasping the thick wood handle firmly. The Sedorne emitted a feral war cry as he lunged at me.

I ducked under his blade and smashed the rake into his face as hard as I could, the strength of my swing limited by lack of space. He staggered and shook his head as I skipped backwards, then he recovered and went for me again. This time I came at him from my right, staying out of range of his sword arm, and swung the wooden shaft sideways, aiming for his temple. It hit true. The wood cracked sharply and broke in half.

The Sedorne crumpled to the floor, where he groaned and rolled over, trying to get up. I bent, grabbed his shorn hair and smacked his face hard into the stone paving. I heard another crack. His nose. Blood spurted from his face and a spike of visceral satisfaction went through me. I smacked his head against the stones once more; he shuddered and was still.

I wanted to hit him again – God, I wanted to – but I didn't have time. Instead I dropped his head and quickly wiped my fingers on my breeches, then straightened, holding on to the splintered remains of the rake. I tucked a cask of pitch under one arm and ran to where the great taper jumped and rippled against the darkening sky. I reached up and thrust the broken piece of wood from the rake into the flame. The splintered end caught immediately.

Holding the burning wood cautiously, I flew back up the stairs and along the inner wall to the lintel above North Gate, where Deo and the namoa behind the door were being forced back. The gap was wide enough for two men to pass through now, and it was only the spears and stakes that were keeping them at bay – in a moment there would be enough space for them to mount a charge and we would be over-whelmed.

I crouched and put the cask at my feet, fumbling the cork out one-handed as I held the burning taper far away from my face. On my knees above their heads, I screamed down at Deo and the defenders, "Get back! Get away from the gate!"

Faces tilted up in angered surprise. Then Deo saw me and let out a great whoop. "*You heard her! Get back!*" he bellowed at the defenders. He grabbed Mira and ran; the other temple people and namoa scattered.

The Sedorne pushing against the gate let out a roar of triumph as it thudded open. I lifted the cask and doused the outlaws beneath me with the pitch. There were a few yells of surprise and disgust. Their charge stumbled to a stop as they looked up at the wall with belated caution. I shoved the taper into the opening of the cask, waited for the soft *whoomph* as the remaining fluid caught, and then hurled it down onto their heads.

The wooden cask exploded as it hit the ground, splattering everyone in range with burning pitch. The flames spread rapidly, racing, blue white, from man to man, wherever the pitch had fallen. There was another *whoomph* as the fire took a great breath of new air and unfolded across the flagstones. Screaming broke out and the outlaws fell back, beating frantically at the fires on their faces, bodies and hair. Some rolled on the ground, shrieking with pain; others swore and cursed as they tried to put out the flames that engulfed their friends. For a second, the gateway was empty.

"Close the gate!" I yelled.

The namoa were already charging forward, leaping over the flaming patches on our side of the wall and shoving the gate closed with a resounding thud. Deo dropped the iron bolt, pausing only to swat out the small fires that smouldered on the wooden door. There was a ragged cheer from the Rua.

"Barricade it!" I shouted. "Keep them out!"

Deo shook a fist at me, already in action. "Get down off that wall before someone knocks you off it, girl!" he called up, pitching his voice over the screaming of the burning Sedorne outlaws.

I realized I was shaking. I heaved myself to my feet, breathing through my mouth so that the smell of charred flesh that wafted up from below would not turn my stomach, and carefully made my way back along the wall. I feared my leaden feet might betray me and send me toppling off, even if no Sedorne had the presence of mind to pelt me with rocks.

As I reached the bottom of the stairs, there was a smattering of applause from the Rua defenders who could spare a hand from their work barricading the gate. I lifted a trembling hand in acknowledgement and tried to smile as I surveyed the inner courtyard.

One or two temple people were occupied in dragging the bodies of fallen Sedorne away from the entrance. Others were with Deo, piling heavy boxes against the gate. Rashna, slumped on the floor with Mira tying a makeshift bandage around a long gash on her forearm, raised her eyebrows as she saw me.

"You never could resist showing off," she said, "but at least this time you managed to make yourself useful while you were at it." Her voice held little resentment. She was grey with exhaustion.

Mira looked worriedly at me as I passed. "Do you know where Surya is?"

"She was in the House a few minutes ago, ordering people into the shrine," I said.

Mira sighed. "Thank God. I hadn't seen her since… I didn't know what to think."

Deo stepped back from his barricade and came towards me, clapping a hand on my shoulder. "It was well done. Well done."

Before I could answer, there was a noise that seemed to make the inner wall shake, and froze us all in our tracks. The noise sounded again – a hollow, crashing thud – from South Gate.

"What in the name of the Mother…?" Mira said.

"It's a battering ram." Surya's voice echoed down from the wall behind us and everyone in the courtyard looked up.

There was a moment of silence, then the crashing

noise filled the air again, making everyone jump.

Surya walked slowly down the stairs. "They're battering the gate. Soon they will bring it down; there's nothing we can do to stop them. North and South Gates were not built to withstand a siege. That was the Great Wall's purpose, and they've already managed to penetrate that."

The noise of the battering ram reverberated through the courtyard again as she reached us.

She continued, "There are two hundred armed Sedorne out there. The only reason we are still alive is that they weren't prepared for us to put up a fight and we caught them off guard. Now that the surprise has worn off, there's absolutely no hope of keeping them out of the House of God. If we try to defend the temple we'll all die. We have very little time."

"Time to do what?" Rashna said disbelievingly. "According to you we might as well commit suicide!"

"Quiet!" Deo barked. "Let the noirin speak."

Rashna subsided, cheeks burning with dark colour in her otherwise ashen face.

"Thank you, Deo." Surya looked around at the people stood in the courtyard. Her eyes lingered for a moment on me, but her expression didn't change. "You have to hide. Luckily we have the perfect place to do so – the shrine of the Holy Mother. I don't believe the Sedorne could ever find the entrances no matter how long they searched, or get through them no matter how long they tried. You'll be safe inside. When they enter the temple and find it completely deserted, they'll think you've escaped through some hidden passageway; and after they've finished looting, they'll leave."

"There isn't enough room," Joachim protested. "Not room for half as many people."

Surya shook her head. "Our Mother is closer to us in the shrine than anywhere else in this world. She will make room for you all. I don't know how long you'll need to be in there – you must have provisions. Mira, I want you to take some people and go into the stockrooms. Gather as much food and drink as you can, and take it into the shrine. Deo, you and Rashna must organize search parties. Scour the temple and grounds and make sure no one is hiding anywhere, too frightened to come out. Check the nurseries and the infirmary for anyone who can't move by themselves. I will go into the tower. As soon as I see the Sedorne breach the gate, I'll ring the bell. When you hear it, you drop what you're doing and run for the shrine, understand?"

Surya looked around one last time. "You have trusted me all these years, my children. Trust me again now. You will survive this. Go!"

There was a murmur of voices – almost drowned out by the rhythmic thudding from South Gate – and general nodding of heads as the groups broke up and went about their assigned tasks. The faces I could make out in the gathering darkness were composed into expressions of grim resolve.

"Zira." Surya's voice was hardly above a whisper, but it caught me as I turned away, intending to follow Deo. I stopped, my back to her, and waited.

"Zira, come with me. To the tower. Let's wait together."

I turned back to see her holding out her hand. I hesitated. Then I reached out to her, and her calloused fingers closed tightly around mine.

"Come," she said, tugging gently on my arm.

I followed her through the darkness to the House. The oil lamps had not been lit; shadows draped the corridors like the folds of a carelessly dropped cloak. Our footsteps echoed as if we walked in an empty place. We passed the octagon room and my little cell, and mounted the winding steps to the tower in the waiting silence, our hands linked. The warmth of Surya's skin against mine seemed the only real thing, the only living thing, in the House.

When we reached the top of the tower Surya released me and went to stand at one of the open, unglassed windows that circled the walls of the round tower room. I glanced up as I crossed the floor, but the shape of the giant bronze bell was hidden by the darkness in the domed roof. Only the rope that dangled down in the centre of the room revealed its presence.

I joined Surya at the window and leaned out.

Someone had set the great tapers against the inner wall burning, and they threw the emptiness of the inner courtyard into stark relief. Between the Great Wall and the inner wall, the Sedorne had lit their own fires. The deep, regular thudding noises from South Gate drifted up to us clearly, but all else was eerily quiet. A chill shot up my spine and I clenched my teeth.

"Why are they doing this?" I whispered.

I sensed Surya looking at me, but couldn't make out her face in the gloom. "Abheron's been waiting for a chance to get rid of us for years. I don't know why now, instead of five years ago or five years hence. It's just ... fate, I suppose."

"But those men are outlaws..." My voice trailed off as I remembered the attack on Sorin.

"I'd be surprised if any of them had their hair shorn more than a week ago."

The chill crept down my spine again. "If their king himself is behind this – what will happen when he realizes he didn't succeed in destroying us?"

She sighed, the sound small and weary. "I don't know, Zira. I don't know. Just concentrate on getting through tonight."

We said no more, and for long moments the ominous sound of the battering ram was the only noise in the little room. Finally I broke the silence.

"Surya, what you said earlier, about my name—"

"No, *agni*." She cut me off so swiftly that I realized

she had been waiting for me to ask. "I know now that I was wrong to tell you that."

"Surya—"

"Please, Zira. Please. God took your memories for a reason. It's not up to me to tell you what I know, but for Her to restore the knowledge to you."

I was silent again, struggling with equal parts anger, disappointment ... and relief. Coward! I scolded myself. Have the bravery to demand an answer. You need to know who you are!

Surya stepped closer to me, one of her hands grasping my shoulder. Her voice was pleading as she spoke. "Listen, *agni*. That night – the night you were given to me – it was as if you were born again, made new in God's fire. From that moment you were mine, my own daughter: a daughter of the flames. Remember that, Zira. You have always been mine, in my heart."

There was a deafening crash from below. Our heads jerked round to see the barricade at South Gate disintegrate – the tip of the ram smashed through the wooden gate in an explosion of debris.

"Surya! The bell!"

She was already turning, seizing the long rope and hauling on it for all she was worth. The rich, laughing tone of the bell rang out, hideously out of place against the undulating war cries and crashing noises coming from below us.

"Go!" she shouted as she released the rope.

I clattered down the stairs with her on my heels, heading for the entrance to the shrine set at the base of the tower. We skidded to a halt before what looked like a solid wall; Surya stood on her tiptoes and pressed two plain stone blocks in the wall over her head, then another one near the floor. There was a sullen grating noise.

The entrance did not open.

The muffled crash of splintering wood echoed clearly up the stairs. The doors to the octagon room! They were in the House.

"Why won't it open?" I cried, staring at the stubbornly closed entrance.

Surya stepped back. Her face had gone blank. "Fate strikes again," she whispered. "You open it."

"What?" I gaped at her for an instant, but there was no time to argue, and I was already stepping forward as the cries of the Sedorne began to echo up the stairs behind us. I pressed the two stones above my head and then kicked the lower one with my foot.

The door grated again. Slowly, grudgingly, it began to open.

"What's the matter with it?" I squeezed my fingers into the narrow gap and pushed with all my might, trying to force it open.

"I don't know, Zira," Surya said, her voice strangely even. "Keep trying."

I glanced back and saw that she had drawn a long

knife from her belt, turning to face the stairs. Shadows were swarming up the steps towards us. They would reach us any moment. Oh God. Holy Mother – open the door!

I strained against the door with all my might. It juddered; the mechanism let out a high-pitched squeal. Then whatever was blocking the runners gave way and it slid back with a loud crunch. I fell forward, steadied myself against the wall and swung round with a sob of relief – in time to see the first Sedorne warriors spill into the corridor. They let out wild howls of battle rage as they caught sight of us. Surya lifted her knife and eased into a fighting stance.

"Come on!" I yelled, grabbing her knife arm.

She tore her gaze from the Sedorne and looked behind her. She froze as she saw the open entrance, her expression disbelieving. "It opened," she breathed.

One of the outlaws leaped forward, his war cry echoing off the walls as he loomed over us, sword raised. Surya wrenched her arm away from me, but too late. Her dagger slid off his blade with a squeal of metal and a trail of glowing sparks. The sword slashed down.

There was a heavy, wet thud.

I heard the breath leave Surya in a hollow whistle. She staggered back against me, knocking me off balance; we both toppled through the entrance to the shrine. I landed against the wall with her on top of me.

The Sedorne stepped into the opening, his sword raised again. Instinctively my foot lashed out. It hit the stone panel in the floor.

The heavy door shot into place, trapping the outlaw's hand against the wall with a horrendous crunching of bones. I heard his scream of pain. The sword clattered from his smashed fingers and his hand was wrenched back out of sight. The narrow gap disappeared and the entrance sealed with a final thud.

I scrambled out from beneath Surya, easing her down onto the floor. She let out a broken, choked cry of pain as I moved. Horrified, I saw blood pulsing from her chest, black in the shadows, spilling over her habit like dark water. The horrible warmth soaked into my breeches as I kneeled beside her, spurted through my fingers as I tried to staunch the flow. She shuddered under my hands, her limbs twitching spasmodically.

"Don't move, Surya... Surya – please, *please!*" I begged.

One of her hands came up and clutched at mine, nails digging painfully into my skin as she struggled to speak. "The price..."

A bubble of blood broke on her lips, and the droplet of dark liquid ran along her cheek to pool under her eye like a tear. She made a little noise: half sob, half cough. It might have been my name. Her fingers lost their grip on my hand and I caught at them as they fell away.

"Surya, no!"

The breath slid from her in a long sigh and she went limp. Her head lolled sideways, eyes glinting in the dim light. There was nothing in them. I stared down at her, the blood warm under my fingers, my heart crashing in my ears.

Then something seemed to burst inside me. A great howl of grief exploded from my lips and I lifted her, cradling her body. She weighed nothing. Her head rolled against my shoulder and her legs dangled over my arm as I staggered down the worn steps to the shrine, keening like a wounded animal.

Before long, light and voices reached me. People rushed out of the shrine to see what the noise was – and then fell back, white-faced and stricken, as they saw Surya, lying in my arms. My voice died as I walked through the crowds of temple people and namoa into the golden light. Silence rippled ahead of me until the shrine was utterly still.

Then Deo was there. He reached out and gently lifted Surya's body from my clutching fingers. His dark, hard face was streaked with tears.

"There, now ... there..." he crooned softly, whether to me or to Surya I did not know.

As her weight left my arms, my knees buckled. Someone caught me as I fell and eased me down to the ground. Blankets were draped around me. I heard Mira talking, but could not make out the words, or even her face. People came and went. They spoke softly to me, touched me. I couldn't make myself respond. I had gone away.

I lay, Surya's blood crusting on my hands and clothes, unable to move, hardly breathing. Perhaps I was dying.

Then a voice came that I could not ignore.

It is time, my daughter.

CHAPTER EIGHT

At the centre of the shrine, the peacock flames erupted into life. I jerked to my knees, nearly falling, squinting against the light as the flames exploded upwards, swelling until they crackled high above the treetops. Shades of shimmering blue, green, purple and gold unfolded through the blaze, colours so pure that the eye could hardly perceive them. I heard a clamour of voices, shouting, cries of joy or fear from the other occupants of the shrine. But that voice – the terrible, beautiful voice that had awoken me – called inside my head, blocking them all out.

Step into the fire, Zahira. Reclaim what is yours.

Barely aware of my own actions, I reached out to clutch the twisted trunk of a lir tree and hauled myself to my feet. As I stumbled forward, my watering eyes made out the shape of a giant woman, her arms raised to the sky, the azure folds of her sleeves billowing like the mantle of the clouds. Then there was a purple and emerald flower, the exquisite petals dilating to reveal a blazing gold stamen. As I reached the pit, the flames became a great iridescent bird that spread its fiery wings until they blocked out the sky itself.

Arms outstretched, I stepped into the fire.

Remember.

...Sunlight turned her hair golden. I lay against her shoulder, under the shining ripples of hair, and watched the way the light glinted through it onto the bodice of her dress. I liked this dress. I pulled happily at the little blue and silver threads until she caught me and brushed my hands away. She shifted me in her arms and then lifted me. Air rushed around me as she swung me up, and I shrieked with laughter at the speed and the little thrill of fear. Her hair fell back and I saw her lovely face, smiling – always smiling – and her eyes. Her eyes were blue, the deepest and most beautiful blue in the world. I got the lovely feeling inside and waved my hands madly.

"Don't ruin Mama's favourite dress, Zahira," she said, laughing up at me.

I understood the words, though she was speaking Sedorne. She always spoke in Sedorne, so that I would know it as well as I knew my dada's language.

Remember.

...Dada. Big hands, brown, like mine; not white, like Mama's. They were not smooth like Mama's either, but hard on the palms and tips, so that they felt like the unpolished wood on the toy ships my brothers carved. They curved around mine gently as he showed me how to use the quill pen. Carefully I dipped it into the ink; a few drops fell onto the paper, glinting strangely in the candlelight, like little black jewels. I reached out to touch, but he caught my fingers and held them to stop me.

"Uh, uh. We don't need to put our fingers there," he said, his deep voice rumbling with laughter. "Concentrate on the letters. Write me your name, sweeting."

My fingers were clumsy, but I wrote my own name: *Zahira Elfenesh*.

"That's beautiful! Good girl. Now, do you think you can do it in Mama's language?"

This was harder. I dripped more ink on the paper, but ignored it as I slowly scratched out the square letters that spelled my name. *Zahira Elfenesh*.

"Well done. My clever girl." He hugged me with one arm as he took the quill and slid the ink bottle out of my reach. I glowed with pride and then looked up hopefully. Dada sometimes gave me sweets when I was good. He laughed again at the look on my face.

"All right then." He set me down on the floor by his desk. "There're sugared almonds in the bottom drawer.

But only a handful – and don't tell your brothers and sister."

"No, Dada," I said, already pulling out the drawer.

Remember.

...Indira. My eldest sibling, my only sister. I sat on her knee, wriggling with impatience as she deftly knotted and plaited my hair.

"Will it look like Mama's?" I said, twitching as I tried to see into the mirror. It was too high up. All I could see was Indira's face, her blue eyes frowning down at her handiwork.

"Not if you don't stop moving," she said firmly. "Sit still."

"But I want to see," I whined.

She laughed suddenly. "Oh, all right. I'm done." She adjusted the mirror so I could see my hair, plaited in swirls around my head, just as Mama wore hers.

"Thank you!" I cried, jumping up and down on Indira's knee in excitement.

"Well, I can't do it as well as Mama's maid," she said modestly, but she was grinning. "One day you'll dance with your hair all braided with pearls and jewels, and wearing a beautiful dress, and all the lords and casadors will fight to be your partner."

"Really?" I breathed. I stared at my own face and tried to imagine how it would look when I was old enough to dance. I had the same blue eyes as my sister, but her skin was paler and her face longer, with high cheekbones like Mama's. My face was brown from the sun, and round. I didn't have dimples either. Would I change when I was fifteen like Indira? Or would I always look the same?

"Of course." Indira interrupted my thoughts. "Now get off, will you? I'm late for riding. Go and play with Kiran and Pallav."

...My brothers. Kiran, tall, and slender like Mama, Pallav, short but broad like Dada.

"You can have this one, Ziri," Kiran said, handing me the smallest boat, with the odd-shaped bow and broken sail.

"I want the *River Spirit*," I said, dismayed, looking at the much larger and better carved toy boat he was holding.

"The *River Spirit* is mine," he said pompously. "And the *River Rat* is yours."

"And the *Wind Rider* is mine," Pallav agreed, not looking up from the fountain, where his boat bobbed happily in the miniature currents and waves.

"Not fair," I muttered.

"Is," said Pallav, not taking his eyes off the *Wind Rider*. "When you can carve your own, then you can have whatever you want."

Kiran nodded. "Until then, you can have the *River Rat*." He turned away and placed the *River Spirit* on the water.

I stared at the *River Rat* in silence, lip trembling, and

then gently put it down on the rim of the fountain. If I couldn't have a good boat, I didn't want to sail.

After a moment, Pallav turned round and looked at me. He sighed when he saw my expression. "Oh, all right. You can have the *Wind Rider*. But only this once."

I clapped my hands with glee and hugged him.

"*Eugh.*" He pushed me off. "Only this once! The *Wind Rider* is mine. But I suppose I can carve you something better than the *River Rat*..."

"You made me carve the *River Spirit* myself," Kiran protested.

"Ziri's only five," Pallav said. "She's just a baby..."

Zahira. Remember who you are.

Screaming – blood – smoke and flames. Nanny has me. She whispers that everything will be all right, but I can hear her heart thudding and her fingers clutch me too tight. She's frightened. Mama – I want my mama! I want my dada!

Then pain. Horrible, screaming pain that throbs and throbs across my face. And my eye – my eye – I want my mama...

I have held these memories safe for you, Zahira, through all the years of your childhood. Now you are a woman in the reckoning of your people. The time has come for you to remember.

Mama! Where is my mama? Where is Dada? Where am I?

Who ... who am I?

When you wake, you will know who you are. Then you must decide what to do. Have courage, my daughter. I am with you.

When I woke, I was lying in the fire pit at the centre of the shrine. Flames the colour of peacock feathers rippled gently against my skin. It felt like warm water. I heard voices, and saw faces, dozens of faces, watching me, arranged in expressions of anxiety and shock. For a moment, through the flickering of the fire, I didn't recognize them. Then I realized they were the namoa whom I had known all my life. They looked different but they weren't. It was me.

I was the stranger.

I reached my hand up through the fire to Deo. He grasped my fingers without hesitation and pulled me upright. With his help, I got to my feet in the stone pit, the fire lapping at my ankles, and scrambled up the smooth bank of grass to where the other namoa stood. They edged away from me, as if they were afraid even to feel the brush of my tunic. Below me, I could see everyone I knew, their faces turned up to watch me. Waiting...

I am the stranger. Where am I? Who am I? A strange, sharp voice repeated the questions in my head.

Whose voice?

Who are you?

Only Deo seemed unafraid. His hand on my fingers

was firm and reassuring – but when I turned my head to look at him, I saw him start in surprise.

"Your eyes," he said. "They're…"

I blinked at him, and lifted my free hand to touch the skin under my eye.

"They're blue, aren't they?" I stopped speaking abruptly as I heard my own voice. It was different. The soft burr of the mountains was gone. Without it my voice sounded deeper, more sure of itself.

I sound like my father… It was Zahira's voice in my mind. My voice … her mind. Who am I?

I staggered as the flood of memories threatened to overwhelm me again. My head pounded with flashing images, faces, lights. Deo put his arm round my shoulder and I sagged into him gratefully, shaking my head.

"What happened?" he asked, his voice low. "We all saw the hand of the Holy Mother reach for you. We saw you step into the flames. What did She say? Why are you different?"

I straightened, steadying myself against Deo's shoulder. "Because … I am different."

I stepped away from him and turned back to look down at the temple people.

Our people, Zahira's voice whispered.

I took a deep breath. "How long have we been in here?" I asked Deo.

"The – the gate was broken a day and a half ago."

"Has anyone been outside yet?"

"No." He hesitated. "We were waiting for you."

Waiting for you? Zahira whispered. Waiting for *us*.

Holy Mother. Am I going mad?

I rubbed my head. "I think it's safe now. Someone should go out and check, carefully."

"Did God tell you this?" He sounded hopeful.

I sighed. I was so tired and my head hurt so much. "Send someone out, would you? Please?"

The namoa murmured and whispered around me as I sat down on the smooth grass, while Deo went out of one of the entrances.

Mama and Dada ... Kiran and Pallav ... Indira. My breath caught and I hid my face in the crook of my elbow, feeling moisture pool against my skin. My family. I had been without a family for so long. In the fire, I had been with them again for an instant. An eternity. Now they were gone once more. Everyone I – *Zahira* – loved was dead. And Surya ... Surya... She was gone too. I still had her blood on me. The one person Zira – I – loved was dead. There was no one left. Nothing left. Except me.

Us.

The Holy Mother had said I would know who I was. I didn't. I didn't know anything. Is she the same as me? Am I her? Who are we?

"They're gone."

I looked up at the sound of Deo's voice. He was staring at me, his face ashy with shock. I had never seen him so pale, not even when he'd seen Surya … Surya, dead.

"What is it?" I asked, climbing to my feet with difficulty.

"They're gone, but…" He shook his head, unable to continue.

"I'll come." I walked past him, through the crowds of people, through the entrance and down the stairs. I heard a tide of voices and footsteps rising in my wake, and realized everyone was following.

The entrance opened onto the inner courtyard; I stepped cautiously through. I was lucky to be able to get out at all. Stone blocks lay everywhere, like gravestones. As the namoa and temple people spilled out behind me, I saw what had made Deo's face go pale.

The outlaws had lifted the stone flags and tunnelled under them to the foundations of the walls. There was nothing left of the inner wall but tumbled piles of rubble. Remnants of the stronger Great Wall stood like rotted teeth in an old woman's mouth. The Great Gate had been torn down and set afire; it still burned sullenly, barely more than charcoal, the metal braces twisted and blackened in the heat.

And the House. The front wall of the House… They had pulled it down. The internal walls and ceilings had collapsed. It was a smoking, gaping ruin.

We can never rebuild this. It has been finished. For ever.

The shock of it hit me like a blow to the face. Our

home. The home of the Holy Order, and the centre of Rua worship for hundreds of years. It had taken our ancestors fifty years to build it, four hundred years ago. The Sedorne had destroyed it in a day and a half.

The temple people and namoa wandered through the wreckage, dazed and weeping. I saw a small group of refugee children shifting through the debris in the octagon room with deftness that spoke of long practice. Rashna saw them too, and drove them away.

"Have you no shame?" she cried, wiping tears from her face. "Get off!"

I felt a touch on my shoulder and looked round to find Mira and Deo standing behind me. It was Mira whose hand lay on my arm. Her other hand, visibly shaking, was pressed to the small bulge of her stomach.

"Zira," she said softly. "I'm sorry. I know you must be exhausted after … after everything. But if God spoke to you – please won't you tell us what She said?" Her gaze left me to stare at the ruin of our home. "We need Her guidance now. We need … something."

Talk to them? I nodded, feeling my shoulders bow under the weight of responsibility. How awful to be the only one who knew what had to be done. To be the one who had to do it.

I looked around and saw a heap of wall blocks lying near by; I stepped onto them and picked my way up to the top, so that I could be seen by everyone in the courtyard.

"Namoa!" I shouted. "Temple people! Hear me, please!"

The devastated people turned towards my voice and began to gather around the pile of rocks. Deo nodded encouragingly at me. I stood still, trying to remember what to do.

Is this right? I don't know.

Is this what we do?

I don't know!

My head swam dizzily as Zira and Zahira warped and twisted together. I couldn't feel where one ended and the other began.

Does Zira end? Does Zahira begin? Are they even different? Who was asking?

Stop talking!

I closed my eyes briefly, then began. "Our Mother spoke to me in the sacred fire. Now I need to tell you what She said." I paused for a moment, hanging, trying to decide. "God... God told me that when I left the flames I would have to decide what to do. When I opened my eyes in the shrine, I didn't know. It was only when I came out here and saw this—" My voice broke. I swallowed. "Then I knew what She meant. We cannot stay here."

I stopped, waiting until the murmuring and whispers died away. "You can all see it. Now that the walls are down, the Sedorne will never leave us alone. Our only hope is to leave, find somewhere safe to stay, until we can return and rebuild the House of God."

"What?" It was Rashna, pushing her way to the front. Her voice shook with emotion as she stared up at me. "What are you talking about? That's lunacy. We can't abandon the temple. It's our duty to protect the sacred fire. It's the duty of all namoa."

"The sacred fire doesn't need our protection," I said quietly. "It's safe within the shrine. We aren't. Surya believed the outlaws were sent by the Sedorne king. What do you think will happen when he realizes we've survived? He'll never leave us alone, not while a single one of us defies him. He'll send more men, and he'll keep on until the Holy Order is completely destroyed. That's why we can't stay here."

"Surya died to protect the House of God!" Rashna shouted roughly. "She would never have abandoned it. I don't believe anything you say. I don't believe God spoke to you at all. Why would She choose you, out of all of us? Why would She set you to lead us?"

I stared at her, and there must have been something in my face that warned her how close to the edge I was, because her mouth closed abruptly, and she stepped back.

"You all know me. My name is Zira. I am an orphan, and I was brought here after the Invasion Fire. You know me. But … but I am also someone else. Something else. My other – my real name is Zahira Elfenesh. I am the youngest daughter of Toril and

Emelia Elfenesh. The last surviving heir to the Elfenesh line. God showed me who I was when I stepped into the flames. That's why I will lead you."

"The reia," Mira whispered.

"The blue eyes." Deo stared at me. "The voice…"

"You? You're the reia?"

"She's the one…"

Before my horrified eyes, Mira began to lower herself to her knees; others in the crowd swiftly followed suit.

"Stop that!" I cried, leaping down from the pile of stones. "For God's sake, Mira, you're pregnant." I grabbed her before her knees could touch the ground, and pulled her back up. The sheer absurdity of the situation struck me and a bubble of hysterical laughter made my voice tremble as I nudged Deo, also halfway to the ground, with my foot. "Don't you dare kneel before me, Deo! Get up, all of you! I'm still the person you knew."

"But, Majesty—"

"And don't call me that either. Just Zira, please." *My name is Zahira*, whispered a voice in my head. I ignored it.

"But…" Mira clutched my arm. "What do you want us to do?"

"I only want you to trust me. That's all. I think I know somewhere we can go to be safe, but you must trust me."

"Where?"

Mira's question was echoed by a dozen voices, and she released me to face the namoa and temple people again.

"I know someone. He owes me a debt. Owes me his life, he said. He swore an oath to me, that if ever I were in need, he would help me."

"Who? Who is this person?" someone asked.

"His name is Sorin Mesgao."

"Sorin? A Sedorne?" Rashna burst out.

"He is Sedorne, yes. But then, so am I. Half Sedorne, anyway."

There was silence. I looked around at the shocked faces.

"He's an honourable man. He has his own reasons to hate Abheron. He won't betray me – or you. All we have to do is get ourselves to Fort Mesgao. Once we're there, those of you with families will be able to go back to them, and the rest of us can try to contact the resistance. But first we have to get away from here, before word reaches King Abheron that his men found the temple empty. Once that happens, we'll have very little time. Will you trust me?"

There was another moment of silence. Then Deo nodded decisively.

"Of course. We will go with you."

There was a general murmur of agreement, and some nodding. A few people – including Rashna –

stood back, unconvinced, but they did not voice their doubts. They were a minority. Looking around me at these people I knew so well, I saw a shining of terrible hope.

The temple people had lost their home and their leader, and now they had nothing left. These people – the ones who had started to kneel, the ones who looked at me with shining faces – would follow me as trustingly as sleepwalkers following a dream. I *was* a dream to them. A dream of the Chosen of God, the lost heir of the rei, who would deliver them from suffering. They were blind to all the flaws I had failed to mention. They would follow, and somehow I would have to lead.

Please, Mother, let me be right about Sorin, I prayed. Or they'll be following me to their deaths.

CHAPTER
NINE

The following week was the worst I had ever endured. Travelling to Mesgao in clear weather in a well-sprung trap with a pair of strong ponies was one thing. Making the same journey with one hundred and eighty-three men, women and children, using only the three ancient nags and one rickety cart that the Sedorne had not seen fit to steal ... well, that was something else entirely.

To make our misery complete, the blossoming of spring we had just begun to enjoy played us false from the first day. We walked, stumbled and fell through a world of treacherous mud, damply slithering mist and clouds so low that the mountains behind us were completely shrouded. We had been forced to leave behind the namoa's thick red robes with their wide hoods:

they were too distinctive. Most of the namoa had very little else to wear, and the Sedorne had not spared anyone's trunks or closets, so none of us had enough warm clothing.

There wasn't much food – only the provisions which Mira and her helpers had hastily grabbed before the attack – so the parents stinted themselves in order to give their children enough to eat. I did the same, not out of any sense of nobility, but because children cry when they're hungry, a kind of high, breathless sobbing that goes on and on. Adults at least suffer in silence.

During the day we split into several groups, so as to attract less attention. One group took the cart and travelled along the main road. The others made their way through the rocks and scrub above as quietly as they could, or split into even smaller groups and walked on the road some way behind. Here, at least, the weather was an aid to us. The mists and rain offered camouflage and reduced traffic along the mountain route. Still, whenever we passed other travellers, the namoa with face tattoos of stars, birds or flames would quietly disappear into the rocks.

Once, a small unit of gourdin surprised us on a sharp turn, and stopped the group of fifteen or so people travelling on the road. They inspected the grubby refugees and insisted on searching the cart, and they weren't very polite about any of it.

Along with a fighting namoa named Kapila, I hid in

the twisted bristlecone tree arching over the road. Rocks clenched in our hands, we waited to leap down onto the soldiers' heads if they showed any sign of violence.

One of the gourdin pulled a toy – a rag doll – from the hands of a little girl and casually ripped it apart, flinging it down into the road when it proved to hold nothing more exciting than sawdust. When the child screamed, the gourdin slapped her hard enough to knock her to the ground.

I gasped, and beside me I felt Kapila brace to drop. But instead of giving the order to attack, I found myself reaching out and grabbing her arm, holding her still. Kapila stared at me in outrage as the gourdin ground the remains of the rag doll into the dirt and then swaggered away. I felt outrage myself – what am I doing? What needs to be done: quiet! – but I could not seem to move my arm. A few moments later, the soldiers finished their inspection and went on down the road.

As soon as they were out of sight, Kapila wrenched her arm away. "Why did you stop me?" she demanded, gesturing down at the still sobbing child, now being rocked in a namoa's arms. "He might have killed her!"

A deep, cold voice that I barely recognized as my own answered, "She's fine. Would you have risked all our lives over a rag doll and a few tears?"

Kapila stared at me in disbelief. "Just what are you?"

"One thing I'm not is a fool."

She flung herself down out of the tree without even looking where she fell, landed badly, and limped away. I climbed down more slowly, my whole body shaking. I felt sick. Inside my head I heard Kapila's question echoing in my own voice. But whose voice was it? Who had spoken? Who had held Kapila's arm? Me? Was Zahira me, or Zira?

Who had made that choice?

Deo approached me a little while later, when we had moved on. "You did right," he said quietly. "It was a hard decision, but a good one."

"Thank you." I touched his arm and turned away before he could see my expression. He didn't understand. It wasn't hard. For me – us – it wasn't hard at all.

At night we gathered again, taking what comfort we could in one another's company. There wasn't much comfort to be had, especially as the days went on.

It was inevitable that the journey would take its toll on our most vulnerable. The first to be lost was old Theri. He was seventy years old and had been confined to the infirmary for weeks before the attack with a weak heart. As dawn broke on our second day of travel, his daughter – brave, reckless Kapila – went to wake him and found that he had slipped away in the night. We buried him by the roadside. Kapila, weeping bitterly, vowed to return and place a marker there before the year was out. Afterwards she stared at me as if I were a murderer. I felt like one.

Esha, a young temple woman, was heavily pregnant when we began our trek. Her birthing pangs started on the third day of the journey, a month early. When the dreadful thing was over, we buried her tiny still-born son under a mountain vetch that was alight with yellow flowers, and then tucked the devastated woman, still weak with loss of blood, into the cart and carried on.

On the fifth day, the worst came. Padma, a four-year-old refugee girl, had been receiving treatment for her weak chest from the first day she arrived at the temple; deprived of that, and in the cold and the wet, she sickened rapidly. The herb namoa told me it was an infection in her lungs, and there was nothing to be done.

Padma had come to the temple as an orphan. She had no family to offer comfort in those final moments. It was me who held her, stroking her shuddering back, rocking her, until her painful, rattling breaths finally stopped. I dug her grave, and built a cairn of pale stones to mark the resting place, praying that the Holy Mother would warm the little girl's cold face and hands in the world beyond. Rashna came to help me, and though I caught her hard, doubting look, I still valued her silent company. There were too many voices in my own head now for me to enjoy conversation with anyone else.

I waited, almost hopefully, for someone to point a finger. For the moment when someone would cry, "She did this! She's responsible! She's not fit to be our leader!" Each day I saw faces that were angry, tired, accusing. I saw people turn from me in bitterness or despair. I knew the first night that someone slipped away under cover of darkness into the mountains, leaving their friends behind because they could not or would not endure our trek; and I knew that it continued to happen every night afterwards. I waited – but the moment did not come. They might weep and rage and doubt, but still … still they followed me.

They looked to me for everything. Comfort, guidance, a sense of hope, a promise that everything would be all right again. Even Mira and Deo treated me differently. It was as if their friend Zira had died – or, worse, as if she had never existed at all. When they looked at me, they saw someone else. I began to realize, with a creeping sense of fear, that I no longer had a single friend. Only followers.

It was at those times, more than any other, that I missed Surya. I missed her wry smile and her teasing. The way that she had read from the Book of the Holy Mother, and made me believe in the words. I had lost her so quickly, so unexpectedly, that I could hardly believe she was really gone, even though I had been the one to wash her body and prepare it for death, and lay her in the ground of the flower garden, under her favourite blue starflower. Grief ached like a rock lodged in my chest.

I missed my family too, almost too much to bear. Anything might stir memories of them. The smile on a woman's face that reminded me of my mother. A stumble in the dirt that recalled my brother's clumsiness. A certain tone in a man's voice as he spoke to his child that sounded for a moment like my father. The young girl playing with her hair, just as Indira had once done. The images were so sharp, and so very painful. Zahira longed for her family, wanted them, *needed* them in a way that Zira had never needed anyone, not even Surya.

I slept little that week. At night, as I huddled against Mira's back for warmth, I stared at the impenetrable darkness of the sky, searching in vain for a star. Whenever I could fool myself that I saw a glint of light, I would beg my family's forgiveness for having forgotten them. Then I would beg Surya's, for the way the pain of her loss had been swamped in the greater flood of my grief over a family that I had barely known.

I had longed for a family all my life. I'd had one, and lost them. I grieved for what I had lost, and I grieved for what I had never had. I felt as if I were swimming through foreign emotions all the time, but the emotions were mine. *Mine*. There were two hearts, two souls, within my body, and I could not figure out which truly belonged to me.

I did not know who "me" was any more.

We reached Mesgao on the seventh day, circling the town warily. Dividing into even smaller groups, we scrambled down the terraced hillside as swiftly as possible, taking cover in the thick foliage offered by the tea fields.

I crouched in the gathering darkness, the wind tugging at my hair, and looked up at Mesgao. The rain had stopped a little while ago, and the sky spread above like a dove's soft grey wing, so close I felt I might reach up and stroke the iridescent pink feathers of the clouds. We had pet doves once; they were soft, and they fluttered so gently in my hands, like a warm heart beating... I blinked, trying to push Zahira's memory down and call on Zira's of Mesgao. That was what I needed now.

The hump of the fort was outlined against the sky; I could see the flicker of firelight behind the oblong openings of the windows, and fancied I could make out the flutter of a pennant against the clouds. The rest was hidden, blanked out in the dimness. As the namoa and temple people began to settle for the night, I went back to my meagre pack of possessions, opened it and drew out two items which I hoped would help bring me success in my task.

The first was a red hooded namoa's robe like the one I had worn that day in the marketplace. I stroked it for a minute, struggling with two sets of memories: Zira's of seeing people wearing such robes every day and wearing them herself, Zahira's of listening to a man in such a robe read stories from a book when she was little. I shook myself free again, trying to concentrate. I thought the status it conferred might allow me to get past the guards.

The second thing was more precious. I had known when I returned to my cell that the wind chime Sorin gave me would be gone. But in their haste to tear down the valuable silver, the outlaws had snapped the fine threads that held the chime together. When I entered the little room for the last time to gather up my blankets, I found a gleaming strand among the debris, still intact. It was a gently curving silver chime, with one tiny mother-of-pearl fish suspended from its tip.

As I stared down at the gleam of silver in my hand, I felt my resolve firming. I couldn't wait another sleepless night. I would go now; then at least we would know all our fate when the sun rose tomorrow. I pulled the warm robe down over mud-splattered, ragged clothes, and tucked the silver chime into one of the pockets.

"What are you doing?" Mira asked, looking up anxiously from the tiny fire she was attempting to build. She was kneeling on a rolled-up blanket, one hand rubbing absently at her back; I could see she was wretchedly uncomfortable. One more reason to get this over with.

"I'm getting ready to go up to the fort," I said. "There's no reason to wait, is there?"

"But – but…" She waved a piece of kindling helplessly. "Surely—"

"Mira." I kneeled before her and took her waving hand in mine. "It's best to find out as soon as possible what choices we have. Don't worry."

Mira turned her head away. "Deo!"

"Yes?" He glanced up from the broken sword strap that Rashna was showing him.

"Deo, Zahira intends to go to Mesgao tonight. In the dark. Alone!" Mira stared at him meaningfully. He in turn looked at me.

"Is that really necessary?" he asked quietly. I could tell that he just managed to restrain himself from adding "Majesty" to the end of his sentence.

"It's better than waiting," I said uncomfortably. I didn't know which was worse, Deo's deference or Mira's mother henning. "And I don't intend to go alone. I'll take … um…" I looked around. "Rashna."

The other woman jumped at the sound of her name. I couldn't see her face very well, but I'd have wagered she was narrowing her eyes at me.

"What's happening now?" she asked. I thought she only just managed to restrain herself from saying,

"What trouble is Zira getting us into now?" Oddly, her attitude was a comfort.

"I'm going to see Lord Mesgao tonight. I'd like to take you as an escort, Rashna."

"Me?" Now I was sure her eyes had narrowed. She hesitated, then said, "You know how I feel about us coming here. But if you want me with you, I would, of course, be honoured."

I smiled at the fine edge of sarcasm in her tone. "Good. See if you can find a clean robe somewhere, and we'll walk up."

"Very well." She turned away.

The walk up the hill, through the quiet town and to the fort was accomplished in silence. I could feel Rashna simmering with objections beside me, but I was too full of tension myself to try to reason with her. Even if I had been utterly calm, I wouldn't have gone out of my way to make conversation. Rashna and I had never been friends and I doubted that we ever would be.

From the time when we were both children, Rashna had always taunted me with the fact that I was the noirin's little favourite, that I received special attention. Of course, it was true. Surya did love me and single me out. I'd always assumed it was the promise she had made to my dying mother that made us so special to each other. Now I realized she had been taking care of the heir to the throne, doing her duty.

Holy Mother, it hurt to accept that. Yet she said she loved me – that I was like a daughter to her. There could be no greater honour than that. To be the daughter of a woman like Noirin Surya – even if only for ten years. I squeezed my eyes shut for a second, pushing the terrible ache of loneliness away.

In any case, Rashna had good reason to resent me as a child – and she had taken revenge by making me miserable whenever she had the chance. Oddly, I had never been able to stir any real hatred in myself towards Rashna, even when she was bullying me mercilessly. I just found her sarcasm tiresome.

As we approached the massive, iron-braced gates of the fort, I glanced at Rashna out of the corner of my eye.

"Keep close to me," I said. "And keep quiet too. I don't know how we're going to be received here."

"Not so confident now, Reia?" she asked, folding her arms. "I assume I'm to intervene if anyone shows signs of harming your precious person?"

I sighed. "I'd appreciate that, thank you."

Before she could speak again, I stepped forward and banged as hard as I could on the door. I rubbed my smarting knuckles and waited for a response.

A moment later, a little door in the bottom of one of the giant gates opened and a gourdin, dressed in casual leather uniform, stepped out, a spiked halberd in his hand. The man was only an inch or so taller than me, but I found myself stepping back nervously. It was something to do with the silhouette of his helmet, with the intricately braided coils of reddish hair beneath it, and the wide, square shoulders of his armour. I had been brought up to fear and hate these people most of my life and it was hard to break that habit.

"I…" My voice wavered horribly and I stopped, clearing my throat to cover my embarrassment. "I need to see Sorin Mesgao. He knows me."

"Does he indeed?" The man smiled broadly. He looked back through the door, presumably at a fellow guard, and called out, *"Esfad e mourns Rua grinei. Mesgao far e maera!"*

There was a burst of laughter from the other side of the wooden barrier.

"There's a little Rua tart here. Reckons she knows Mesgao!"

I frowned as I realized that I understood the foreign words – and then gasped with anger as the name the man had called me sank in. I was dressed as a namoa, and he called me a tart? I stepped forward again, thrusting my face up into his. The light from the torch burning above fell full on my face and the soldier blinked as he met my furious eyes and saw the scar glaring at him from my cheek.

"Watch who you're calling a tart, soldier," I hissed in Sedorne.

The man gaped at me. The laughter behind him stopped abruptly.

I continued, still in the foreign tongue, "Take this to Mesgao – he'll see me, I promise you." I pulled the silver chime from my pocket and held it up to the light.

The gourdin reached out and took the chime from my fingers. "I ... apologize, sister," he said awkwardly in Rua. "I didn't realize. I'll take this to my lord at once."

I nodded sharply and stepped back. He disappeared through the door with surprising speed for such a large man, leaving the entrance open.

"Not bad," Rashna said grudgingly. "Never seen a gourdin move so fast. Where did you learn their language?"

"From my mother."

She pulled a face as if she had bitten down on a piece of gristle, and said no more.

There was a commotion somewhere behind the gates and the sound of hurried footsteps. Then the door, which had slowly begun to drift closed, was thrown open hard enough to slam against the wood behind it, and Sorin Mesgao stepped out.

CHAPTER TEN

He stopped dead when he saw us, the silver chime in his hand. "Zahira."

"I... You remember me," I said stupidly as I stepped forward. I felt again that disorientating sense of recognition as I looked at him. The gold of his hair, and the slanted deep blue eyes, even the shape of his face. He reminded me of my mother...

His expression as the light revealed me changed from astonishment to outright shock. "Of course I remember. Dear gods, Zahira! You look like ... well, death is putting it politely. What happened to you?"

He reached out cautiously, as if he thought any sudden movement might frighten me. His big hands settled on my shoulders and he patted me softly, as one might comfort a child.

"I can't explain now. I need to know – will you keep your promise? Will you help me?" Despite all my efforts, my voice trembled.

He gave me a worried look, and I realized I was even less coherent than I'd thought.

"What do you need? Are you sick? Hurt?"

"No." I pushed his hands away. "No, you don't understand. My people need your help."

"Your ... *people*?"

"A week ago outlaws – Sedorne – attacked the House of God. Most of us managed to hide in time, but they destroyed the temple. Our home. We've nothing left. Nowhere to go." I gulped in a breath that sounded perilously close to a sob.

"The House of God? Why would anyone—" He broke off, his expression changing.

"Please." I swallowed down another sob, and my pride with it. "I've got a templeful of refugees hiding down there in the tea fields. My friends. Women and children. They expect me to save them, but I can't do it alone. I need – I need help."

I put my hands up to hide my face and felt the chill of tears against my palms. Please, someone help me.

He put his hands on my shoulders again and I felt his hair brush against mine as he leaned over me.

"Stop now," he murmured. "It's all right. We'll look after them."

"You will help us?" I asked, my words muffled by

my fingers. I didn't dare look at him.

"You have my oath. You knew I would."

"Thank you." I felt such a surge of relief that my stomach churned. New tears welled up, hidden in my hands. "Thank you. I – I must go back. I have to tell them…"

"I'd advise you to wait a moment and sit down, before you fall down. When was the last time you ate?"

I shrugged, struggling to calm my breathing. I scrubbed my hands over my face roughly, erasing all traces of moisture – I hoped – and finally looked up. "I don't remember."

"I thought so. Send your friend back."

"My—" I remembered Rashna mid word, and turned to find her leaning nonchalantly against the fort wall. Her expression, however, was anything but bored – a fine mixture of disbelief and disgust.

"I suppose so," I said, sighing. My legs had gone alarmingly wobbly, but I hated to think what tales Rashna would take back to the camp with her.

Before I could say anything, Sorin spoke to Rashna. "Just get them to gather everything up and come. It's safe to use the road if you have wagons. I'll have the gates opened for you."

Rashna nodded, then bowed beautifully – the bow of servant to master. She turned and walked out of the light without a word.

"Oh no." I rubbed my face again. "We offended her."

"Yes, she looked the type," Sorin said, straight-faced, as he took my arm. "Come on. I was having some tea when you arrived. I think a cup would do you good."

"I have to be here when they come," I said, stopping abruptly. "Otherwise they'll be worried."

"Very well." He tugged me forward and guided me through the door. In the flickering taperlight I saw a square courtyard, surrounded by walls with high arch-ways leading into the building. Above, a mezzanine level with a wooden roof overhung the area. To my surprise the place didn't look warlike at all; there were flowering trees in pots around the edges of the court-yard, and I thought I could hear water, as if from a fountain. I couldn't see anyone around.

Sorin led me across the front of the courtyard to a little wooden hut that sat next to the gates. He pushed the door open, revealing a trio of gourdin sat inside. The men were intimidatingly large and dressed in leather armour – but they looked up rather nervously as Sorin appeared.

"Clear out," he ordered. "Open the gates and make ready for a large number of guests. Ask Gita to prepare tea and something to eat, would you?"

The men saluted and shuffled past Sorin sheepishly. I didn't understand their worried air until I recognized one as the man who'd called me a tart. The soldier made the Sedorne nod of respect at me as he passed. I thought, with no little satisfaction, that it would be a long time before any of them dared insult a Rua woman again.

"Come and sit here." Sorin held the door open for me and I walked past him into the dimly lit hut. I selected a chair at the table in the centre of the room and fell down into it, resting my elbow on the table and my head in my hand. He pulled up a seat next to mine and sat with a sigh.

"You'll be the first thing your friends will see when they come through the gates," he said.

I nodded in thanks, letting my eyes close for a moment. They were dry and sore, as if they were full of dust. My back ached. And my head felt funny…

I woke with a scream. Nightmares of smoke, darkness and fire had me jerking upright before I realized where I was.

I sat, gasping for breath, with the last remnants of remembered pain – Zahira's pain – fading from Zira's face. It was light; morning sun dripped like clear honey through the shutters at the window. I was in bed, in the centre of an unfamiliar room. Bright tapestries hung on the walls and the ceiling was high, though the room itself was small. Soft blankets and furs had fallen around my waist as I sat up. I was still in my cotton tunic and leather breeches.

"Are you all right?"

I jumped and twisted to see Sorin seated in a chair behind the bed.

"I..." Rubbing the back of my neck, I stared at him. "What...?"

"You fell asleep in the guardhouse last night. One of your people – Deo? – carried you up here and we let you sleep. You must have needed it. It's nearly noon."

"Oh no! Is everyone all right?" I asked, stricken. What must they have thought?

"They're fine. Mostly sleeping, now – it was a hard journey for all of you. Wait a moment." He got up, opened the door, and spoke to someone on the other side. I heard footsteps moving away before he closed the door again. "Breakfast will be here soon," he said, turning back to me. "Now I'll ask again. Are you all right?"

I looked away, feeling my face burn. Holy Mother. Could I have made a bigger fool of myself?

"I am, thank you. I'm sorry about my behaviour last night," I said stiffly. "I didn't mean to impose on you."

"I enjoyed it actually. It's not every day that pretty girls fling themselves into my arms."

I gritted my teeth. "I think that's in rather poor taste."

He slapped his hand to his heart. "You wound me, my lady."

I realized – belatedly – that he was only teasing, and managed a weak laugh at the expression of mock suffering on his face. "Oh, all right. I'm sorry again – for being an idiot this time."

"Worth it to get a laugh out of you. I shall mark the date in my diary." He grinned.

There was a quiet knock on the door. Sorin, still grinning, opened it and took a tray from the Rua woman on the other side. Her round face wrinkled into a smile, so that the faded tattoo of flowers around her left eye disappeared into a lacework of fine lines. She bowed deeply and backed away, her eyes not leaving me.

Sorin nudged the door closed with his foot and carried the tray over to the bed. The grin had been replaced with a speculative look.

"That was Gita," he said as he sat on the edge of the bed and placed the tray before me. "She's the head cook. She doesn't normally bring trays up herself. She doesn't normally bow to my guests either."

I picked the tray up and feigned great interest in the contents, cursing the loose tongues of the namoa and temple people. Someone must have said something about me – and a rumour like that would spread as quickly as flames through a funeral pyre. What had they thought they were doing? It could put us all in danger. I wasn't ready for it. It was bad enough when my own friends, people I had known all my life, treated me like their reia. How was I supposed to handle being reia to every Rua I met?

"If you don't want that, I'll eat it," Sorin said.

I blinked and focused on the plates in front of me. There were two golden herby omelettes, still steaming and folded in neat triangles together. Flaky pistachio and date pastries filled another plate, along with a generous pot of jam. There were also two bowls of fried dumplings: sweet ones made with cinnamon and pomegranate seeds and savoury ones made with olives and diced lamb. Two cups and a pot of what smelled like mint tea were crammed into the last available space.

"Not on your life," I said as my stomach let out a low rumble. For someone who'd been living on stale bread and crumbs of goat's cheese for a week, this was heaven. I cut a chunk of the first omelette and devoured it, sighing blissfully. "You can help if you like, though," I said as I swallowed, already lifting another piece of omelette.

"I should hope so." He poured two cups of tea and handed me one. "You'll make yourself sick."

I laughed at that, gulping down the scalding, sweet tea. "Possibly. But keep your hands off that jam."

"Oh." He replaced the pot, crestfallen.

"You like Rua food?" I asked, as a memory came of my poor mother grimacing her way through the Rua banquets she'd been forced to attend. I broke a dumpling apart and blew on it, speaking again around my first mouthful. "I think many Sedorne find it too highly spiced."

"I've lived here since I was fourteen, Zahira." He bit into a pomegranate dumpling. "I grew up on Rua spices. I eat Sedorne from time to time, but Rua is my favourite."

I managed a smile, but found myself wishing that I could divide Rua and Sedorne as neatly as he did. When I had been just Zira, I'd done it without even thinking. Now I couldn't remember what that felt like.

Who are we? No – who am I? Oh, that damned question again…

Something must have shown in my face; Sorin put down his teacup abruptly.

"What's wrong?" he asked.

I couldn't answer his question any more than I could answer my own. I avoided his eyes, nibbling on a pastry. "I don't know. I suppose I'm still worried about my people. What will happen to them now? And what about you? Surely Abheron will find out about this, from gossip or spies."

"No, he won't. I have a small staff here. The building can hold twice as many – which is a good thing at the moment – but it's kept half empty because I'll only have people I know and trust under my roof."

I thought about the sneering gourdin last night and nodded doubtfully.

Sorin raised an eyebrow. "Do you believe anyone you've brought here might betray you?"

"No!" I said indignantly.

"Then allow me the same knowledge of my own people," he said calmly. "You and your refugees are safe; I'll make sure they're looked after." The smile faded from his face and he gazed at me seriously. "I don't think that's what's really bothering you. I don't think that's what has you screaming in your sleep."

I looked away from him again. "I don't know what you mean."

"Yes, you do. You're different. Dear elements, those eyes nearly knocked me off my feet, not to mention your voice. You spoke Sedorne to my guards. When did you learn that? Then there's the fact that you now seem to be noirin to your people when less than three months ago you told me you were a novice. What's happened to you?"

I carefully picked apart layers of pastry, and said nothing.

"It would be a good idea to trust me," he added.

I looked at him in silence. He looked back. I felt something shift inside, an emotion that both parts of me shared.

"Sorin, you're acting as if we … as if we know each other. Really we've only just met. I've already trusted you more than is wise or even safe. I have to decide what to do next and what risks I'm justified in taking."

I stopped, then whispered, "Please. Let me think."

He sighed. "Zahira, you've asked for my help – my shield and my sword arm – and I will lend them to you with all my heart. But if you insist on sending me into battle blindfolded, I become a danger not just to myself, but to you and everyone you're trying to protect. Think on that."

Before I could react, he got up and left the room, gently closing the door behind him.

I sat there, blinking at the space he'd left behind.

A moment later, there was another knock at the door and Mira came in. My head was spinning so fast that I had to look at her for a full minute before I recognized her.

She was wearing new clothes: a fitted red tunic open over a white shirt, which emphasized the bulge of her stomach much more than the baggy robes she'd been wearing when I last saw her. A night of proper rest and some good food seemed to have done her enormous good – she was shining with health. She'd also taken the time to rebraid her frizzy black hair, taming the various wisps which had escaped over the past week and stood out around her face, giving her a frazzled air. She was carrying a pile of clean clothes.

"Hello," she said softly, closing the door behind her. "Lord Mesgao said you were awake. How are you feeling?"

"Why must everyone ask that? I am perfectly well,"

I said irritably, moving the tray and swinging my legs out of bed. "What about you and the baby?"

"We're perfectly well too." She put the pile of clothes down on a chest of drawers and came to stand in front of me.

"Reia, I must say this. You were right to bring us here. Mesgao is a kind man, and this is a good place. I'm sorry we doubted you."

I looked at her in surprise. "You never expressed any doubts, Mira."

"No, but I had them. We all did. We let ourselves listen to those without faith, and we questioned your wisdom. I'm sorry for it. We should have known better than to think you'd lead us into danger."

I laughed shakily, running my fingers through my tangled hair. So they don't believe we're all-knowing and all-seeing after all, I thought. Is that a relief, or a disappointment? And how close did I come to dealing with an open rebellion out there on the road?

"Never mind," I said, a shade too quickly. "We're here now." I looked down at my mud-splattered breeches, happy to have something else to concentrate on. "I really need a bath and something else to wear."

She smiled. "There's a bathhouse downstairs. And the servants – even the Sedorne ones – have been so wonderful. They've lent us all new things until we can make or buy our own."

"Yes. Um. Mira, speaking of the Rua here," I began

cautiously, "just what have you been telling them about me?"

"Nothing, Reia," she said, shocked. "Honestly. Why?"

"Because I've had the head cook, Gita, up here delivering my breakfast. And she couldn't take her eyes off me."

Mira bit her lip. "I can't believe anyone would be so stupid as to gossip about you. We need to keep your identity a secret until you're ready to challenge the king."

I felt my eyes widening at that casual announcement. Holy Mother, they were already planning an uprising? No, no – leave it for the moment. I don't have the energy to deal with it now.

"Er … that aside, though … would you speak to everyone, Mira? Make it clear that gossip could put us all in danger."

"Of course."

"Thank you. Now – a bath."

I got up, pleased to find that my legs were strong enough to hold me again, and picked up the pile of clean clothes.

CHAPTER
ELEVEN

After being guided to the bathhouse, I washed off a week's worth of grime with blissful relief at the luxury of hot – hot! – water. When I emerged into the main courtyard – clean and dressed in fresh clothes – the area was filled with people. They sat on benches under the potted trees, talking, sewing, watching the children play. Quite a lot of them were namoa, but I could see unfamiliar Rua there, and a few Sedorne too. I was glad to see that no fights had broken out yet.

As I skirted the area I realized that my eyes were skimming the crowd for Sorin. He wasn't there. Obviously he had more important things to do than wait for me to arrive. I wondered what he was doing. Was he angry at me for not trusting him? I shook my head as if I could shake the plaguing thoughts out, and went to talk to Dumeetra and Ajit about their new baby, who had a nasty cough.

I spent most of that afternoon talking, trying to make sure everyone was happy and had everything they needed. No one else offered an apology like Mira's, but there was an extra depth in many bows and an extra strength in many handclasps that told their own stories. People seemed content, for the moment, just to relax and recover from their ordeal.

There was a strange holiday sort of mood among some of the temple people and namoa, as if they could hardly believe they had arrived in a place like this – a place of warm clothes and plentiful food and sunlight. As if they had forgotten, in that terrible week, what such a place felt like, and they were only now remembering. They didn't want to ask questions about the future. They were afraid of the answers.

There were conspicuous absences. The people who had left us on the journey and others who had arrived in Mesgao but somehow never made it into the fort. Still others, like Rashna, Kapila and – to my sorrow – Joachim the garden master, hung back, their eyes watchful and wary. They did not trust the Sedorne; they did not trust me. I did not know how to reach them. How could I convince them that everything was well now, that we were all safe, when I didn't really believe it myself? We had found shelter for the moment, but I could hear the storm still raging outside.

Eventually we would have to brave it again.

After the evening meal, I went wandering through the quiet halls of the fort. I didn't really know what I was searching for. It certainly was not Sorin Mesgao. I had not looked for him all day, or wondered at his absence.

But even though I was not looking for him so determinedly, I failed to come across him anywhere. After being asked by the second polite servant whether I was lost, I began to feel aggrieved.

"It's ridiculous," I muttered to myself. "How are we going to discuss my people's future if he's never anywhere to be found?"

I was distracted from my irritation by the echo of a voice calling out. The sound was just beyond the range of my hearing, and teasingly familiar. I could not make out the words. Was it my name? Was someone calling me? Insensibly I found my feet speeding. Who was calling?

When I rounded the corner, there was no one there. Everything was quiet again. There was an open doorway opposite, and the warm glow of firelight spilled through it into the corridor. I hesitated for a moment, then went forward.

The room was large, with two rows of wooden benches, and tapers flickering at regular intervals along the walls. At the head of the room there was a stone pit, very like the one at the centre of the holy shrine –

except that the banked embers glowing happily at its heart were red and gold, natural in origin.

For a moment, I almost thought I had stumbled into some kind of shrine to the Mother. It couldn't be. It was all wrong. Apart from the House of God – built hundreds of years ago – the holy places of the Order were usually little stone huts or cairns out in the open, with scraps of colourful material and God charms tied to the outside by those who visited them. No temple built by the Order would ever have housed the thing that sat on a recessed shelf above the fire pit.

It was a statue of a woman, carved from golden marble and inlaid with amber and garnet. She was seated cross-legged, arms raised to the sky, with her beautiful face lifted. Hair curled around her face like flames. She looked so much like my vision of the Holy Mother that I was riveted, moving closer almost against my will. The Order would never make an image of God like that. I was in a heathen – no, not heathen, just Sedorne – temple.

I looked around. There was no sense of wrongness, no feeling that I was in a forbidden place. I hadn't much idea of the way that Sedorne religion worked – I couldn't remember Mama being very religious – but it seemed to me that if the Sedorne were worshipping the element of fire here, then in a way they were also worshipping the Holy Mother.

I walked to the front of the room and sat down on

one of the wooden benches. It was padded with soft embroidered cushions and very comfortable – definitely not like a Rua temple. I leaned back with a sigh, and watched the glow of the embers.

I must have fallen into a light trance, or perhaps merely dozed off. Whichever, it was some time later when a shadow moved to my left. I started, and looked up to see Sorin in the process of sitting down next to me.

"I've been trying to find you," he said quietly. "What are you doing?"

"I was just watching the embers. I'm sorry – shouldn't I be here?" I kept my voice low too. He returned my gaze evenly and I realized, with some relief, that he wasn't nursing a grudge.

"I can't see any harm in it," he said. "But you do know you are watching the embers of Ioana, goddess of fire, don't you?"

"They're still flames. That means they belong to the Holy Mother."

He smiled. "Typical Rua stubbornness."

Sedorne stubbornness, Dada would have said...

There was a moment of silence. Then I spoke, "Can I ask you a question?"

"Of course."

"How does this, er, this religion work?"

He whistled softly. "That is a question. You know of the four elements?"

"Earth, air, fire and water?"

He nodded. "We believe everything that exists is formed of a combination of those four elements. The world itself was created when they came together. Each of the elements is embodied by one of our gods – Ioana, goddess of fire; Tiberiv, god of air; Ovidiv; god of water; and Iosee, goddess of earth. They are present in all things and all people, and exist all around us."

"Are there temples for the other elements in the fort?"

"No. Each person is born to serve one of the elements – just as every animal and plant owes allegiance to one of them. When a baby is born, our priests consult their holy scrolls, examine the baby and decide to which element the child belongs. I was a child of the flames. I offer respect to all the gods, but I worship Ioana and she watches over me."

"A child of the flames?" *Daughter of the flames*, Surya had called me...

"That's right."

I looked away from him, into the fire pit. God had sent us to this man of all men – this man who truly owed his worship to Her. Perhaps She had even guided me to the temple at this, the right moment. Or perhaps She had lifted Her hand from me in the sacred shrine, and my decisions and actions were my own. What then?

I made a series of rapid judgements. Every instinct I owned told me that Sorin was a good man. I had seen for myself that he had both honour and kindness, and I was sure that he was at odds with Abheron. Despite all that, he was still Sedorne. It was one thing for him to deplore Abheron's viciousness and shelter the raggedy, harmless victims – quite another to harbour the missing heir to the Ruan throne, who could topple his king from power. If I told him who I was, he would have to make a choice between his own honour and loyalty to his people.

I couldn't believe that he would betray us.

I turned back to him, hesitated. "Sorin, you and I ... we barely know each other."

He looked at me calmly, apparently unphased by the change of subject.

"You said that before, Zahira, but you're only talking about time, not knowledge. Some people spend years with each other without ever really knowing one another. Our acquaintance has been very short, but in that short time you have been a friend to me. I may not know everything about you, but I know enough. You have to decide if you know enough about me to trust me with whatever is going through your head."

My mouth was dry. I stared at the glowing embers of the fire pit as if they would prompt me to speak, and began.

"I've lied to you, Sorin. From the very first time we

met. I told you that my name was Zahira, because I wanted to keep you at a distance. And when you made me promise to come to you for help, I lied then too, for I had no intention of taking you at your word. But the Mother has an odd sense of humour. Though I believed I lied, She made what I said into truth. All the things I believed were truth were lies instead. The name I believed was mine, wasn't. The life I thought was mine, wasn't. I was someone else." I shook my head at the tangle of words I'd made. "Do you understand?"

"Not really," he said, and I could hear the frown in his voice.

"My mother and father and my sister and brothers were killed in the fire at the rei's palace. My nanny carried me from the building and through the hills to the House of God – sacrificing her own life to save mine – and gave me to Noirin Surya. I think Surya put me into the sacred flames. I know that the Mother took all my memories of my life before the fire, so that I might not betray myself. From then on – for ten years – I was brought up as the noirin's daughter. She called me her little *agni*, her daughter of the flames. She kept my real identity secret – even from me – in order to keep me safe."

"Safe from what?"

I lifted my eyes away from the fire pit to look at him. "Safe from the ones who killed my family. Safe from Abheron. Sorin, I am the lost reia. I am Zahira Elfenesh."

He went very still. I licked my dry lips and waited. Suddenly he grinned. It was an ironic expression – and he shook his head as if he had been slapped – but it was a smile nonetheless.

"Well, I wasn't prepared for that." There was a moment of silence. Then: "So that's why Gita deigned to leave the kitchen and bring your tray herself. And your people – they really are *your* people. I see now. Thank you for telling me."

As suddenly as it had appeared, the smile was gone. He looked at me gravely. "Now there's something I have to tell you."

"If it's that you're about to call the gourdin in and have me arrested, I'd really rather not hear it," I said quickly.

"No, it's not that – though it's good to see how deeply you trust me. Zahira, when you first told me that the House of God had been attacked, I knew Abheron had to be behind it; and I could think of only one reason why he should, after a decade of ignoring them, suddenly declare war on the namoa. There must have been a spy in Mesgao that day, when you intervened on my behalf. The report of a namoa helping me must have goaded Abheron into action. He's obviously decided the Order is a threat he has to eliminate."

I gaped at him, shattered. "Then … I'm responsible?"

"No," he said sharply. "You might as well say that

I'm responsible for being attacked in the first place. The one responsible is our king. Our king…"

He took a deep breath. "I have to tell you, Zahira. Your mother was Emelia Luminov. And Emelia Luminov's brother was Abheron Luminov. The king."

I felt as if he had poured a bucket of cold water over my head.

"Then he – he's my uncle," I said as the coldness crept down over my whole body. "He killed his own sister? His own niece and nephews?"

Uncle Abheron?

"Yes."

"You accepted such a man as your king?" My voice was high-pitched, dangerously close to hysteria.

Sorin grabbed my shoulder and held me still when I would have leaped up.

"No, I didn't accept him as my king, Zahira. That's why he's trying to kill me."

I breathed deeply, trying to calm down. I didn't know what reaction I'd expected from him, but it wasn't this round of new revelations.

"Then it was his – my uncle's – men that day in the bazaar?"

The king is my uncle. Abheron is my uncle. The king…

"Yes. Zahira, I'm sorry – I know this is a horrible shock. But please, listen to me. If Abheron ever found out about you, he would stop at nothing to kill you.

You are incredibly dangerous to him: you have a true blood claim to the throne of Ruan. The Rua would rally to your cause. The problem is that the Rua alone could never defeat him. Now, Abheron wants me dead, because two generations ago my grandfather was the Sedorne king. He was killed when the Luminov family seized power, and they've been trying to get rid of us all ever since, because we have a true blood claim to the crown of Sedra. Some of the Sedorne would answer my call to rise against Abheron, but not enough to succeed. Do you understand what this means?"

I was only half listening to him, searching Zahira's mind for any trace – some memory, some image – of King Abheron. Surely there had to be something. He was my uncle, Zahira's own blood relative. He killed my family. Mama and Dada and everyone. He killed them all.

I blinked, tried to focus on him. "I don't; I'm sorry."

"It means that if you and I were to unite our claims, we would have a stronger blood right to the throne of Ruan *and* of Sedra, than Abheron. If Rua and Sedorne were to join together against him, there would be a real chance – probably the only chance – of deposing him."

"Sorin…" I said slowly, my attention suddenly snapping back to him. "What are you suggesting?"

"I'm asking you to marry me, Zahira."

I stared, unable even to speak. Then I reached up

and began trying to prise his fingers from my shoulder.

"Let go of me," I said loudly.

"Zahira—"

"No, I'm not listening any more. You're insane."

"You've said that before, and you were proved wrong."

"That was lunch, not marriage!" I almost shrieked. I couldn't believe the pain that was clawing inside me. He only wanted me for his ambition's sake. For power. I had thought there was something … something real. It was all lies, calculated and black.

"Do you honestly expect us to shackle ourselves to another Sedorne tyrant? Do I look that stupid? Why in the name of God would I allow you to use me like that?"

"I don't want to use you, Zahira! Stop and think for a moment. Think about what I've said."

"I have thought! Maybe you're right, that together we could get rid of Abheron – though that's a highly questionable assumption – but to what end? It would be a big sacrifice on my part, and much as I hate that murdering Pig, I don't really want to give up my life to get revenge on him, especially if it would only result in another Sedorne ruler on the throne."

"I don't want another Sedorne ruler on the throne. I want a reia there. You."

"Oh, how charitable—"

He let out a laugh of sheer exasperation. "Would

you let me speak for five seconds, or must we sit like this all night?"

I hissed between my teeth, "Fine, speak."

"Thank you." He cautiously released me. "Zahira, you came here when you had nowhere to go, and gave your people's lives into my hands. You've trusted me with your real name. So I hope you feel for me some part of what I feel for you."

"And what is that?" I wanted to bite my tongue as the question slipped out.

"Admiration. Respect. Trust."

"Oh." I looked down at my hands. Don't be pathetic. Concentrate on what's important.

"If you do feel those things for me," he continued, "then you should be able to listen to me with an open mind. Forget 'Rua' and 'Sedorne'; it shouldn't be that hard – you're half Sedorne yourself. Look at it this way. It would be bringing together two peoples in a common cause, with the best interests of both at heart, in order to remove a bad king from power."

"What would happen then?" I said, my voice hard. "Even if we managed to unite Rua and Sedorne, and our two forces didn't kill each other, and didn't get butchered by Abheron's army, and somehow we managed to get rid of him … what then? I can't be reia if you're king."

"Why not?"

"Because the first thing any reia did would be to rid

Ruan of the Sedorne. You took this land by force, and you occupy it by force. Even you, Sorin, rule lands which do not belong to you – lands stolen from their rightful casador. You don't belong here."

"You're missing a crucial point, Zahira."

"Really? Do tell," I said with weary sarcasm.

"*You can't get rid of us.* We've been here for a decade and we've sunk our roots too deep. The only way to get every Sedorne out of Ruan would be to rip the land apart with bloody civil war. We'd all end up killing each other – and for what? This nation is big enough for us all to share."

"That's not the point."

"Then what is?"

I leaned forward, my voice trembling with intensity. "My people deserve freedom from servitude. From fear. They deserve their homes and their lives as they were before the invasion. They deserve happiness."

He spoke seriously. "There's no reason they can't have that, if we work together."

I shook my head in disbelief. "And your allies would be willing to change? To give up their lands and their riches to the Rua they've been grinding under their feet for ten years?"

"What about the Rua casadors who've allied themselves with Abheron?"

"What about them?" I almost wailed.

"What would you do to them if you became reia?"

"I'd strip them of lands and titles and execute or exile them," I said flatly.

"Then give *their* lands to the Sedorne who earn them by working with us against Abheron. Let the lands held by the Sedorne who stand with Abheron against us go back to their original Rua owners once they've been exiled," he said with seemingly boundless confidence. "That's if those Rua owners are still in the country. Many fled and left their people to their fate. I know several men – good men – who are lord over lands that have no rightful casador. Unless you'd let those cowards return and take up their titles again?"

"I wouldn't, no. But—"

"What I propose is a union of equals, Zahira. You and I would rule together, share power equally. We would repeal Abheron's laws, stop the persecution of the Rua and begin anew. No more force or intimidation. A second chance for Ruan. For Sedorne and Rua to live as one people."

I put my head down in my hands, cradling my forehead as if I thought I could quieten its mad buzzing with the touch of my fingers. He makes it sound so real, so right. He makes it sound easy, but it isn't. I can't believe I'm considering this. But … I am…

If what he was proposing actually worked, the dreams we had all cherished all our lives would come true. There would be a reia on the throne again, and peace, safety. Surya would have been right. But how could I possibly marry him?

"What about you and me?" I found myself asking, my voice barely above a whisper.

There was a moment's silence.

"Look at me." His voice sounded a fraction deeper than normal.

I peeked between my fingers. His face was utterly serious as he spoke.

"We have respect and affection between us, Zahira. We can be friends, which is more than many a wedded couple are. In time … perhaps there will be more."

"But – if this is to work – it must be *real*. We must have heirs…" My voice went horribly high on the last word, and I cringed.

"Yes." He tilted his head, trying to make out my expression behind my hands. "Zahira?"

"You said there were different types of trust," I whispered.

"I did. That would be an important one."

Slowly, I forced my hands away from my face and sat up to look at him properly. "You think … you know me?" I asked, the words quavering.

"Yes. I do." He held out his hand. I took it, and held on hard. "Do you know me?"

"I think … I think I do," I said.

We sat for a moment, hanging on to each other's fingers. I felt warmth spreading through me, replacing the terrible chill that had seized me earlier. We could

do this. We could really do it. We could make everything worth it, all the pain and the loss. We could
make a dream real.

I said, "All right. I'll marry you."

CHAPTER
TWELVE

Of course, Mira and Deo – as my unofficial second in command – had to be told first. I sat them down in Sorin's bright study, with jasmine tea and sticky pastries – the pastries were Sorin's idea – and I explained, very seriously, what we had decided. Sorin, at my request, made himself busy elsewhere.

With shaking hands and desperate enthusiasm I poured out all my reasons, all my ideas. Sorin and I had sat up through the night in the temple, discussing our plans in minute detail, and I explained it all. How a united Rua and Sedorne force had the only true chance of defeating Abheron. How we would redistribute wealth and lands fairly. How we intended to draw up a new charter of equal rights and fairness.

When I finished, there was a minute of shocked

stillness. Then Mira got up from her seat and came to kneel at my feet, clutching at my hands.

"I don't understand." Her eyes were filled with tears, and she brushed them away impatiently to hold my fingers again. "You don't have to do this. No one could ask it, Zira – Zahira. Reia. There are other ways!"

I looked at Deo. He said, firmly, "Lord Mesgao has been good to us; he has our thanks for that. But he's not one of us, Zahira. To ask us now to entrust our people, our nation – you – to a stranger... No. This isn't right."

"Haven't you heard a word I've said? This is our chance, Deo. Mira, you said yourself you trusted Sorin. Can't you see this is the only way?"

"No!" Deo's voice burst out of him and his hand thudded down on the arm of his chair hard enough to make a cloud of dust rise from the upholstery. "He's Sedorne! He's not one of us!"

I felt something cold and horrible stir inside me. I pushed Mira's hands away. "Deo ... I'm not one of you either."

Mira choked on a sob. Without another word Deo rose and helped her to her feet, and together they left the room. I sat where they had left me, frozen with anguish. I could not believe what had just happened.

To them, Sorin was Sedorne, and that was that. Even after what he had done for us, there was no possible meeting point. All my bright, warm confidence had gone. I had said all I could. They had listened, but not understood. For the first time in my life, my gift had failed me. My dearest friends thought I had lost my mind. I agreed with them almost. It was madness. Complete insanity. The fact that I had told a Sedorne – a lord – who we were was bad enough. To wish to marry him? After knowing him for such a brief time? It was inconceivable. Yet I had agreed to it.

Against all reason, I believed in it.

Sorin's words had lit a fire inside Zira and Zahira. From the moment I had left the House of God, I had been desperately seeking answers. Struggling each day, trying to understand why I had been saved, what I was supposed to do. Now I thought I knew. This was the reason. This was my purpose. Something to fight for; something to believe in; something real, and wonderful. Perhaps, with my fractured mind and mixed-up memories, I was the last person anyone would imagine to save Ruan. Perhaps I would never really know how to accept that I was the reia. Yet I believed what Sorin spoke of, could be.

The fire inside me was hope. I had to keep it alive. But how could I do that if I couldn't convince anyone – not even my friends – to help?

After a while I left the room and wandered down into the main courtyard. The area was more or less deserted. A few people moved in the shadows under the arches, and I could hear voices from the mezzanine above my head, but no one I recognized. I didn't want to see anyone at the moment, especially not Sorin.

I removed the rather fancy embroidered jacket I was wearing and rolled up the sleeves of the linen shirt. I took off the soft leather boots and fine stockings, and let my toes wriggle on the smooth marble flagstones. Then I eased myself into a balanced stance, and began to go through a series of warming-up exercises, stretching the neglected muscles in my arms, back, shoulders and legs. I had had no interest in practice during our journey – and Deo had left me be for the first time in my life – but as my body fell back into the familiar rhythms of movement I realized how much I had missed it.

With my right leg I began a sequence of side kicks, low, higher, highest, and was dismayed at the stiff pull of the ligaments. I swapped sides and went through the drill again with my left leg. Next came side punches, fist and palm, both sides. Then spinning kicks. Then punches. When my body was warm and glowing from the exercise, I started practising flips and jumps, throwing myself backwards, sideways, spinning and cartwheeling. Blood surged through my veins like thunder; sweat ran along my arms and back and legs and broke out on my face. I could feel my lips stretching into a fierce grin. I executed a perfect triple backflip and landed with my arms spread and my face turned up to the sky.

The grin slid off my face. Deo stood in the darkness of the arch opposite me, arms folded.

"I've let you get overconfident, Reia," he said, voice flat and expressionless. "It's time to show you how far you have to go."

"What?" I let out a ragged sigh. "Deo—"

"Don't talk. Fight." He erupted out of the shadows, his right foot lashing towards my face. I dodged sideways and deflected his fist with my forearm as it flashed out.

"I don't want to fight, Deo!" I panted.

He responded with a roundhouse kick that caught my side like a hammer. I lost all my breath with a whimper and stumbled to my knees, arms falling from their defensive positions to clutch at the injury.

Deo stepped back. "Is that the best you've got, Your Highness?"

I forced my hands away from the throbbing bruise, and rose to my feet. We stared at each other for a moment.

"Very well." I barely recognized my own voice. It was like a razor. "We'll fight."

I went forward and he came to meet me.

Deflecting another punch, I seized his extended forearm, turned my hip into his body as I yanked his elbow past my collarbone, and threw him over my shoulder. He landed hard, rolled and came up fast but slightly off balance. I twisted sideways, curling my left leg up into my chest and lashing out with a powerful kick to his stomach.

He dodged back, but the blow landed with enough force to send his breath huffing out. He turned the backward movement into a spin and went at me with another roundhouse. I slid underneath it and went down, sweeping out my own leg to hit the back of his knee and send him crashing back again. I heard something crack sharply as he fell. I refused to wince. This wasn't the soft dirt of the training ring, but he had chosen the battleground and he had started the fight. I got up and waited.

Deo rolled over with a muffled groan, but didn't get up. His hands had gone to the back of his head and his eyes were closed, white teeth biting down on his lower lip.

"Deo?" My hot blood chilled. What had cracked in that fall? "Deo? What is it?" I kneeled down next to him and put out my hand.

His eyes flicked open. I pulled back a second too late. He grabbed my wrist, jerked me sideways and rolled until he was kneeling on my chest, elbow lodged against my throat.

"You are not invulnerable," he ground out, voice barely above a whisper. "You are not always right. You have a soft, stupid heart and it will trip you up every time. Do you understand?"

I couldn't move my head to nod. I couldn't even breathe. I blinked, and he eased his elbow away, shifting until he kneeled over me instead of on me.

"You cheated," I said hoarsely, coughing.

"Your enemies will cheat, Reia. They'll break any promise, chance any deception, to bring you down. If you don't learn that, you will be dead."

I sat up cautiously, feeling all the bruises, scrapes and bumps I had gained clamouring for my attention. "But that's why I need you."

He bowed his head. "Reia."

"No, Deo!" I leaned forward and grabbed his shoulder. "I don't need you to be my subject; I need you to be my friend. Please trust me. Please help me. Please be my friend again."

I heard him sigh. Then his big, brawny arms were around me, squeezing hard enough to crack a rib. "All right, girl. I'll go along with you and your crazy scheme. God knows where we're going, but I'll go along with you. To the end."

I hugged him back. "Thank you."

"And no more neglecting your practice. That sideways kick was pathetic."

I snorted and let my head fall down on his shoulder. "Yes, namoa."

"That's my girl."

I stood at the narrow window and looked down into the courtyard below. In the gathering darkness people were still laughing and dancing, if rather unsteadily after all the wine and ale they'd consumed. Someone was singing a Rua wedding song, not solemnly and beautifully as it had been sung earlier today, but bawdily, stumbling over half the words. I realized that it had to be a Sedorne singing it – the flat, slurred pronunciation could not possibly belong to a Rua. I leaned forward to try to see who it was, but the shadows and the slenderness of the window opening defeated me.

Deo and Mira had participated in the ceremony at my request. It couldn't have taken place without two Rua witnesses to sing the appropriate songs, and I would have been hard pressed to find anyone else to agree. But I had seen Mira's eyes begging me to reconsider until the very last moment, and Deo's unhappy resignation. The temple people and other namoa did not know what to think. Some of them quite clearly believed I was being forced into the marriage, and had to be persuaded not to object forcibly. Others just looked lost and miserable. The boisterous enthusiasm of Sorin's people hadn't helped.

The first part of the plan Sorin and I had agreed to was complete. I knew we would have to undertake separate Sedorne and Rua wedding ceremonies in order for the marriage to be recognized by everyone, and since Sedorne weddings were horribly elaborate and took almost a whole day, we had agreed to have the Rua wedding as soon as possible, for everyone in the fort to celebrate and enjoy. Ha. The impressive Sedorne ritual was being saved for later, when all our potential allies were here to be impressed.

Looking down into the courtyard again, I just hoped the people below remembered that the reason for this celebration had to be kept secret. Since I had no idea if there was still a spy in Mesgao town, the truth had to be kept within the walls of the fort for as long as possible, until we could arrange for everyone we needed to convince – Rua resistance and Sedorne lords – to arrive here and begin negotiating.

I leaned my head wearily against the rough, pale stone of the wall, unable to distract myself any longer.

I was married.

Every trace of the certainty and confidence I had felt when I ordered this wedding was gone. It had evaporated when the gaggle of laughing women – made up of both Rua and Sedorne – had surrounded me downstairs and dragged me into this room. Sorin's room. When they had produced the lacy white nightgown they expected me to wear. The moment, the very instant, I had seen one of them sprinkling flower petals on the bed.

Sorin's bed. My bed. Our bed.

Dear God, what had I thought I was doing? He was Sedorne.

What have I done?

The nightgown lay on the edge of the bed, untouched. I was still fully clothed in the trousers and over-robe I had worn for the wedding, the silky green fabric embroidered at hems and neckline with a pattern of peacock feathers. The emerald-encrusted tortoiseshell combs Sorin had given me for a wedding gift still gripped my hair. Zira wasn't lacy nightclothes and jewelled combs. And Zahira had never even kissed a boy.

I tried to remember how I had felt during the ceremony. A surge of happiness had rushed into me as Sorin and I, led by Deo and Mira, had joined our voices in the wedding song. I'd chosen my favourite of all the songs, a complicated two-part harmony with several verses, only realizing when it was too late that it would be incredibly difficult for Sorin to learn in a day.

He hadn't stumbled over a single word, a single note. Our voices had soared together as Mira and Deo had fallen quiet. It had felt right then. I thought I knew what I was doing.

Oh God. I was a fool. I have no idea what I'm doing.

I heard the door open, and forced myself to turn.

The firelight shied from the doorway; he was no more than a shadow. A tiny glint of light dared reflect from his eyes, another from the strand of hair that had fallen over his forehead, but that was all. I couldn't see his face. Something icy brushed along my back, raising the tiny hairs.

Calm down. Stop this. Sorin had shown me kindness and respect. He was a good man. He was a friend. It was ridiculous to fear my friend. Wasn't it? Suddenly it came to me that he *wasn't* my friend any more. He would never be my friend again. He was my husband now. This man, this foreigner, this pale-haired stranger. He was my husband.

And I was afraid of him.

He let the door shut behind him and took a step forward. My body jerked as if he struck me. I only just managed to keep myself from backing away.

He froze mid step. "Don't!" he said, his voice harsh.

I stiffened, feeling every muscle bunch and knot as I stared at the wall behind him. I couldn't bear to meet his eyes. My fingers curled into fists at my sides.

"Don't. Please," he said more softly, coming towards me again.

I couldn't answer him. I couldn't move at all, not even when his hands reached out to draw me against him, and his arms closed around me.

"Don't be afraid of me, Zahira. Please don't be afraid of me," he whispered.

I can't help it! I wanted to wail the words, but pressed my lips together desperately. No. I won't humiliate myself.

For long moments I stood rigid as Sorin held me. His grip did not loosen, and he said nothing. I inhaled his clean, familiar smell. He was warm, making my cold, tense muscles unclench, one by one. Gradually I began to relax, and allowed myself to lean against him.

"I'm sorry," I mumbled, at length. "I... I didn't know you."

"It's all right," he said, his voice rumbling against my ear.

I heard the relief in his voice, and realized that he had been afraid too – perhaps of this very reaction from me, and how he would deal with it. That comforted me.

"This is no good, is it?" he said finally.

"What?" I stiffened, pushing back from him so that I could see his face.

He let go of me reluctantly. "I've rushed you. I did it on purpose. I was so sure, and I wanted you to be sure too. But for all my fine words about the difference between time and knowledge, we haven't had the chance to get used to each other yet. You haven't had the chance to get used to me."

I slumped back down into the window embrasure, the sudden rush of relief making me feel weak and shaky. "Are you – do you – you don't mind if we wait?"

"All I know is, I don't want you to look at me like that ever again. I want ... this part ... to be something good, for both of us. We're going to be around each other a lot. For the rest of our lives. We have time."

"Thank you." I leaned my head against the stone and smiled at him. It was a good smile. I didn't want him to guess – didn't even want to admit to myself – that amid the relief there had been a funny squeezing sensation in my stomach. A feeling like … disappointment.

Holy Mother, act like a grown-up. This is what you wanted. He's being wonderful. Just stop it.

Stop it!

Then he leaned forward, put his hands on my shoulders and kissed me. His lips were warm and soft, parting mine gently, and I sank into him, grabbing hold of the front of his tunic to stop myself sliding right out of the window embrasure onto the floor. When he drew back I had to draw in several deep breaths before I could speak.

"What was that for?" I managed

"All part of getting to know you." He carefully uncurled my fingers from his tunic and raised them to his lips. "I intend to get to know you very well, Zahira."

He let go of my hands, turned, and walked away, closing the door softly behind him. Then I did slide out of the window onto the floor. I sat with my head against my knees, listening to my heart bumping. I couldn't stop it.

I'd fallen in love with him…

CHAPTER THIRTEEN

Two weeks later, I woke abruptly from a dream – a terrible dream – about Surya. The bedroom was close and still, darkness lying against my skin as clammily as the sheets twisted around my legs. I made a tiny noise of misery as I tried to force the images of death from my mind. I was panting, covered in sweat. Sickness rolled greasily in my gut.

Cautiously I pulled myself up into a sitting position. The room shifted dizzily around me as I moved – then my stomach heaved and I only just had time to drag the pot from under the bed before I vomited messily.

When the heaving stopped I was slumped over the side of the mattress, shuddering, sweat trickling along my hairline, disgusted with myself. I pulled the sleeping tunic over my head and wiped my mouth on it – it made little difference, as the cloth was already splattered – then screwed it up and threw it away from me as I slithered down onto the cold floor. Groggy as I was, I now realized that this sickness could not be the result of a nightmare, however horrible. I was ill. I hated being ill.

I crawled on hands and knees to the chest at the end of the bed to pull out a pair of half-length cotton trousers and a fresh tunic. Once I had fumbled them on, I climbed up the nearest bedpost like a puny vine and then, desperate to get away from the vile smells of sweat and sick, staggered across the room to the door.

A sharp intake of breath made me jump as I stepped out onto the covered mezzanine overlooking the courtyard. I squinted through the darkness to see one of Sorin's gourdin leaning idly on the mezzanine rail, his helmet under his arm. He was probably supposed to be patrolling the area outside my and Sorin's adjoining rooms. He certainly stood to attention very quickly and saluted me snappily. I straightened up, hoping the darkness would hide my damp, pasty face from him, as it hid his expression from me.

"Alrik, is it?" I croaked.

"Yes, my lady. Is everything all right?"

"I just need some fresh air. Don't mind me." I walked carefully away. I could feel his gaze on my back, and concentrated stubbornly on placing one foot before the other, until I rounded the corner out of his sight. Then I let myself lean against the rail as he had done, breathing slowly, deeply, trying to suppress the bubbling that wanted to rise up in my throat. Holy Mother, I hate being sick.

Gradually the cool, fresh night air began to work on me, and the shivering and nausea began to subside a little. I could smell night-flowering jasmine from the courtyard below, and the warm straw and manure scent of the stables. My eyes had adjusted to the darkness now, and I absently traced the lines of wall, roof and paving that were not quite familiar to me yet.

In a minute I would go back to bed. Or maybe I would go next door and wake Sorin up. The least he could do was offer me his company in my hour of need. And perhaps a cup of tea... I smiled as I imagined his indignation at being disturbed in the middle of the night and sent off for tea. Yes, I would definitely go back in a minute.

A sharp cry – a sound of fear or pain, hastily choked off – jerked me upright. The ground seemed to shift under my feet and I caught my balance against the wall. The voice had come from my left, beyond the curve of the mezzanine. The gourdin?

I opened my mouth – and hesitated as instinct flared like a blue flame, warning me against calling out. Something was wrong. My memory darted to the night Surya died. Zira had felt this way then. Oh God ... not again.

I swallowed hard as I began to move back along the mezzanine, shoulder blades pressed to the wall, ears straining against the quiet. I couldn't see the gourdin as I rounded the corner. Had he moved on?

My foot hit something hard. I looked down.

It was Alrik's arm. He was slumped face down on the floor. I dropped to my knees beside him, sickness lurching through me again as the hot metallic stench of blood filled my nostrils. I slid my arms under his torso and heaved him over.

Holy Mother of Flame...

I had a stomach-clenching flashback to Surya and a strangled sob forced itself up out of my lips. I knew Alrik was dead before I saw the wound gaping wetly above his mail surcoat. His throat had been cut. His eyes glinted, opaque, as his head slipped off my forearm.

My breath sawed painfully in my throat as I eased him down and clawed my way back up the wall. I left dark, wet handprints on the white plaster. I was right next to Sorin's bedroom door. It was open.

Sorin. Sorin will know what to do... Blindly I stumbled through the entrance – and froze.

I took in every detail in an instant. Muddled shadows and moonlight resolved into lumped-up pillows and blankets; the silky swathe of Sorin's hair spread over his back; the dark figure leaning over the bed, raising the weapon in a practised killing arc; the knife blade flashing almost liquid through the darkness.

I screamed.

The noise shrilled through the deadly quiet like a stone shattering glass. The dark figure jerked round in shock, pulled his arm back and threw the knife at me.

I ducked just barely in time. The blade buried itself in the wall above my head with a *thunk*. I screamed again, so loudly this time that my throat burned. On the bed, Sorin didn't stir.

Oh God – oh, dear God, please let him be all right...

The dark figure came at me. I ran.

The quick, light footsteps were terrifyingly close as I pounded down the mezzanine, rounded the corner and flung myself onto the stairs to the north tower. The gourdin kept watch in the tower. Have to get away from Sorin... Gasping and sobbing for breath, the world heaving around me, I scrabbled up the stairs, legs like weights that wanted to pull me back into the murderer's grasp.

I skidded into the tower room a couple of steps ahead of my pursuer – and saw with an absurd sinking of shock that it was in darkness. Empty.

I had made a mistake.

There was only a chair and a bare splintery wooden table beneath one of the high windows. Nothing I could use to defend myself. Weak as a newborn calf, no weapons, nowhere to run – *trapped*. I spun in a mad circle of confusion and caught sight of the shuttered windows again. I threw myself at one, shoving the wooden shutter back. A blast of cold air hit me in the face. Oh, please, *please*...

There was a rush of movement behind me. I swung round, grabbing the flimsy table and raising it like a shield. I only saw a shadow, marked by a long line of shining, razor-sharp metal. Then the dark figure smashed into the table shield hard enough to thrust me into the wall. I pushed back, shoving the table forward as hard as I could. The attacker reeled away with a harsh huff of breath, the knife skittering to the floor.

I swung the table again, with all my strength. My assailant gave an agonized grunt as the edge caught him square in the stomach. He lost his balance and hit the opposite wall. The table collapsed into splintery fragments in my hands. I dropped the pieces and turned to scramble onto the chair, feeling the ancient wood groan warningly as I caught the windowsill. Panting with effort I heaved up so that I hung half in, half out of the window, peering down. I couldn't make it... My arm muscles shuddered and I felt the chair begin to give way, buckling underfoot. No more time. Teeth gritted, I managed to pull myself up to crouch in the opening.

I looked back for a second. The shadowy attacker was gathering himself beneath my precarious perch, the dim light glittering from his wicked blade as he drew it back to throw. I was a sitting target here. Only one way out. Closing my eyes on a prayer to the Mother that my memory of the outside of the tower was right – that I hadn't made another mistake – I twisted up until my legs were outside the window and dropped.

The night wind pushed me back and I found myself plastered against the tower wall, shivering and weak with relief, my feet planted firmly on a narrow stone ledge. I sucked in a deep breath, thanking God for giving me an accurate memory this time. The fort was spread out beneath me in a muddle of rooftops and shadowy drops. I couldn't see anyone moving. Surely my screams had woken someone!

"Help!" I shouted. The wind ripped my voice into feeble shreds and scattered them.

I looked up. The window was about a foot above my head. There was no sign of the murderer at it. I thought he was at least a few inches shorter than me – and he didn't have the chair. How long would it take him to get out? What would I do when he did?

I felt myself sway helplessly for an endless second. Then I was pressed against the stone again, fingers clutching convulsively at the rough blocks. I blinked away tears from the stinging wind and looked up at the window. Still no sign of my pursuer.

Sweat slid coldly down my face as I began edging round the side of the tower. If I could get down onto the curtain wall, then maybe I could make it onto the mezzanine roof below. God only knew what I would do then – but at least it was slightly closer to the ground. I came to the outer corner of the tower and carefully craned my head to look down. About twelve feet below me the curtain wall came to a corner as well, the wall at its thickest. If I dropped here … maybe I'd land all right.

And maybe I wouldn't.

Another wave of sick dizziness washed over me and I snapped my head back against the wall with a thud, sweat prickling all over my body as I gasped for air. I'd never been afraid of heights before, but sacred flames, I didn't think I could do this. If only my head would clear…

The wind's howl quietened for a second, and I heard a stealthy scraping noise to my right. My eyes snapped open. The murderer was halfway out of the window, dangling by his fingers as he felt for the ledge with one foot. Looking up in the moonlight, I could see that his face was covered by a wrapping of dark fabric, even concealing his hair. His eyes alone were revealed. They were like death – completely without mercy.

I didn't have to worry about Sorin, I realized sickly. It's me he's really after, and he's not giving up until I'm as dead as Alrik.

I gulped down a mouthful of bile, straightened my body, inched forward – and let myself fall.

I landed on the curtain wall with a bruising impact

on my hip and shoulder and rolled back from the edge, shredding the skin of my palms as I clutched for a hold. The wind screamed through my hair and in my ears, deafening me for a moment before dying down again. I groaned with pain, terrified that if I tried to stand the dizziness would fell me as easily as the murderer's knife.

I heard the murderer land more gracefully behind me and managed to get onto my back in time to see him straighten up. No choice now. I bent forward and, carefully, carefully, got to my feet, feeling myself wobble as I spread my arms for balance. How would the killer react if I vomited at his feet?

"Who are you?" I screamed. "Why are you doing this?" I didn't dare move.

The shadowy figure stepped cautiously forward, spreading his arms too. He didn't have illness as an excuse – he was less confident at heights than I was. His hands were empty. Had he lost the knife scrambling out of the window?

"Come on then!" I taunted breathlessly. "Are you too frightened, without your knife? Coward! Murderer!"

I didn't expect an answer – but neither did I expect him to drop his arms and rush at me.

We collided with mutual grunts of pain, teetering on the edge above the mezzanine as I grappled, feet sliding, hands scrabbling for purchase, punching, tearing, kicking at each other, snarling and yelping like animals.

I jabbed at his shoulder with a disturbingly weak elbow, taking a punch to the face that made my teeth ache. I wavered back and then latched on to his wrist, sinking my teeth into the forearm to taste blood. He seized a handful of my hair, yanking it out by the roots as he tried to pull me off, his other hand smashing down on my neck, making my left side go numb. I kicked out and felt the crunch as my heel connected with his ankle.

Then we were plummeting from the wall together, our screams echoing into one voice.

In mid fall I realized: I know that voice.

We hit the steep roof in an explosion of shattering terracotta. The roof buckled under our weight and I rolled sideways, flailing fingers grasping hold of a section of coping at the top. I heaved myself across to lie on an unbroken section of the roof as my attacker slid down with the tiles below me. The dark figure grappled with the cascading debris and then wrapped arms around a wooden beam, partially exposed by the lost tiles. For a moment we both hung on, panting, bleeding and exhausted, only feet apart.

I stared down at the murderer. "Kapila?"

Her head snapped up. The concealing cloth had been ripped free and the sight of her familiar face – scratched, bruised, grey with weariness as it had been on our trek through the mountains here – made my heart contract as if God had reached in and crushed it.

"Yes." She laughed bitterly. "Are you pretending to

be surprised? My father is rotting by the wayside because of you!"

"Kapila, I…" I shook my head miserably, closing my eyes against her accusing face. "I did what I thought was best. The only thing I could do. I didn't – I never meant…"

I heard her grunts of effort as she began pulling herself up along the beam towards me.

"We've lost everything! Our home, our lives. Everything that was good. Esha's baby – I can still hear Esha screaming. And poor little Padma."

Shaken and sick, unable to move, I heard her scrabble across the section of tiles next to me, and her grunt of relief as she grabbed the coping above it. We would be lying nose to nose – if I had the courage to face her. I squeezed my eyes shut more tightly.

"Why did you bring us here? Why? We could have stayed where we were safe, where we belonged. We could have rebuilt and carried on. But no, you had to prove you were the great leader. You sacrificed our own people to do it! Do you think of that when you get into bed with that filthy Sedorne husband of yours? Do you?"

"You were my friend once," I said weakly. My fingers, numb with hanging on to the stone, spasmed and twitched. She's going to kill me, I realized weakly. I don't know how to stop her…

"I was Zira's friend," she spat. "Zira died in the

House of God. Who asked you to be our reia? Who are you?"

A fleck of Kapila's spittle hit my cheek. I flinched.

I felt dizzy again – a different kind of dizziness this time. Something was changing inside me. Distantly I heard Kapila ranting bitterly about her plan. How she had drugged the food Sorin and I ate tonight so that we would sleep soundly through our own murders – which would have worked if my body hadn't reacted so strongly to the drug. How she had sneaked up on the unprepared guard on the mezzanine to kill him. But my attention was no longer with her.

Something … something was coming…

There was an echo of a voice – a terrible, fiery voice that burned my ears, and made my eyes sting with joy – calling out the question that had haunted me.

Who are you, Zira? Who are you? Who are you Zahira? Answer!

Me. Not Zira or Zahira. Just *me*.

Deep inside, I felt an almost physical shift. It was as if all my bones had been slightly dislocated, and they had suddenly snapped into place. There was a flare of glowing blue light behind my eyes, a sense of endless joy, and of love.

Then the feeling was gone, and I was alone.

I sucked in a deep breath, tightening my grip on the stone and wedging my foot into a gap in the tiles so that I couldn't fall. The dizziness eased away and I opened my eyes to look Kapila full in the face.

"Stop it," I said sharply, cutting her off. "Stop lying."

She gasped in shock. "Lying?"

"Yes. You are lying, to me and yourself. Who asked me to be your reia? *You*, Kapila. All of you. You followed me. You *made* me your reia."

"We were frightened and desperate, but that doesn't make it right! Those graves by the roadside—"

"Are the price," I cut her off again. "You wanted *me* to make the decisions for you – I did. You wanted *me* to keep you safe – I did. You wanted to believe in *me* – I let you. But you have to pay for what you want, Kapila, and you can't change your mind now."

She let go of the coping and flung herself on top of me with a scream of rage. I felt the tiles beneath us start to crack as her hands went around my neck. I choked and squirmed, my hands tightening desperately on the post stone as I pulled my free leg up and kicked hard into her chest.

Her hold on my neck broke and she fell away from me, sliding down in another avalanche of tiles. She rolled once, screamed, and caught at the very edge of the roof, dangling helplessly. I looked down into her face, into her eyes, burning like black coals with desperation and terror. She didn't cry out for help. She hung on, waiting.

Kapila had been my friend. Before everything shattered, before grief and anger warped her into a killer, she had been a good woman. She had gone mad, and maybe that was my fault. If I let her die without even trying to save her, what would that make me?

The reia.

My people needed me to survive.

I watched as Kapila kicked and struggled madly to get back onto the roof. As she gasped and swore and fought to keep her hold. As her fingers began to slip. And, finally, as her grip failed, and she fell away into the darkness.

Then I just held on and waited for someone to find me.

CHAPTER FOURTEEN

Lord Tiede found the king in his private armoury. The room had a towering ceiling that seemed to amplify noise tenfold – he believed the old rei had used it as a music room or something, before the invasion – and the violent ringing of swords made him flinch as he stepped through the doorway. He recognized the king's opponent as the captain of the palace gourdin unit, and felt a small sting of pity for the man. Still, one of the junior palace surgeons stood to attention in the opposite corner of the room, so the captain would receive excellent care.

Tiede hoped there wouldn't be too much blood.

He averted his eyes from the almost hypnotic slide and slash of light on the long blades, and examined his king more closely. Lank reddish-gold hair had escaped from a simple braid to curl around his face, which was damp with exertion. Sweat plastered the thin lawn shirt to his well muscled body. That was good. If he was exhausted then he might be less excitable…

Tiede flinched again at a particularly loud scream of metal, but schooled himself to calmness. Perhaps this little scene was a blessing in disguise. The languid manner and elegantly tailored wardrobe made it easy to forget that the king was a great warrior. It was best not to forget things about the king. Tiede glanced at the king's right hand holding the sword, and then at the heavy duelling gauntlet on his left hand. He shuddered, and looked away.

A few moments later, Tiede heard a shout of pain. He looked up to see the captain crumple to the ground, a crimson stain spreading across his shoulder. The surgeon rushed forward immediately and covered up the wound with a large pad of folded cloth. Tiede sighed with relief. He really hated blood.

"Good match, Captain Marin. Excellent." King Abheron saluted the man on the floor with his sword, carefully wiped the blood from the blade, and then turned to place it in one of the racks on the wall.

"Ah, Tiede." He raised an eyebrow as he caught sight of him. "I hope you bring me good news?"

"Ahem." Tiede clasped his hands together. "Perhaps it might be better to discuss it in private?"

The king glanced back at the collapsed captain and

the surgeon. "I think they're somewhat busy to eavesdrop, Tiede. But by all means…"

He waved Tiede ahead of him into his sitting room and summoned a blank-faced Rua serving girl. "Send another surgeon into the armoury," he ordered. "With a stretcher. Then bring me some wine." The girl disappeared noiselessly.

The king sat down in one of the armchairs, rubbing his face with a soft towel. "Proceed," he said.

Lord Tiede didn't wait to be invited to sit – he knew that wouldn't happen. Instead he took up a position before his king and cleared his throat.

"I have had the reports back from the gourdin who carried out your orders on the House of God, Your Highness. I am afraid it did not go as expected."

"I'd gathered that from your less than celebratory expression," Abheron said, flinging the soaked towel aside.

Tiede managed to restrain his panicky desire to pace. "The gourdin penetrated the outer wall of the House through trickery, killing two gatekeepers and a number of other holy people. However, there was also an inner wall, which the namoa barricaded. When, after some minutes, the gourdin managed to break through, the temple was, most unfortunately, empty."

The king regarded Tiede in silence. "Empty?"

"They found one woman. Whom they also killed," he added hurriedly. "They believe the holy people had some hidden exit which they used to escape."

"Didn't the men consider surrounding the complex before attacking it?" the king asked in tones of mild interest.

"It is apparently not possible to do this, due to the mountainous terrain. The men destroyed both the outer and inner walls and as much of the main building as they could, leaving it uninhabitable. The namoa will not be able to return there."

The king heaved a sigh. "Then where will they go, Tiede? Where *did* they go?"

"I ... don't know, Your Highness."

"Surely it is not possible for several hundred people to simply wander about my countryside without anyone noticing? Surely the regular patrols picked up some trace of them?"

"There was nothing, Your Highness. Gourdin in the area did report a slight increase in the number of refugees travelling along the Mayanti road – but none of them were wearing those funny robes or had tattoos with the correct symbols to be holy people."

"Not all namoa are tattooed, Tiede. And I imagine they'd have taken some pains to disguise themselves." Abheron sighed. Suddenly he straightened, sitting forward in his seat. "The Mayanti road? The road to Mesgao?"

"Er, yes, I believe that road does lead to Mesgao."

"So." Abheron sat back slowly. "It is entirely

possible that rather than shatter the connection between the Order and Sorin, we have driven them into each other's arms. The move was badly played, Lord Tiede."

The king's pale eyes fixed on him. It took every nerve in Tiede's body not to back away. He watched as the king began plucking at the fingers of the leather gauntlet on his left hand.

"Something's coming, Tiede," Abheron said softly, unblinking. "I can feel it."

Tiede didn't even dare nod. He stood absolutely still, and prayed to Ovidiv that something – anything – would distract the king before ... before...

There was a tiny noise at the door. It was the Rua girl, with the wine. Tiede watched her desperately as she set the silver tray down on the table at Abheron's elbow, curtsied, and then crept from the room again. As she closed the door behind her, Abheron blinked. The intensity of his gaze dimmed, and he pulled the gauntlet back into place before raising a hand to rub his forehead.

"You have, on occasion, been a useful spymaster, Tiede. I think it may be time for you to retire, and spend more time with your grandchildren. I can find someone else to handle these delicate matters for me."

"Yes – yes, Your Highness. I am most grateful," he stuttered, blinking frantically as tears of relief prickled behind his eyelids.

"But first I must give you a chance to redeem yourself, mustn't I?" The king reached out and poured himself a glass of wine. "I wouldn't want your failures to play on your conscience, Tiede. That wouldn't be fair."

Tiede's heart sank. "Your Highness is very kind," he said, trying to keep the bitterness from his voice.

King Abheron looked up from his inspection of the fine red wine in his glass. "Be careful, Tiede," he advised quietly. "My patience does have limits. Now – I want every spy, every contact, every informant, to converge on Mesgao immediately. Get someone inside the fort; I don't care how. Find out what Sorin is doing and who is with him. Report back to me as soon as you have something. And that had better be soon. Understood?"

"Of course, Your Highness. As it happens we – we already have a spy in the fort. I took advantage of a most unusual opportunity not long ago. Her first report is due at any time." Tiede clenched his shaking hands at his waist again.

"Good. Very good. Send my secretary in on your way out. I need him to begin preparations."

"Preparations?"

"Yes, Tiede. I have a plan…"

By the time they found me and brought me down from the roof, I had already heard the screaming and shouts from the town below, and seen the bloody red taint of fire in the sky. I knew, before they told me, what had happened.

Half of the namoa and temple people – half of my friends, my family – had fled Fort Mesgao in the night. They had taken the Sedorne guards by surprise and beaten them, stolen provisions and, on their way out of town, had set fire to any Sedorne property they had come across.

My own people had turned fire – the weapon of the Sedorne – against me.

We had been welcomed into the fort like honoured, trusted guests. They had run from it like prisoners escaping. That night, as I watched the flames leap against the sky, consuming the homes and businesses of innocent people, I realized that no matter what I said, no matter how they were treated, this was how many of the Rua would always feel. They could not trust the Sedorne. They could not trust me. I just didn't see it until it was too late.

I did not know if Kapila's attack on me had been part of their escape plan, or if she had seized the opportunity to act on her own. I hoped the latter. I hoped that my friends, even if they had not been able to agree with me, would not have wanted me murdered in the night.

I would never know for sure.

I insisted that Kapila be buried decently, and her grave marked – but the marker was nameless. Kapila's name was black now, the name of a murderer and a traitor, and nothing I could do would change that.

Mira and Deo had stayed. They had slept through the whole thing in their room – drugged. I thanked God the drug used was a less potent one than Kapila had fed Sorin and me, or else Mira would have miscarried her baby. When Deo finished turning the air blue with curses, he pulled me into a hard hug and held on to me for a long time. Mira took his place when he finally let me go. I hugged both of them back fiercely.

Joachim had gone, along with half the fighting namoa and many of the other temple people whom I had not known as well. Most of the children had been left behind. To my shock, Rashna had stayed too.

"I have unfinished business here," was all she would say. I didn't know whether this was a promise – or a threat. At that point I was really too tired to care.

The drug had affected Sorin much more strongly than it had me. Mira told me that the mixture of herbs was well known as one the Sedorne were particularly susceptible to. Kapila had obviously decided to forget that I was half Rua when she administered it. Her wilful blindness had saved my life.

Despite all Mira's skill, it was two days before Sorin woke. When he did, his limbs were frighteningly numb and he found it hard to talk. It was awful to watch him struggle to sit up, even hold a cup on his own. I never left his bedside if I could help it, but all

I could say to him was "I'm sorry."

The first words he managed in return were "Don't be stupid."

That evening, after Sorin had managed to get down a cup of nutritious broth and a herbal drink of Mira's, I sat by the window looking out at the fires that still raged in lower Mesgao. We had been forced to evacuate the homes there; the blaze was beyond control. Now a whole new lot of refugees, most of them Sedorne this time, were staying in the fort.

"How could they?" I whispered, looking at the veins of fire leaching up into the clouds like streaks on poisoned flesh. "How could they burn people's homes? The Rua have never used fire like this."

"The Sedorne ... have," Sorin said slowly. "You can't ... blame ... the Rua, for ... turning ... our own weapons ... against us."

I whipped around, suddenly furious. "Fire took my family, killed my parents, destroyed everything I knew and loved. Fire nearly took my eye, scarred me for life! Fire robbed me of my own name for ten years. Fire is death and suffering. It is not a weapon; it is a curse. How could they? How could they turn fire against me? My own people!"

He leaned back against the headboard of the bed, his breathing laboured as he looked at me. "Zahira ... this is not ... your fault."

I stared at him, my eyes burning. "Mira says

you may never recover full feeling in your hands and feet. You might not walk again. If I hadn't come here, hadn't brought all of them *here*—"

"Not your fault!" he croaked, smacking his hand weakly against the side of the bed.

"I am the reia. Everything my people do is my responsibility. It *is* my fault."

"Come ... here." He held out his hand in the familiar beckoning gesture. It shook in the air. I ran forward to take it, unable to bear the sight.

"Sorin—"

"Quiet," he commanded as his fingers closed over mine. "If you ... will stop blaming yourself ... for everything ... I will walk to our wedding. Promise." His fingers tightened slowly, until my hand was almost crushed in his grip. "Promise?"

I lowered my face to press my forehead against his hand, hiding my tears from him. "I promise."

"We will ... go on." He panted with effort as his fingers loosened. I wrapped my other hand around them, to keep them in place. "We will always go on ... together. No ... matter ... what comes."

PART THREE

CHAPTER
FIFTEEN

Sorin kept his promise. Before a month had passed he was on his feet again. He did not have his previous mobility back yet, and he might always need a cane to help his balance, especially when he was tired. But he would walk to our second wedding.

Since the poisoning we had slept in the same room, in the same bed. Sorin was so ill, and I was so very tired, that our sleep had been as chaste as that of brother and sister – but I could not bear the thought that he might have died without my ever knowing how it felt to lie at his side. It would take a great deal to prise me away from his bed now, I knew.

He left at midnight the night before the ceremony. There was a custom that bride and groom must not see each other on the day of their marriage until the wedding itself, in case it brought bad luck. I pointed out that most Sedorne brides weren't already married to their grooms, but I'd made the rather endearing discovery that Sorin was superstitious – he even refused to touch cobwebs in case they gave him bad luck – and so I wasn't surprised when he insisted we observe the old tradition.

He dressed slowly and gingerly in the dark. I heard his fingers fumbling with the buttons but I did not offer to help. He didn't like that. When he had finished, he leaned carefully over to press a kiss to my forehead.

"Go back to sleep," he said, pronouncing the words precisely, as he always did now. "I'll see you in a few hours." Then he slipped out of the room.

After he had gone, I lay alone in the bed, running my hand over the cooling place where he had lain. I realized with an odd lurch of my stomach that it didn't feel right now, without him in it. I'd got used to his breathing next to me. I pulled the blankets around myself more tightly and rolled over, but instead of closing my eyes I lay awake, the past month running back in my head.

For weeks now, important figures from the Rua resistance and potential allies from among the Sedorne lords had been arriving in Mesgao. We had met and talked with them in their separate groups and together, trying to convince them that what we proposed could work. It had not been easy, and not for the reasons I had feared.

The Sedorne lords had astonished me with their willingness to listen. Not one of them had even questioned my identity. When I learned that this was because, despite my colouring, the lords saw a strong resemblance between me and King Abheron, I felt a small chill of disgust – yet I had to admit that the hint of anxious deference they displayed was useful. It was clear that they all had the greatest admiration for Sorin.

But I had been unpleasantly surprised at how pedantic and downright stubborn many of the Rua men and women had been. While most of them accepted me for who I said I was, they had been dismissive of Sorin. The person I had been counting on to support me, Casador Fareed – the man whom Surya had been at such pains to introduce me to, and to whom she had told my real identity all those months ago – seemed to positively enjoy baiting Sorin, though what he expected to gain if Sorin lost his temper, I did not know.

In any case, there was no danger of that; it had been Sorin who restrained me when I was on the verge of exploding. He had nothing to prove to them. We had to remember, he said, that the casadors had already been dispossessed of their rightful place once. Of course they would feel threatened by the idea of co-operation with their conquerors. His patience with them shamed me; at the same time, it gave me a glow of pride in him. He's mine – my husband.

Eventually we had reached a deadlock with the Rua, Fareed at their head. They would not talk to me seriously if those talks included Sorin – and I refused to negotiate without him present.

In the end, it had not been patience which had ended the impasse, but a drifting memory from my childhood. As I listened in mortification to Casador Fareed squabbling with Sorin over the freshness of his morning tea, I suddenly remembered sitting on my father's knee as he presided over a council meeting very like this one, and how he had acted to end the arguing of his petitioners. That memory fused in my mind with a vision of the raggedly Rua orphans that we had taken in at the House of God. They acted aggressively, but their aggression hid fear and confusion. What they really needed was discipline. When they had it, they settled down.

Before I realized what I was doing, I'd smashed my hand down into the low table at which we were all sitting.

"*Enough!*" I yelled. "This is childishness. I will not listen to any more. Leave my presence and do not return until you are willing to remember your duty to your reia and your country."

Out of the corner of my eye I saw Sorin's hastily hidden look of astonishment, but it was too late to back down now. The casadors were gaping at me, Fareed's face turning slowly purple with outrage. I met his dark, angry gaze with every bit of determination I had. There is only one rei in this room, Fareed – and it is not you.

Finally his eyes dropped. He nodded jerkily at the other leaders. One by one, they rose and meekly filed from the room. Sorin's look of astonishment returned as they went, then transformed into a huge grin.

The next day, the Rua men and women had appeared when summoned, listened to what Sorin and I said, and offered no more insult to either of us. Fareed took care not to meet my eyes again. It was well worth the severely strained wrist I'd sustained when I hit the table.

This made things a lot easier when we eventually brought the Rua and Sedorne together. There were still arguments and muttering between them, and several important points which had to be clarified for the benefit of all, but I believed that together Sorin and I had managed to convince our peoples that we could truly get rid of Abheron. They were willing to follow us. Follow me.

Only, not until our union was official. The Sedorne wedding had to go ahead, and it had to be witnessed not just by those we wanted as allies, but by others, ordinary people who would then act as unofficial emissaries when they spread the story. It was our public declaration of unity – and our first challenge to Abheron. Once the wedding was over, we could act.

The ceremony had to go perfectly. It had to. As I had

done a hundred times since I began to learn about Sedorne wedding customs, I cursed the complexity of the ritual. So many things could go wrong. Most of them weren't even under my control.

The namoa and temple people who had fled from Mesgao had gathered their own followers in the mountains above us and were experimenting with small acts of terrorism up and down the countryside. They had borrowed tactics from the Sedorne lords who had once raided Ruan's borders, attacking swiftly and in small numbers, robbing and even killing where they met any opposition. Sedorne farms, merchants, some of the smaller towns with Sedorne populations – all suffered. They screamed to Sorin for help, but there was nothing to be done, except increase the patrols of gourdin in the area. The Rua raiders were swift and skilful, and they did not make many mistakes.

Casador Fareed admitted that the leaders of the raiders had tried to contact the local resistance, but had been repudiated. Observing minutely, I thought that if the resistance had not been in talks with us at that moment, they might have welcomed the efforts of this new guerrilla band with open arms. There was no way to predict what the band of ex-temple people might do in protest at the wedding.

I hesitated, then opened my mind and called out to the Holy Mother.

Please, God, guide me through this. Help me.

I waited, eyes open, tensely expectant of some sign that God had heard my prayer. There was none. I didn't know whether to feel relief or disappointment.

All my life I had believed, blindly and lovingly, in my God. Despite everything, I knew that if I had remained only Zira, I would have clung to that devotion until my dying breath. Since God had reached out and touched me, since I had truly known Her presence and learned the fearsome beauty of Her voice … somehow it had become incredibly difficult to keep to my faith. So many had died in order for my transformation to take place. Surya, Padma, Theri, Esha's little boy. Finally Alrik, and Kapila. I no longer believed only in the Holy Mother's love, but in Her power. I feared it.

I feared what I had become, under Her hand.

Defiant orphan and child princess had both perished in the heat of the sacred flames – had merged somehow to become Zahira, Lady Mesgao, the reia and queen of Ruan. I knew exactly who and what I was.

No one should know exactly who they are. It is terrifying. And I have to live with it, for the rest of my life.

Sighing, I closed my eyes at last, burrowing deeper into my pillow.

A very short time later I felt sunlight on my face and smelled jasmine tea. I opened my eyes to see steam twisting gently up from a cup on my bedside table, and Mira sat in a chair by the bed.

"What time is it?" I croaked, sitting and reaching

gratefully for the cup.

"Still early," Mira said, her hand making gentle patting movements on the generous curve of her belly. "I held Anca back for a few minutes. It wasn't easy – she's almost beside herself with excitement."

I thought about the little blonde Sedorne maid who had been coaching me in the marriage ceremony and supervising the fittings of my wedding costume. She was at least four years older than me, but acted in a way that I would normally associate with a small child. Her giggling got on every nerve I possessed.

"Thank you," I said fervently, sipping the tea.

I looked down into the pale golden liquid in my cup and ran through the wedding vows in my mind. My knowledge of the Sedorne tongue, which had been so clear when the Holy Mother first touched me, had become less acute as the weeks passed. Likewise I'd found many of my childhood memories fading almost as soon as I recalled them – as if they had been with me all along, and had diminished with time. This had made it a lot more difficult to commit the complicated verses of the ceremony to memory, but I thought that with Anca's and Sorin's help, I'd finally got them right. I was more worried about the wedding dance.

I slurped the rest of my tea quickly and threw back the blankets and furs to get up. I bent to touch the floor near my feet, did a few stretching exercises and a slow backward bend, and then nodded.

"All right. Call her in. Have her bring the monstrosity with her."

Mira smiled as she heaved herself up and went to the door. "It's really not a monstrosity."

"Would you ever wear a gown that weighs more than you do?"

"There isn't a dress that weighs more than me," Mira said, patting her swollen stomach again. "Now don't hurt her feelings." She pulled the door open.

A full two hours later I stood before a mirror of polished metal – an extravagant buy from the local merchant that Anca had assured me was vital – and surveyed my appearance.

The Sedorne wedding dress had remained unchanged for centuries, and every detail held meaning. The colours were chosen according to the birth element of the groom, so in my case they were red and gold. The embroidery was the plainest pattern I could argue for, but the curling golden flames rioted over more than half of the material. The bodice was so tight that I had to wear a special contraption made of ivory ribs and silk beneath it, and it was cut low and square so that most of my chest was displayed to the world. The billowing skirt and sleeves had two layers, the red overdress parting at my elbows and hips to reveal a golden one underneath. A short red cloak – with a golden lining – was anchored at my shoulders with cloak pins shaped like ducks, which, I was informed, were a symbol of fidelity.

My jaw-length hair had been twisted and pinned so tightly I was surprised it hadn't dropped out in protest, and over the top a headdress made of red choris flowers and golden charms dedicated to Ioana bobbed and jingled cheerfully.

Anca was teary-eyed with pride. Mira was avoiding my gaze, but her lips were twitching suspiciously.

"If you dare laugh…" I threatened.

"Never, Reia," she said gravely, but spoiled the effect rather by clearing her throat and turning quickly away.

I rolled my eyes and returned my attention to my reflection. All in all, I decided, I would probably never look more ridiculous in my life. But at least there was one thing I could be happy about.

I had given in to everything else, but I had stood fast when it came to veiling my face. Anca had been shocked speechless by my – to her – inexplicable decision. A Sedorne bride simply did *not* show her face. It was a gesture of disrespect to her would-be husband, and his family. She had pleaded and cajoled and argued with me until she had to go and lie down for half an hour to recover. She had even tried to enlist Sorin's support. Unfortunately for her, Sorin had taken one look at my defiant expression and refused to get involved.

So now, in the midst of the ridiculous cake of a

wedding dress and the stupid headdress and odd braided hair, I could meet my own eyes and be sure that it was still me under there. My face. Scar and all. My left hand twitched, but I held the fingers down with an effort of will. Not today.

I lifted my chin. "I'm ready."

An audible gasp rose from the people below when I stepped out onto the mezzanine level. I gritted my teeth, kept my eyes above their faces, and walked down the stairs just as Anca had told me. Stately. Graceful. Serene. The onlookers – Rua and Sedorne, the temple people and namoa who had stayed with me, fort servants, townspeople – parted for me, clapping and shouting my name and throwing choris flowers at my feet. I could almost feel their goodwill lapping at my skin, rising up like the sweet smell of the blossoms that crushed under my slippers. Someone darted forward to touch the trailing ends of my dress and was shooed away briskly by Anca. The feeling of an invisible wave of caring buoyed me up and pushed me along across the courtyard to where the gates of the fort opened wide.

The grey horse that I was to ride stood by the gates, Deo holding the reins. It had flowers and ribbons braided into its long white mane and tail, and looked very pretty. It tossed its head nervously at the movements of the crowd and chewed on its bit with a loud *glunking* noise.

I eyed it with apprehension. I'd never been taught to ride, and there had been little time to practise after I was told it was expected of me for the ceremony. I'd had more important things to concentrate on. I looked at Deo, who smiled reassuringly.

"Easy. Just like we did yesterday," he whispered as he helped me to mount and sit side-saddle on the mare.

I kept my curses at the process quiet, for the sake of the people around us, even when the skirt bunched up awkwardly beneath me and the embroidery scratched at the back of my thighs. The long sleeves of the dress thankfully hid my glaring red and white knuckles as I clutched at the horse's mane. Deo thoughtfully kept a firm hold on my skirt as he led the horse through the gates. The animal snorted and jigged a little under me; I wobbled but managed to keep my balance as we walked slowly down the road into upper Mesgao.

The wide road sloped gently, lined with cheering spectators. The horse jigged sideways again, and Deo muttered at it. Its ears pointed curiously and it settled a little. The air was filled with falling red petals; looking up, I saw people hanging out of windows and sitting on roofs in their finest clothes, throwing down handfuls of flowers.

Then the road curved and brought us to the centre of upper Mesgao. A circular dais sat in the open area, six wooden poles around its circumference, each of them blooming with dozens of long red, gold and yellow ribbons. On the far side of the dais, through drifting petals and fluttering ribbons, I saw a dapple-grey horse – and there was Sorin, waiting for me.

He looked at me intently for a moment, then winked. I pressed my lips together to preserve my solemn expression, and winked back.

Deo got me down off the horse and then I was walking through the rain of choris blossoms towards the dais. Sorin moved towards me, using a long ebony cane tipped with silver. The clapping and shouting died away, leaving ringing silence in its wake. I stepped up at the same time as he did, and we met at the centre of the dais. We looked at each other for another long moment. I saw his chest expand as he sucked in a deep breath; then he gave me a tiny nod, and we began.

First we spoke the three vows of loyalty, obedience and love. Then we each walked a half-turn round the dais and stood where the other had been standing, and repeated more vows: honesty and fidelity. Another half-turn and the third lot of vows: compassion, understanding and tolerance.

We separated and went to our opposite ends of the dais – Sorin carefully laying his cane down so that it wouldn't get in the way – and each selected a handful of ribbons from the pole behind us to begin the final part of the ceremony. The wedding dance.

The intricate steps were taken to an ancient, compelling rhythm; the ribbons and how each of them braided together needed constant attention as we worked around the dais, towards, around, past, and then towards each other again. I tried to ignore the weight of the gown, the stupid jingling of the damn stupid headdress, the trickle of sweat down my back, weaving in and out of the poles. I tried not to worry about how Sorin's legs and arms were holding up, and if he was as tired as me. We knotted, pulled and twisted the ribbons into a multicoloured wall that enveloped us within its circle, blocking out the world outside in a symbolic representation of the bond of marriage.

Sedorne girls and boys practised this dance many times a year on festival days, from childhood – I'd had only one month to learn it. Any tangle or hole in the woven curtain of ribbons was said to be a terrible jinx on the luck of the wedded couple. We couldn't afford to have our people think us jinxed. I had to get this right. I wiped sweat from my face with my forearm and carried on.

Up, in, around the pole, twist the red ribbon, grab a new yellow ribbon, turn, pull, down, around the pole, up, twist the gold ribbon, duck to pick up a new red ribbon, then down, around the pole again… My back aching, breath coming hard in my throat, I danced for what seemed like hours. I couldn't spare the time to look up and check – or take the chance of losing the rhythm. I just had to dance.

Then suddenly my hands were empty. There were no more ribbons. I turned to see Sorin, looking as dazed as me, on the other side of the enclosure we'd made. He staggered a little, and I leaped forward to catch his arm and keep him upright.

"Did ... did we?" I stammered.

He turned his head, inspecting the flame-coloured barrier that enclosed us, then laughed incredulously. "We did! It's perfect! Not a mistake in sight!" He wrapped his arms around me, and we kissed in a burst of relief and happiness.

I distantly heard a surge of noise outside the ribbon barrier. We broke apart and stood, hand in hand, as the people outside undid the woven wall, carefully cutting the barrier apart with short knives and throwing the ribbons up into the air with wild yips and shouts. Young Sedorne women and girls ran forward to snatch up handfuls of the gleaming scraps: good luck when sewn into their own wedding gowns. The town elders – four ancient Rua – stepped up onto the dais to embrace us both and bless us. One bent, with some effort, and handed Sorin his cane.

I looked up at him. "I can't believe it's over. We did it!" I whispered.

He didn't reply. His eyes were fixed on something over my head. I watched his face turn to stone as ominous quiet dropped over us. Out of the corner of my eye I could see the Rua resistance leaders hastily backing away and disappearing into the heaving crowd. The Sedorne lords were doing the same.

I turned.

On the edge of the cleared area a large party of heavily armed gourdin on horseback were forging through the crowd. Ahead of them came others on foot, brandishing cudgels and shoving people aside, spreading through the crowd to surround the area. When the horseback soldiers reached the edge of the dais – only a foot away from where I stood – they peeled back to reveal a figure seated confidently on a tall blood bay stallion.

The shock of recognition ran through me like lightning.

Even on horseback it was obvious that the man was tall and well muscled. He was also extremely good-looking, with coppery-blond hair braided intricately around his head, and smiling grey eyes. He looked at Sorin with an expression of fond amusement, and then swung down from the saddle to stand before us. He was about two inches shorter than Sorin – only a little taller than me.

"Well?" he said, his pleasant voice bright. "Don't you have a welcome for me?"

I felt Sorin tense with rage. His fingers tightened around mine until my bones ground together – and I knew without a shred of doubt that he was about to throw himself at this man and try to kill him. I also knew that the other man was braced for exactly that. So were the sixty or more armed gourdin surrounding us. Sorin couldn't even grip a knife and fork properly, let alone a sword.

"Yes," I said, prising my fingers free of Sorin's grip and stepping down from the edge of the dais. I dropped a little curtsy, looked up into those pale, laughing eyes, and held out my hand.

"Welcome, Uncle Abheron."

CHAPTER
SIXTEEN

The king seemed to freeze. Then he took hold of my bare hand and clasped it firmly between his gloved ones, staring at me in what appeared to be genuine shock.

"Emelia..." he whispered.

"I beg your pardon?"

Traitor. False king. Murderer. My skin crawled until I imagined it rippling and twitching in his grasp. I clenched my teeth against a swell of sickness that made my head spin. God, if only I had my knife.

He smiled, a devastatingly attractive, rueful smile that reminded me horribly of Sorin. I swallowed against the bile rising in my throat.

"You have remarkable eyes, my dear," he said quietly.

Suddenly Sorin's arm was round me, drawing me back. I pulled at my hand. To my surprise, Abheron let it go without a fuss. I leaned gratefully into Sorin, clenching my hands in my skirt.

"You are not well," he said roughly. "Someone bring a chair!"

"She's white as a cloud," Abheron said in apparent concern.

There was a bustle of activity near by, and then Casador Fareed emerged, carrying a wooden stool. He placed it down with a bow and I plopped ungracefully onto it, uncaring of the crushing of my silk gown. Sorin kneeled slowly and painfully beside me, dropping his cane again to chafe my hand.

"I'm sorry," I said, keeping my eyes down on my feet. "I don't know what's wrong with me." Apart from a sudden, overwhelming desire to slash and rip and tear my uncle open and smell the hot metal smell of his blood. He killed my family – my whole family...

"Shock," Abheron said briskly. "I do apologize, my dear, for the lack of warning. I was travelling to the summer palace at Lake Jijendra when I was stunned to receive word that our noble cousin Sorin was to be married – and to a woman called Zahira Elfenesh. I'm afraid I became unspeakably eager to intrude upon the blessed event, and didn't think to send word ahead."

I looked up to see him studying me with every evidence of concern. He gestured expansively, and I saw that he had removed the glove from his right hand. The diamond ring of office on his forefinger caught the sun and glittered like unshed tears.

"You must know that I believed both my nieces to be dead, killed in the same fire that stole the life of my beloved sister. But there can be no doubt as to your identity, not now that I've seen you. What a joyful surprise it is to find you alive, my dear, after all these years of mourning."

"I—" My voice cracked. I was still reeling with the darkness of my own emotions. Not since the day when I had watched Surya die had I felt myself teetering on the edge of control like this. I couldn't deal with his clever wordplay. Sorin squeezed my hand in a silent warning, then, picking up his cane, rose carefully to his feet to face Abheron.

"It is indeed a joyful surprise, Your Majesty, for all of us. We never expected you to honour us with your presence."

"No, indeed. Especially as I was not honoured with an invitation." The king raised an eyebrow.

Sorin smiled blandly. "In my experience, Your Majesty, you rarely wait for an invitation."

There was a short, stinging silence as the pair stared at each other. The ranks of gourdin behind the king were worryingly still: braced for action. Fareed gave me a look of desperate appeal.

I drew in a sharp breath, then said, "I feel much

better now. Could someone help me up, please?" I cringed inwardly, despising myself for the feigned note of helplessness.

Abheron and Sorin broke eye contact and looked at me again. There was a relieved rustle of movement in the cleared area. Thankfully Sorin was closer and reached me first. I dug my fingernails into his forearm as he leaned down and glared at him. I didn't know what was happening – or why we weren't already dead – but if Sorin provoked Abheron again, there were sure to be bloody consequences. If *I* could restrain myself, then so could he.

Still pretending to hang on to Sorin's arm, I made a production of testing my legs and shaking out my skirt, while I composed my face. Then I looked up at Abheron again, praying that my expression did not give away the thudding in my chest.

"Your colour is back," he said, nodding. "Excellent. Dearest niece, of course I understand your husband's wish to enjoy a small, intimate wedding. But now that this has been accomplished, I must claim you for myself. I have an uncle's right, after all. I insist that appropriate celebrations take place, befitting your rank. You must come to the summer palace. Half the court is there already, you know – the heat in the lowlands is dreadful this year. I will throw a ball in your honour and arrange delightful entertainments to amuse you, and in return I will have the pleasure of introducing my newly discovered niece to the court, and of getting to know her better myself."

Trapped. The gleam in his eyes – and the watchful expressions of the gourdin – told me that he had us. He knew it. The only reason we weren't dead was that it amused Abheron to play this game, whatever it was. I tore my gaze away from his expectant face, and looked up at Sorin.

"An invitation we could not think of refusing," Sorin said, lips quirking. Only I could see it in his eyes: the horrible realization that our plans were in ruin, and that we were now in mortal danger.

I forced my lips to stretch into an answering smile as I looked back at Abheron. "Thank you, uncle. We would be honoured."

He laughed. "Wonderful! Leave everything to me. And now – though it pains me – I must leave you for a short while. I will travel on to the palace with all possible speed, make everything ready and wait there to welcome you. I expect you'll need the rest of the day to prepare for the journey – I wouldn't want you to arrive exhausted – but I shall expect you by the end of the week." The flat warning in his voice belied the casual words as he smiled. "I shall of course leave my special guards behind to escort you. There are far too many dangerous elements roaming my kingdom to trust your safety to anyone less than the best."

"Who will protect you, on your journey?" I said,

knowing it was useless.

"Oh, I can look after myself, my dear" he said quietly. "Don't worry, though – I left another unit of gourdin on the outskirts of the town. They will accompany me."

Sorin inclined his head. "You are, as always, perfectly prepared, Your Majesty."

"Of course." Abheron stepped forward. "Now, before I leave, I must embrace the couple and bless them. I believe that is the Rua custom?"

"No!" I burst out. "No, I'm afraid not, Your Highness. In fact, it is considered very bad luck for a relative of the bride to offer a blessing. It – er – might encourage ... bad spirits."

Despite our dire straits, out of the corner of my eye I saw Sorin press his lips together to hide a smile. "Yes. Bad spirits," he agreed, nodding seriously.

"Oh." Abheron tilted his head. "Well, that is unfortunate. But I presume I may still embrace my niece?"

Before I could think of anything else to say, he had put his arms around me. It took every drop of self-control that I possessed to stand still. Nausea rolled in my stomach as a lock of his hair brushed my nose, and I swallowed frantically. Let go, let go – *let go of me...* Then he brushed a kiss to my cheek. My scarred cheek.

I flinched back with a wordless cry of revulsion, planted my hands on his chest and shoved him away. We stared at each other, inches apart and tensed like opponents in a battle. For a split second, I thought I saw something in his eyes, a flare of some darkness unfolding behind the glassy irises. Then he blinked and it was gone. That charming, rueful smile curved his lips again.

"Until we meet again, Zahira," he said softly.

Then he turned and swung up into the saddle, wheeling his mount and trotting away through the crowd without a backward glance.

The unit of foot gourdin spread quickly to surround us, effectively separating us from the crowd. Our allies seemed to have disappeared; there was no sign of them among the anxious faces that I could see through the gaps in the soldiers' ranks. Even Fareed had taken the opportunity to slip away.

Sorin turned to me, ignoring the presence of the gourdin. "By Ioana, woman." His face was grey and suddenly he looked exhausted. He leaned heavily on his cane. "You've more courage than sense."

"What are we going to do?" I whispered.

"I don't know, Zahira. I don't know."

With firmness that held little pretence of courtesy, Abheron's gourdin escorted us back to the fort. They marched through the open gates like a conquering army, taking Sorin's unit of ten lightly armed men by surprise and overwhelming them easily. With the Mesgao guards locked in their barracks, Abheron's gourdin made all exits secure and took up strategic positions throughout the building. No one was to enter or leave without their permission – by order of the king.

The shock and outrage on the faces of our people as the intruders took over told us that the slightest sign from Sorin or me would be enough to start a battle. But the fort's inhabitants stood no chance against the heavily armed force of elite gourdin, our so-called allies had disappeared, and any attempt at resistance could only end in a massacre.

Our plans were destroyed. There was nothing to be done.

So we walked composedly into our bedroom – ignoring the gourdin who stationed himself outside it – and closed the door. I pushed down the bolt on the inside, more from defiance than the idea that it would keep anyone out.

Sorin sank onto the bed. "I should have seen this coming," he said dully. "You tried to tell me – to warn me about spies – but I wouldn't listen."

I sat down next to him and jabbed him sharply in the arm. Panic made my voice sharper still. "Stop it. You don't get to wallow in self-doubts and guilt. I need you to stay alert and reasonable and, most of all, alive."

"Ee–ow." He rubbed clumsily at the area I had poked.

"I'm sorry." I pushed his hand away and rubbed his arm myself. "Just don't frighten me. This is bad enough."

"Bad enough, she says." Sorin laughed feebly. "Some thing of an understatement. Come here."

He drew me against his side and kissed me, the warmth of his lips finding the spot of icy cold on my cheek where Abheron's had touched. I leaned my head against his shoulder. After a moment he sighed deeply, disturbing the fine hairs on the back of my neck. A tiny, involuntary shiver went down my spine. Suddenly I was very aware of how close he was. We were curved into each other, our thighs touching, my breast pressed against his chest.

I hid my face in his doublet self-consciously, and felt his breath quicken. His hand lifted from my back – leaving a glowing imprint where it had rested – and cupped my cheek, tilting my face up. His fingertips were slightly rough against my skin. I looked at him. Tentatively, keeping his gaze on mine, he touched my scar.

I arched against him like a cat, gasping in surprise. His fingers traced the puckered line of flesh, barely grazing the surface of the skin.

"Is this all right?" he asked softly.

I swallowed, turning my face wordlessly into his touch. His fingers slid into my hair. He pressed a kiss to the ruined lobe of my left ear. I felt a starburst of sensation as his lips moved, moistly, against my skin.

I breathed in the warm smell of him, and reached up to touch his cheek as he had touched mine. His stubble prickled on the palm of my hand as I cupped his face.

"Yes," I said.

CHAPTER
SEVENTEEN

The next day we left Mesgao for Lake Jijendra. The whole town turned out to watch us go. The silent, grim-faced people who lined the road were very different from the cheering crowds of our wedding day.

They knew they might never see us again.

The rattle and clank of the gourdin's armour surrounding the carriage was grating. It almost drowned out the thin wail of a small child somewhere behind us as we came to the outskirts of lower Mesgao. Poor baby, I thought as the high-pitched cry stretched on. Woken before dawn, probably not even fed yet. Take the child home, for the Holy Mother's sake – there's no need for it to see this.

I leaned forward to look out of the window. The rising sun had not reached the fort yet; the building was hidden against the hillside, a square hump of shadow. I stared at the shadow, wishing desperately for the sun to rise a little higher, so that I might catch at least one glimpse of the place before we left. One last glimpse, before I was gone. If the sun reached the fort before it disappeared, everything would be well...

Then we rounded the curve of the road, and the fort was hidden from sight.

As the great grey Subira mountains marched west across Ruan, they met the smaller, greener peaks of the Arphat range curving up from the Bluecaps in the south; and where the two crossed briefly, there was a great valley, sheltered from the harsh winds and heat of the lowlands. It was here that the River Mesgao had its source, in Lake Jijendra, the largest body of water in Ruan.

Five hundred years ago, a rei had built a summer palace high on the west bank, overlooking the lake. The term palace was an affectionate one rather than factual, for the building was low and built of intricately carved wood, its airy windows and open verandas designed for comfort and coolness rather than stateliness. Over the years a little village had sprung up around it, at first inhabited only by the artisans, tradespeople and merchants who were required to maintain the palace. But as the centuries passed, the village had grown and spread down the bank and a lively fishing trade had drawn more people into the valley, until the village had become a town, and then a city that was strung out along the west and north sides of the valley. Most of the casadors had built their own homes there – far grander than the palace itself – so that they could follow the rei on his summer journeys and the court and business of governance could continue.

The Jijendra valley was a lush, green place. Trees grew tall and straight, towering above the banks and overhanging the water with vast spreading canopies of silver and purple leaves. The water itself was the colour of the night sky, so deep a blue that it was almost black. When the sun set over it, it turned milky pale, shot with lights of orange and kingfisher blue like a living opal.

Of course, I didn't remember any of this until we had been travelling for four days – until the moment when our carriage rattled down the road and broke through the lush forest that surrounded the lake. Looking out of the window, I saw the late afternoon sun spray through smoky shredded clouds and down on the summer city, setting the pale walls of the palace above it alight, and turning the lake into a glowing pool of liquid fire. The mountains rose up behind, black in the golden sky, their shapes suddenly as familiar to me as my own face.

Vivid images began to flood my mind; I was

bombarded by a million remembered smells, tastes, sounds and emotions.

Figs, picked from the tree and still warm from the sun, sweet and soft, juice running down my chin...

Squealing with laugher as Kiran splashed me with lake water – then guilt as Mama scolded him for wetting my dress...

Cool, moist mosses under my bare feet as I walked along the bank, looking up at the trees towering over the water...

I clutched at my head, gasping.

The high, hoarse barking that sounded from the forest at nightfall – fear of the strange noise, then comfort as Dada showed me the tiny auburn-haired monkeys that made the sounds...

Distantly I heard Sorin's voice, harsh with concern, but I was lost in a whirlpool of sensations.

The smell of the waxy white starflowers that grew around my window as their bell-shaped petals unfurled at dawn...

"Stop it!"

There was a stinging pain on my cheek and I jerked out of the well of memories like someone waking from a dream, my breathing sawing in my throat. I found myself on Sorin's lap, clasped hard against his chest. I looked up into his face and found him staring at me with a mixture of anger and concern.

"It's all right. I'm all right now," I said, my voice

rough, as if I had been screaming. Had I been screaming?

"Thank the goddess," he muttered, closing his eyes in relief.

I raised my hand and rubbed at the hot aching place on my cheek where he'd slapped me. "Ow."

"I'm sorry," he said, his tight grip on my shoulders loosening a little. "But you didn't seem to hear me."

"No. No, I didn't. Thank you."

I sat up properly and slid off his lap to sit next to him, by the window. I took a deep breath, braced myself, and peeked through the opening again. Nothing new came. The memories seemed to have settled into place now. It was a new layer of knowledge: an important one, fresh and clear.

"What happened to you?" he said, voice still low with emotion. He put his arm round me, and I could feel him shaking.

"I remembered this place. You know things often come back to me – memories – of the time before the fire. But this was like … like the first time, when the Holy Mother spoke to me. It hurt."

"Why would your memories hurt you?"

I had tried to describe my walk into the sacred fire to him, but I had not been very successful, partly because he did not worship the Holy Mother and it was hard to talk around the parts I wasn't allowed to mention, and partly because … well, the experience seemed beyond words.

Still, I tried to explain. "Because there were so many of them at once. Too much. It was like drowning in memories. Sorin, the summer palace was where I lived. Mama couldn't stand the heat in Aroha, so we spent nearly all our time here. I hadn't realized. Practically every memory I have of my life before is of this place." I turned to look out of the window again. "This was my home. Look!"

There was a flash of spotted brown and gold fur among the trees and then a splash of water, and I laughed in shock and delight.

"What was that?" Sorin asked, surprised.

"It was a tamul!" I said, leaning forward to try to catch another glimpse. "They're a type of antelope, but they can swim underwater for minutes without coming up for breath. They eat the fruit that falls out of the trees onto the lake bed. This is the only place in Ruan where they can live." I sobered suddenly. "My father taught me about them."

Sorin rubbed my shoulder. I sat back with a sigh, realizing that the tamul – and the brief moment of happiness – was gone.

"Well, I'm glad, even if the territory belongs to the enemy, that it isn't completely unfamiliar," he said.

"No. I know this valley as well as any place on earth." I paused. "We should have made Deo stay with Mira."

Soirn smiled. "Short of cutting his legs off, I doubt

we could have managed it." He leaned his head back against the squabs tiredly. "He loves you, Zahira. He couldn't let you go into danger alone. In any case, Deo will be very helpful to have around, and Mira supported his decision to come. We need all the help we can get."

"I know. I just hope Rashna is having some luck."

He smiled again, and this time the smile held a hint of its old arrogance. "That woman doesn't need luck. We'll probably arrive to find that she's taken the palace herself and tied Abheron in a bow for us."

I snorted with laughter. I could just imagine the look on Rashna's face – half smug, half disdainful. The laughter died as I realized I couldn't imagine anyone besting Abheron, not even Rashna.

When Sorin had suggested that we send a couple of agents ahead of us to the summer palace, to pose as servants and try to discover Abheron's plans, Rashna had been the last person I'd expected to volunteer. Especially as it would involve working with a Sedorne man, picked for the task by Sorin.

"Why do you want to do this?" I asked her seriously.

"Why do you think, Reia?" She tapped her foot impatiently. "You're walking blindly into a trap. God knows what the Pig has planned for you. You need a secret weapon, and I'm the best person for it."

"Rashna..." My voice trailed off uncomfortably as I tried to think of a way to ask my question without offending her. Why do you care?

"Look," she interrupted, "you know what I think of you, and I know what you think of me. But that has nothing to do with it. I may not like you much – or that cocky Sedorne you married – but you're the only reia we've got, and we can't afford to lose you."

I blinked. "Very well. Thank you."

"You're welcome." She bowed – her graceful, sarcastic bow – and turned to leave, but I said her name as she reached the door.

"Um... Don't get killed or anything, will you?"

"I'm perfectly capable of looking after myself, thanks. You worry about yourself."

I sat back, put firmly in my place, and she disappeared through the door.

She'd gone that night disguised as a bent old namoa whom Abheron's men had dismissed as harmless. Riding a pair of the best horses in Mesgao, Rashna and Stefan – Sorin's man – had crept out of the town, intending to ride hard for Jijendra. She should be there by now, hopefully blending in with the rush of servants that the palace would have to hire to pull off this impromptu ball in my honour. Please, God, she would find some way of helping us.

If only we could figure out what Abheron was up to. His actions, contradictory and apparently impulsive, made no sense. If he intended to kill us, then why not just do it? Why this elaborate charade? What did he hope to achieve? Unless even he didn't know...

"Sorin." I picked absently at the embroidery on my blue skirt. Mira had persuaded me into Sedorne dress for this journey, telling me that it would put Sedorne men at their ease in my presence, causing them to underestimate me. I knew her argument had merit, but I still felt horribly overdressed and uncomfortable.

"Yes?"

"Why is he doing this?" I asked. "All this – it isn't his normal behaviour, I know that much."

Sorin sounded as frustrated as I was. "You're right that it's out of character. Abheron's not a sadist. He's a murderer and a traitor, yes; but I've never heard that he enjoys playing with his victims."

"I don't think what's happening now is part of any clever plan. I think he intended to kill us but he changed his mind."

"What makes you believe that?" He looked at me intently.

"It seems to me that he's constantly playing a part: all that languid hand-waving and the clever wordplay. It's a cover for the intellect underneath, and it's deliberately unconvincing because he knows that it keeps people off balance. But when he looked at me that first time – when he took my hand – and then again, after he kissed me ... I could swear I saw something in his eyes. Something real."

Sorin frowned. "Real what? Emotion?"

"Yes. He was shocked, angry. And there was something else. I could feel it, pushing at me – and it made me frightened. He was hanging on to his control by his fingertips."

Sorin rubbed his hand over his face. "If you're right that we've upset his plans, then it could be a good thing – give us a chance to escape before he decides what to do with us. But I don't like the idea that he's teetering on the edge, Zahira. I don't want to think about what Abheron might do if he ever really lost control."

There was a moment of quiet – except for the rattle of the wheels on the road, and the creaking of the carriage roof, and the clashing armour of the gourdin unit escorting us. We leaned against each other, and didn't say anything else for a long while.

Tiede was enjoying a late and intimate meal with his mistress when the king's page scratched on his door.

After hastily readjusting his clothes, Tiede followed the page through the unfamiliar corridors of the summer palace, wondering why he had been called to the picture room. As far as he knew the chamber was not in regular use – the portraits of the previous occupants having long since been removed, leaving the walls bare – and besides, the king had only just arrived from Mesgao. In his place, Tiede would have been soaking in a hot bath.

Tiede was never confident when he was summoned to see the king. To allow oneself to fall into complacency was a fatal mistake when dealing with His Majesty, and one that Tiede had never committed. Mainly because the king terrified him, and always had.

On this occasion, however, Tiede felt, if not at ease, then at least not uncomfortable. He had been given a chance to make up for his recent lack of success, and he had done it. He had provided the king with the exact details that had been requested, organized everything just as the king had wished, and had even accomplished the feat of turning one of Sorin's own household to the king's use, something no previous spymaster had ever done. He very much hoped that on this occasion, the king would have only words of praise for him.

Two gourdin in light travelling armour were posted outside the door. Tiede was too preoccupied to notice that the men did not salute him as he passed, as would have been normal etiquette. The long, narrow chamber was blazing with lights, mismatched candelabra crammed into every available niche in the walls, and some extra even placed on the floor. The walls danced with shadows, highlighting the paler squares left when all the paintings had been taken down.

The first thing Tiede noticed was that, today, one of the portraits had been restored to its original place. It depicted a blonde Sedorne woman with vivid blue eyes, dressed in outlandish Rua clothing and with her hair arranged in an unattractive Rua style. She looked vaguely familiar, but Tiede only spared her one curious glance. He was more surprised to see His Majesty, still dressed in dusty, sweat-stained riding clothes, slumped in a chair placed directly before the painting.

Tiede bowed low – as low as he could, with the first two courses sitting undigested in his stomach – and murmured, "Your Majesty summoned me?"

Abheron didn't answer, never taking his eyes from the picture before him. If Tiede hadn't known full well that the king never drank to excess, he would have thought the man was drunk, lolling in the chair with his legs flung out, and his head resting on the back of the chair as he stared up at the portrait.

Tiede waited. He thought of the delicious dinner he had ordered, and which was congealing as he stood there, and the luscious young woman no doubt growing more drowsy and bored by the second, and felt a slight ruffle of annoyance pass over him. Perhaps the man *was* drunk. He was the first to admit that the king was nothing if not unpredictable.

He cleared his throat noisily. "Your Majesty summoned me?"

Abheron stirred. "Yes."

The word was flat and without any trace of the normal drawl that coloured the king's speech. Tiede's annoyance was instantly replaced with the cold brush of anxiety. What now?

King Abheron continued to stare at the picture. Tiede suddenly wondered if he had seen His Majesty blink since he entered the room. He was uneasily convinced he had not. He flicked a quick glance at this apparently fascinating portrait, trying to figure out why the woman, with her odd clothes and hair, seemed familiar.

"Repeat to me the report you gave on Sorin's new bride," the king said abruptly.

"Well. Er…" Tiede cleared his throat again, then pulled himself together and began. "The girl calls herself Zahira Elfenesh, apparently claiming a relationship with the deceased Elfenesh royal line."

"No. Not that," the king interrupted. "The physical description."

Tiede huffed out a short breath, now thoroughly unnerved, and began again. "Approximately five feet nine inches tall. Quite mannish in appearance, with short black hair and dark skin. She is said to have a very ugly scar – possibly from a burn – on the left side of the face. No tattoos or other unique features known."

"So much detail, Tiede. Yet none of it at all useful. Tell me – do you recognize the woman in this picture?"

Tiede moved uneasily from foot to foot. "I'm afraid I do not, Your Majesty."

"I'm not surprised." Abheron stood slowly and reached out a gloved hand, brushing his fingers gently over the painted curve of the woman's face. His voice lowered to a whisper. *"Emelia."*

They both stood silent, the king staring at the painting, the lord staring at the king.

"I do not believe you are a stupid man, Lord Tiede," Abheron said eventually. "Yet you have all the subtlety and perception of a lump of rock. Again and again, amid your endless reports and details, you have managed to miss the one truly important fact. Again and again, you have failed me. You did not tell me, faithful spymaster, that Zahira Elfenesh has her mother's eyes…"

Caught off guard, Tiede broke his own cardinal rule and began to babble. "I – I apologize, Your Majesty. The information was not in any report – I could not have known—"

"I don't care, Tiede. It's too late now to undo the damage. This is the last time you will send me blindly against my fate. The very last time."

At those words, Tiede heard the clash of the gourdin's armour directly behind him. Gauntleted hands closed on his shoulders and forced him to his knees. Terror, all the worse for being completely unexpected, rose in his throat with a sick, burning taste like bile. He struggled feebly under his captors' hands, breath sobbing.

"No! No – Your Majesty, please! How could I have known? Please, in the sweet goddess's name, have mercy!"

"Mercy?" the king repeated.

Suddenly his shoulders began to jerk, and a low, rumbling laugh broke from his chest, echoing hollowly from the high ceiling of the room. It was a bitter, joyless sound. The gourdin holding Tiede shivered.

After a moment, King Abheron sighed. "Take him away, for pity's sake. Get him out of my sight, and don't let me see him again."

The gourdin needed no further urging. They dragged the pleading, struggling man away. Abheron waited until the last, desperate noises of his former spymaster grew distant and eventually ceased. Then he leaned forward to pick a candle out of the holder near his foot. He raised it up before his face, so that the heat of the flame beat against his skin and blocked the picture from his sight with its hypnotic yellow movement.

"I'm sorry, Emelia," he whispered. "I didn't know what to do."

Slowly, slowly, as if struggling with an object a hundred times heavier, he lifted the candle so that its dancing point touched the edge of the picture frame. The gold paint began to blister and blacken. Abheron's tongue flickered out to wet his lip. His hand shook.

A long rivulet of wax spilled over the edge of the candle and onto his skin.

With a hiss of pain Abheron dropped the candle, and the liquid wax doused the flame as it fell to the ground. He stared down at the smoking wick, and then at the ruined corner of the picture frame. He blinked, as if waking from a trance.

Then he buried his face in his hands and wept.

CHAPTER
EIGHTEEN

Sorin told me that under Abheron's rule the summer city had enjoyed more popularity than ever before. The pale-skinned Sedorne people, used to cooler weather in their native Sedra, found it impossible to stand the heat in the lowlands. Still, the main part of the population – living in small wooden houses close to the waterline – remained Rua. And somehow they knew who was in the carriage travelling along the road to the summer palace that afternoon.

Everywhere we looked, people were clustered, staring at the carriage, running along after it, trying to catch a glimpse of us through the windows. Their faces were alive with curiosity and fearful hope. I was too used to that look now. When gourdin peeled away from the column around us to break the gatherings up and force the crowds back, I almost felt grateful.

The road climbed steeply, zigzagging back and forth along the steps of the terraced riverbank towards the palace. The building seemed to glow ahead of us, pearly and luminous. As we drew closer I saw that carved lanterns hung from the peaked roofs – an incredible extravagance so early in the day. Dada had loved the cool green shadows under the trees, and would never have banished them.

We drove slowly past the east wing of the palace and into the central courtyard. The carriage jerked to a stop before the entrance.

The doorway was not grand, but the wooden frame and lintel were beautifully carved just as I remembered – images of pygmy monkeys, leaping tamul and parrots with their wings spread wide. Three low steps, inlaid with blue and yellow tiles, led up to the simple wooden door. The archways of the verandas on either side were covered with the climbing starflower vine, the bell-shaped blossoms closed now.

There was a moment of stillness. Sorin and I looked at each other.

"Well," I said. "We're here."

The door of the palace opened and a small elderly Sedorne man, grandly dressed, appeared. His steps as delicate and precise as if he were taking part in a dance, he came down the stairs to the carriage door and opened it. He unfolded the coach steps with his own little hands, and then reached out to me.

"My lady," he whispered, his voice papery and dry.

Reluctantly I reached out and took his hand; it was as papery and dry as his voice. He made a production of helping me from the carriage, though I was perfectly capable of climbing down on my own. Then he stepped aside to allow Sorin to disembark too. I looked around and realized that, somehow, without me noticing, the second carriage with our luggage and servants, including Deo, had disappeared. The courtyard was empty except for us three, and the unit of gourdin who had been our constant companions throughout the journey. They formed a loose crescent around us and the carriage, apparently happy to hand us over to this harmless-looking little man.

I gazed down at him with some misgiving. What was happening now? Beside me, Sorin was braced and waiting, gripping his cane below the heavy silver cap at the top. I realized he was getting ready to use it as a club.

"Lord and Lady Mesgao, I am the master of palace ceremonies, His Majesty's personal servant," the man began, his breathy tones addressed respectfully to our feet. "He has instructed me that you are to be treated as his most honoured guests. There is an amusement planned for you tonight; but for now, he wishes you to rest and recover from your hard journey. If you would consent to follow me…" His voice trailed off and he waved his hands towards the entrance.

I looked at Sorin in confusion. Honoured guests? I didn't know quite what I was expecting, but it certainly wasn't this.

Sorin shrugged, his shoulders relaxing a little. He let his cane drop down into its normal position in his hand. "Into the lion's den, my love?"

He held out his free arm – a peculiar Sedorne gesture that I didn't believe I would ever grow used to. I laid my palm on his arm, and we walked up the low steps. I heard muffled boot falls as two of the gourdin fell into step behind us, and was surprised to find the noise slightly reassuring. It reminded me that no matter what games Abheron played, we were still prisoners here.

As I passed through the doorway I found my free hand reaching out to the frame at about waist height – and there, on the nose of one of the tiny carved monkeys, the smooth place that I had stroked each time I entered this door as a child. It had been at eye level back then. My finger slid off the wood, and then we were inside.

I felt another echo of recognition as the cool shadow of the hall fell over us. There were no lamps burning here; the dim shapes of the archways around us were quiet and mysterious. I made out the geometric patterns of the yellow and blue tiles underfoot more through memory than sight.

The little man stepped up beside us. "A suite has been prepared for you," he said. "Your possessions and servants should already be there. If you would care to come this way…"

He led us to a large room, where there was a very formal, very Sedorne arrangement of chairs and reclining couches. I looked in vain for a comfortable cushion anywhere.

"I will leave you here," he said, gently sculling his hands in the air. "Arrangements will be made for you later on." He slid gracefully out of sight.

"Whatever that means," I muttered.

The gourdin who had followed us took up positions on either side of the door. Sorin smiled wryly and we passed inside. On one side, light flooded in through doors opened onto the garden; and on the other, I could see another room dominated by a large bed. In the centre of the room, golden-haired Anca stood over a pile of trunks and cases, directing several Sedorne servants to unpack them.

When I had told Mira that she would not be coming with us, she had insisted that I would need a maid, and to my surprise, Anca had volunteered. Even after my warnings about possible danger she had stood fast. Her lady would need someone, she said, and she knew how to do the job properly.

She curtsied when she saw us. "Deo is caring for your horse, my lady – the one who pulled up lame. He said he would come later and report to you."

I smiled at her in gratitude. She knew I hadn't the faintest idea about horses. She was reassuring me that Deo was well and would come and see us when he could.

"Thank you, Anca," Sorin said.

"Would you like me to order refreshments?"

"Um ... not for me," I said. The idea of food made me feel a little queasy. Suddenly I was very tired.

"No, we ate on the journey," Sorin said. I could feel him gazing at me with concern. Always trying to look after me, I thought guiltily. I should be looking after him.

"I think we should rest," he continued. "Whatever ... amusement Abheron has planned, it would be best to attend with clear heads. I imagine we'll need them."

When I woke, the bronzy shadows told me that dusk had fallen. I lay still on the bed, listening to the peculiar quiet that holds the world still as it passes from day to night.

Sorin was sprawled beside me on his stomach, pale hair lying in a long curve along his spine, face relaxed into a secret smile. I reached out and stroked a few stray strands back from his cheek, careful not to disturb him. I liked to see him quiet like this. When he was awake his face could change as swiftly as clouds in a storm, alive with emotions both real and assumed –

whatever would help him to convince people of his point of view. At other times he could look blank and impassive, his features a mask that only I saw through. I liked to watch him when he slept, and remember that he was only eight years older than me.

But the quiet, rather than lulling me back to sleep, stirred a vague itch of restlessness. I stretched, pointing my toes and hands. My muscles felt stiff and my bones creaked ominously. Too much waiting around; too much sitting in carriages. I lay still again, but it was no good. I had slept my fill; I needed to be up and moving.

I burrowed under the draped muslin – arranged over the bed to keep out stinging flies – and emerged to stand beside the bed. Anca had folded my dressing gown over the footboard. The gown was gorgeous, heavy watered silk in my favourite shade of blue. Sorin had given it to me as a surprise a week before we married the second time, and I loved it. It seemed far too fine to be worn casually but I could never resist putting it on – it made me feel like a child playing in a queen's robe. I pulled it on over my shift. The hem, heavy with blue beads, swirled majestically around my feet as I tied the beaded belt at my waist. I kicked the dusty, creased travelling gown, which I had flung down on the floor in disgust earlier, out of my way and opened the door into the sitting room.

I found it empty as I had expected, with the doors

to the garden closed. I looked at the square, formal Sedorne furniture. The low ceilings and windows were not meant for such tall objects – they made the room seem out of balance. My restlessness increased and I began to pace the walls. Something wasn't right. This room was blank, empty of memories. I'd probably been here as a child, but it looked so different now that it failed to touch anything in my mind. I wanted familiarity and comfort. This place only off-ered strangeness.

Then a memory came – the nursery where I had played with my brothers and sister. The room where I had once slept. Without thinking, I was at the door and opening it.

I half expected the gourdin to block the exit, but they stood back, not even glancing at me at the door swung inwards. I looked at them suspiciously, wonder-ing what their orders were. If all the exits were guarded in a similar fashion, perhaps I was allowed to move freely within the palace. I paused on the threshold, looking around. There was no one to be seen in either direction, and when I stepped out, the guards still did not move.

Caution warred with curiosity. Was this some kind of trap? How could it be, when Abheron already had Sorin and me just where he wanted? God only knew what the madman had planned, but it didn't seem that close supervision was part of it.

I wanted to see my old room. I wanted to meet the memories in private. This might be my last chance.

I closed the door experimentally behind me. The gourdin stood motionless. That seemed to settle it. They would not interfere. Decided, I walked purposefully along the corridor, leaving the guards behind. My feet – bare, as they had usually been when I was a child – instinctively found their own way, leading me round a long bend in the corridor, down some low steps, and then…

I walked in, shutting the door silently, and looked around. I had thought that seeing the nursery now, it would seem smaller. In fact it was bigger – a vast, echoing expanse of a room. Empty.

The childhood clutter of toys, tables and books was long gone. The floor was bare, the shutters tightly bolted. Things were heaped haphazardly against the walls and covered with white sheets. Like winding sheets, I thought morbidly. When I tugged at one, it came back to reveal Sedorne furniture – disused and damaged pieces that had been piled here out of the way. There was nothing familiar.

"Well." I sighed to myself, disappointed. "It has been nearly eleven years."

I went to the place where I remembered my bedroom's entrance being. It was almost hidden behind another pile of sheet-covered furniture. I scrabbled and pushed until I opened up a little space, enough to get at the door.

With a shock, I realized another reason why everything seemed so alien to me now. There had been no wooden doors here when I was a child, only curtains, beaded at the bottom to hang straight. Abheron must have gone through the whole palace and had doors fitted into every entrance, even where the rooms were disused. An odd, compulsive thing to have done.

I reached for the handle – feeling the slide of dust under my fingers – and turned it, squeezing through the narrow gap into the room beyond.

Here, as in the nursery, furniture and junk were piled everywhere, but no one had bothered to tuck sheets around these discarded objects, and dust lay in a thick bluish-grey layer over everything. The large windows in the right-hand wall, which had often served as doors to me and my siblings, were shuttered, leaving the place in melancholy gloom.

I gathered the full skirt of my gown around me and picked my way through the mountains of old furniture, looking for anything familiar. I found a book on the floor, its pages rippled and rotted with damp so that I could not tell what had been written there. The painted pictures were streaks of washed-out colour. Had it been a story I knew? A book I loved? There was no way of telling. The pages crumbled under my fingers, releasing a musty, sick smell.

Near the far wall I found my old bed. It was nothing more than a box of polished redwood with a fanshaped headboard and a stylized pattern of dancing monkeys carved into the sides. I remembered tracing the pattern at night as I drifted into sleep. My fingers were too big now to fit into the grooves and bumps. I crouched beside the bed for a long moment, stroking the polished wood – thinking about stories read to me by my nanny and my mother, the way the sun fell through the windows in the mornings in long silky bars of gold, birds and monkeys calling, and the distant splash of water that had lulled me to sleep...

Then I heard something that made me jump: laughter.

The laughter was masculine, and close – someone was outside the window. I got up carefully, stepped over a fallen chair, and put my hand on the shutter beside my bed. To my surprise it was only pushed shut, not bolted; I eased it back, looked out – and froze in shock.

Just outside the room, the cliff on which the summer palace was built extended on a long promontory of rock out into the lake, like a natural pier. From the end of the rock it was possible to see the whole of the lake and forest, and two low wooden benches sat there for people to enjoy the view. As children, my brothers and I had left food there, and watched from this window as the shy tamul climbed out of the water and crept up onto the pier to eat the fruit.

Now Abheron was there. Dressed in casual clothes and with his long hair in a simple braid, he crouched on that finger of rock, hands full of fruit and scraps of bread. A tamul stood before him, its golden spotted hide and tiny pale horns shining in the last of the light as it delicately picked the food from his fingers.

He laughed again, softly, as if the tamul was tickling his skin, though one of his hands was gloved. The little creature shied away at the noise, but returned to snuffle the last pieces of fruit from his hands. Then it trotted away from him to the edge of the stony bank. Swift and sure-footed, it disappeared over the side. A moment later, I heard a quiet splash in the water.

Abheron straightened, his back to me, and stared out over the water for a long minute. I couldn't take my eyes off him. What I had just seen was ... was *wrong*. Abheron, vile murderer, feeding a wild creature from his own fingers?

"You can come out now," he called suddenly.

I jumped, started back, and tripped over the fallen chair behind me, sending the shutter banging loudly shut. As I shoved the chair away, the unlocked shutter drifted open again to reveal Abheron standing just outside the window, looking at me.

Too fast, I thought, blankly staring at him. This man moves too fast.

"I could feel you watching me," he said calmly. "I hoped you might decide to join me of your own volition. It's a lovely evening."

I brushed the hair out of my eyes and climbed slowly

to my feet, praying that my face didn't reveal anything. I had no choice but to gather the shreds of dignity stiffly around me and step over the low sill of the window. He moved back, studying me with narrowed eyes. I jerked my chin up, and he smiled.

"I thought I'd be safe from you, you know," he said. "Foolish of me."

"What?" I said warily.

He looked away from me, over the water again. "You really are very like your mother."

"I can barely remember her," I said icily. Some reckless spirit made me add, "I'm told that I'm very like you, though."

He looked back at me. "Whoever said that was mistaken. You're nothing like me, Zahira."

There was a moment of quiet, filled with currents of emotion from him that I could not decipher. I could feel that menacing swirl of darkness unfolding, pushing at me. It was all I could do to remain still.

Finally, unable to stand it any longer, I burst out, "Why did you bring us here? What do you want?"

"The answer to both questions is the same," he replied, unperturbed. "I wish to seek redemption."

"Redemption? You dare speak of redemption to me?"

"Oh, yes. Yes, I do."

Night was beginning to draw in, and over the lake, swallows and martins swooped and wheeled, scooping up the insects that gathered at twilight. They swarmed above us, filling the air with a kind of noiseless rushing, the breath of beating wings. I could feel my heart thundering almost in rhythm with them as I stared at him.

"I've done great harm to you and your family, Zahira. I never intended to, you must understand that. It is my fate to destroy all that I love."

"Excuses, Uncle?" My voice was high-pitched and shrill – even I could hear it. "There is no fate. We make our own choices for our own reasons, and we must accept responsibility for them."

"You're young yet," he said with a touch of weariness. "You will learn, as you get older, that destiny is a crashing tide. It picks us up, carries us away. No matter how we struggle and fight, there is no escaping it."

When I didn't reply, he sighed. "I beg your patience for a short while, my dear. The truth – like fate – is a bitter thing. We must learn to swallow both."

"Go on," I said, folding my arms.

Abheron settled himself on one of the wooden benches. "I suggest you sit. No? Very well. The story begins with my birth. My mother died having me – the first in a long line of deaths laid on my account. I'm sure you know of the Sedorne custom that every child is dedicated to a particular element? As heir to the throne, obviously my dedication was very important. Unfortunately, after the priests had chanted and prodded and conferred over me at length, they declared themselves baffled. Finally they called in their most revered priest to examine me. The old man had one sniff and reeled back in horror. He announced that I was cursed, doomed – for none of the gods would claim me. The fate that awaited me in life was this: just as I had killed my own mother by being born, so I would destroy every person whom I might ever love.

"My father – the king – threw all the priests out in a rage, but he could not quite ignore what they had said. A cursed heir was surely worse than no heir at all. On the other hand, he was then in middle age, and had only managed to beget two children – myself, and my sister, six years older. He desperately needed an heir. And so he came up with a plan."

Abheron paused for a moment, shifting to prop his left ankle on his right knee. He rested his left hand, still gloved, on his thigh. "Are you sure you wouldn't like to sit?" he asked. "I'm afraid this tale goes on for some while yet."

Reluctantly I moved to sit on the bench across from him, rigidly straight, with my hands in my lap.

"Carry on," I said evenly, determined not to let my interest show. I knew that I shouldn't believe a word he said. But he had mentioned my mother more than once now. Horrible as it was, this man – this man who had killed her – was the only person who'd known her well enough to tell me more.

"Your grandfather was one of those men," he said,

"who believe that love is a kind of weakness – a flaw which afflicts women and children, but to which men are not prone. So he reasoned that if I were to be taken away from his home and isolated from my family until I became a man, when I returned, everyone would be safe from me. Of course, servants, tutors, nannies and such would have to go with me, to raise me as a king's son, but it mattered little if any of *them* were to fall victim to my curse.

"So I grew up in a wilderness far from anywhere, cared for by a succession of servants who went out of their way to ensure that I hated them. I'm sure you can understand that I grew into rather an odd sort of young man, with strange ideas and preoccupations. But all in all, my father's plan might well have worked, were it not for one thing."

"What was that?" I asked.

"That he was a stupid, dried-up old idiot who knew nothing of love." He laughed, but the sound held no humour. "I was summoned back to the bosom of my family on my twenty-first birthday, to find a bewildering occasion in progress. This, I was told, was a joint celebration of my return and of my sister's engagement to the ruler of a neighbouring country.

"As I walked into the ballroom to meet my family for the first time, I saw a woman. Though she was not the most beautiful woman in the room, though her face seemed sad and still, when she looked at me … I fell in love with her. Truly in love. And I love her still, though I have not seen her in many long years.

"Unfortunately for both of us, that woman's name was Emelia and she was my own sister. Your mother."

CHAPTER
NINETEEN

My skin turned to ice. I sat in frozen silence as he laughed again, bitterly.

"What a coil! I had never loved anyone before, you know, and so I became very afraid – I knew I might cause Emelia to die, simply by caring for her. In the following weeks as she prepared to leave, I avoided her completely. I ran when I saw her coming, hid when I heard her voice, took care that we never exchanged a single word.

"But fate – as I have told you – must have its own way. Which was why, on the night before she was to leave for her new home, Emelia sought me out. She had a soft heart, my sister. She wanted to speak to me at least once before she left. Seeing her then, being alone with her, I lost my noble ideas about protecting her, forgot how afraid I had been. I embraced her, and told her that I loved her – and when she understood what I meant, she looked at me, my dear Zahira, just as you are looking at me now, with horror and pity. She kissed me, just here" – he brushed his forehead with one gloved finger – "and told me that she wished me well. Then she walked away.

"I must admit that at first there was a good deal of relief mixed with my sadness at watching her go. She would surely be safe, so far from me – because, of course, absence would cause my love for her to die away. Soon I would barely remember her. She would be safe.

"Time did pass. My father grew feeble and ill, and the underclasses of Sedra – merchants, tradesmen, politicians – grew in power, until the warrior caste, the true Sedorne, were no more than figureheads, power-less and ignored. Until my father was no more than a puppet king, despised by all. And, despite my every effort to extinguish it, my obsession with Emelia did not die. I lived in daily fear of the report that would come, to tell me that I had killed her. But years came and went and still Emelia lived on.

"Eventually my father died, and with his passing I began to see the world differently. There was no curse; there never had been a curse. It was a lie that had cost me the woman I loved. I was arrogant enough, you see, to believe that I could have made Emelia love me –

that, if I had wished it, our relationship of brother and sister would have not mattered and we would have been happy together. Instead I had let her go.

"At the same time, I was also struggling to deal with the events that were taking place in Sedra. The Sedorne were being taxed and persecuted to the point that in order to survive, many of my lords were making raids on wealthy neighbouring countries. Including Ruan, the land where my sister had made her home. I was powerless to stop it.

"Eventually an ambassador from Ruan came to me, asking me to put a stop to the raids – to return with him as an honoured guest and negotiate with Rei Toril. I hardly know how to describe my feelings to you, except that the chance of seeing Emelia again blinded me to everything else. So I gathered up an honour guard of loyal lords and gourdin, and travelled to Aroha, and met with my sister's husband. It went well, I thought. We talked. I asked for Toril's advice, and he was kind enough to give it. I even managed to avoid staring at Emelia too much. Then night fell…"

The shades of evening were thick now around us, and I could barely see his face – only a white glint of light in his eyes and a reddish one from his hair. But I was sure that he was not looking at me any more, I could get up and walk away and he would barely notice.

"I had been given a suite in the family wing – for

I was family, of course. I couldn't sleep. I got up and wandered out onto the balcony that ran around the outside of the palace. It was there that I found Emelia. Perhaps she couldn't sleep either. I called out to her, but she went white and fled back into the building. I thought I knew why. So I followed her into her private room.

"She must have been reading, because there were lights burning everywhere. I remember the way our shadows warped and flickered on the walls as I tried to talk to her. To tell her that I had realized the curse was nonsense, and that she was safe from me. She wouldn't listen. She didn't care about the curse; she'd never cared about it. She was frightened because of the feelings I had, which were so unnatural, so repulsive to her.

"When I realized that, I became angry. All the bitterness that had been festering within me for so long spewed out. I grabbed at her – whether to strike her or kiss her, I do not know. We struggled. A lamp fell and set fire to one of the curtains. Then Toril came in; he must have heard the shouting. He saw the fire, saw Emelia trying to get away from me, and... Elements only know what he thought. He lunged at me, drawing his knife. He wounded me, here." He touched his right shoulder.

"I reacted on instinct. I took the knife from him and killed him with it. By then half of the room was in flames. I tried to grab Emelia again, to pull her out to safety. She ran away from me. She ran through the flames to her husband. I saw her one last time, kneeling over his body. She wouldn't leave him, even though he was dead. She loved him. *She loved him.*"

He stopped abruptly. When he spoke again, he was talking to me, not to himself. "I ran out onto the balcony, shouting for help. The wound I had received was bad, and I was losing blood very quickly. I collapsed. I know little of what happened next except that my men, finding me wounded, assumed treachery. They got me out and left the rest to burn. When I woke, everything I had loved was destroyed, just as the old priest had warned."

I sat for a moment, images pulsing horribly in my mind – fire, smoke, screaming. Then gradually they drained away, leaving me cold and ill, head aching. My breath shuddered in my chest.

"You tell the story," I began haltingly, "as if you were nothing but a helpless victim. Do you believe that?"

"Oh no, Zahira. It was all my fault. I accepted that years ago – accepted the curse," he said evenly. "But perhaps I could be forgiven, if it were not for what I did next."

"Next?" I said numbly.

"You know what happened after the Great Fire. You know what I did. Finding myself, suddenly, the sole relation of the dead rei, I seized control of his country, and made myself king. A real king, not a puppet, as I had been in Sedra. I have clung to that power with every fibre I possess in the years since."

"Then why?" I asked, bewildered. My eyes were stinging, and I lifted my hands to rub them fiercely. "Why any of this? You had a second chance here to begin anew. Why order the deaths of innocents? Why persecute the Rua and take their homes? Why have the House of God destroyed?"

"Because it is all I can do," Abheron said simply. "It's all I can be. If I am a murderer, a tyrant and a despot, then I am a successful one, the best that ever lived. But if I am simply a man … then I have nothing. I am nothing."

Finally I whispered, "What do you want?"

"I want you."

I gaped at him, finally managing to choke out an incredulous, "What?"

"It is impossible for me to put right all the evils I have done. But I can put you back in your rightful place, Zahira. I have no children, nor do I ever intend to have any. But you could have been my daughter. And like my father before me, I need an heir."

"I don't understand."

"I cannot live for ever. When I die, you will be reia. You can do whatever you will with this country. Create a paradise on earth, if you wish – I don't care. Emelia's daughter will sit upon the throne, and I will have made some reparation for all my sins."

I shook my head slowly. "I don't … I don't believe you. If you intend to simply give me what I was fighting for, then why all this? No." I got to my feet. "I don't believe you. There's something you're not saying."

He sighed, coming to stand before me. On the uneven ground we were eye to eye. "You're very acute. There is a catch to this bargain. Let me lay the terms before you. While I live, you will not interfere in the running of my kingdom. You will reside with me as a member of my family but I will rule Ruan until I die, and you will support me. And … there's one more thing. Your husband. You will have to agree to let him go."

"Let him go?" I echoed sceptically. "What exactly do you mean by that?"

"I beg your pardon; I was attempting to be delicate. You will have to agree to his death, my dear."

I let out a sharp laugh. "I'll never agree to that. You know I won't."

"I'm afraid you must. It's part of the bargain. I cannot rule with him undermining me. Even if he could be induced to agree to this – which is doubtful – he'd challenge me to a duel of kingship as soon as he could. I'm surprised he hasn't already."

Sorin can't fight any more… No, I would never admit that to this man. "Sorin is honourable. If he were to agree to any bargain, he would keep his word."

"Of course. A duel of kingship is a very honourable thing – it's a traditional Sedorne method for the nobility to get rid of a bad king. Once the challenge has been issued in public, there is no going back. The gods must decide on the winner. Make no mistake, my dear, it would be the first thing he'd do. He really hates me, you know, and not unreasonably."

I stared at him incredulously. "If you want Sorin dead, then why not have him killed? In fact, why not have both of us killed? You've had ample opportunity. Why this elaborate production?"

"I don't want you dead, my dear – and if I had your husband killed now, you would never forgive me," Abheron said with incongruous gentleness. "This must be your decision, Zahira. The good of your country versus the good of Sorin Mesgao. Your choice."

"It's a choice I'll never make," I said harshly. "Nothing good, nothing worth having, could be founded on the murder of an innocent man. And the bargain you offer is fatally flawed, Abheron. I would never agree to support you in your persecution of my people. You may live for another fifty years. I will not watch Ruan suffer under your hands for that long."

He nodded. "I knew this would be your first reaction. But what I propose is your only option, Zahira, the only way that you will live to see your people free. You can't hope to defeat me, or get rid of me in any other way. Once all this is over, you'll see that I'm right."

"You're mad. Completely insane," I said evenly. "I won't betray my husband. I won't betray everything that I believe in. I'll die before I agree to any of this."

"You won't die, my dear," he said softly. He plucked at the fingers of the glove on his left hand, pulling it slowly off. "I won't let you. I intend to take very good care of you from now on."

I jerked in shock as he revealed his left hand. It was horribly burned – a mass of twisted scar tissue that made my own scar look like nothing. His two smallest fingers were missing, and the others were twisted into bent claws like a hen's foot; he must have had wires in the fingers of his glove to make his hand seem normal.

"I got this trying to save your mother. Earlier I said that you and I were nothing alike – but we do have certain things in common." He raised the claw-like hand to my face and lightly stroked my scar with his bent fingers. I stood like a stone pillar under his touch.

"The longer you hesitate, the more painful it will be, my dear. You'll walk this path, even if I have to line it with fire. It's the only way."

He turned and strode away along the top of the cliff, pulling the glove over his ruined hand as he went.

I stood completely still, watching him out of sight. Then I bent down and vomited, my stomach heaving convulsively long after it was empty. Finally, shaking so badly that I could hardly stand straight, I staggered through the window into the palace.

It felt like hours since I had seen the comfortable, quiet suite Sorin and I had been given – I could hardly believe that Sorin was still peacefully asleep in the bed when I reached it. I flung off the heavy dressing gown and crawled under the muslin nets to curl, shivering, next to him.

After a moment, he stirred, turning over to put his arms around me. I burrowed into him, pressing my face into his shoulder.

"Where have you been?" he murmured sleepily. "You're freezing."

"I've been talking to Abheron."

I felt him tense as he came awake.

"What has he done? What did he say to you?" he demanded.

"Horrible things, Sorin," I whispered, closing my eyes. "Horrible things…"

CHAPTER
TWENTY

About half an hour later, a servant brought tea and
bowls of sweet couscous to our suite and informed us
that His Highness's entertainment would begin soon.
Fresh hot water had been pumped into the tanks of our
private bathroom next door, and we had just under an
hour to get ready. The servant also brought a large
wooden box – a gift, he said, from the king to his
niece. He wished me to wear it tonight.

Sorin and I stared at each other as the door closed
behind the man. Then I kicked out viciously at the gift
box, which had been laid at my feet, sending it skid-
ding against the wall. Anca was nowhere to be found,
and Deo had not come to see us. There was no word
from Rashna or Stefan.

"Do you—" I broke off, kicked the box again, and

forced myself to finish. "Do you think Abheron has killed them?"

Sorin took my hands between his and held them, saying nothing. I sighed unsteadily, breath jerking in my throat as I struggled to keep control.

"We should never have brought them," I said finally. My voice broke on the last word, and I gulped.

He rubbed his thumb over my wrist, gently soothing. "No."

"What about Rashna? Stefan?"

"I don't know, love. He seems to know what we think before we do. I – I'm sorry I've brought you to this."

"Please don't. We're in this together. We have been since the start and we will be at the end. You said that to me. You have to believe it."

"Zahira…"

I knew what he was about to say. "No!" I said loudly, straightening my back.

He lifted his head to look at me, and I saw the despair in his eyes. "If there's the slightest chance that he'd keep his word—"

"No," I said, more quietly. "No, Sorin."

I pulled my hands out of his and touched his face. After a moment, he lifted his own hand, and laid it on my scarred cheek. I wondered if his numb hand could even feel my skin. We stood together for a minute. Then Sorin cleared his throat and went over to where

Abheron's gift lay on the floor.

"Let's see what he's sent you," he said, kneeling down carefully to pick the box up.

His fingers fumbled with the lid; it fell off to reveal a white gown in the Sedorne style, with sumptuous gold embroidery on the tight bodice and underskirt, and waterfall sleeves.

"This must have cost him a small fortune. He has style," Sorin said ruefully. "You have to give him that."

"No, I don't," I said firmly. "I don't have to give him anything. Since Mira's not here to bully me, I will not be trussing myself up in that monstrosity. I'll wear something comfortable – something that makes me feel like myself, not a sacrificial offering on Abheron's altar."

Sorin snorted with laughter, though the noise did not hold its usual exuberance. "Well, whatever you intend to put on, we'd better hurry. I don't want his guards dragging us out of the bath if we're late."

"Don't worry," I said, taking the dress from him and flinging it back in the box. "I won't be long."

While Sorin bathed, shaved very slowly, and laboriously plaited his hair into one of the simple braids that were all he could manage these days, I went through a rapid series of warm-up exercises, kicking and punching the air, bending and stretching and, after I'd pushed the chairs back, flipping. Once the blood was pumping, I searched through the chests stowed against the wall until I found a suit of clothing that I'd had made in Mesgao.

The full trousers and knee-length tunic, slashed to the hip, had hardly creased at all. They were completely plain, the only hint of decoration in the sash, which was embroidered in silver with a pattern of leaping fish. The beauty of the suit was in the fabric – rich peacock blue silk, the same shade as the sacred fire. The same shade as Sorin's eyes.

I laid the clothes out on the bed, and found the boots that went with them, soft grey suede. By Sedorne standards they were insultingly informal. At least, I hoped so. I bathed quickly after Sorin, pulled on the tunic and trousers, and then rummaged through Anca's box of tools – make-up, hair ties, ribbons and waxes. My hair was already curling wildly from the steam of the bathwater; I rubbed in some wax and twisted it up haphazardly into a dozen ribbons.

Leaving my hair to set, I wrapped the sash around my waist, knotting it intricately at my hip, and hanging from it the silver chime and mother-of-pearl fish that I had hidden among my possessions. Then I borrowed a stick of Anca's blue eye kohl and a hand mirror. I hesitated, remembering Abheron's claw-like fingers caressing my scarred cheek. The kohl would disguise the scar. Not completely, and not all of it, but it would hide some of the ruined skin. Then I shook my head. No. I had nothing to hide, nothing to be ashamed of.

Defiantly I drew a mock tattoo on the right side – the good side – of my face, stylized flames, curling under my eye and along the line of my brow. Finally I pulled the ribbons out of my hair. It sprang into a halo of wild crinkly curls, standing straight out from my head. The mad hair, the dark swirls of the pattern I had drawn on my face – like a mirror image of the pale slashing scar on my other cheek – combined with the dangerous glitter in my eyes, gave me a feral look. I nodded in satisfaction.

Sorin, when he saw me, laughed in amazement. He looked the very picture of a perfect lord, his dove-grey and lavender clothes beautifully embroidered, his hair neatly braided and simply gemmed with mother-of-pearl beads large enough for his fingers to grasp. We couldn't have looked more different if we'd tried. Somehow that seemed right. Let everyone see that Rua and Sedorne *could* unite – *could* learn to love each other, and work together. Let them see, and be jealous.

"You'll strike terror into their hearts," he said, reaching out curiously to touch my hair. "And I'll watch them run."

There was a quiet knock at the door, and the master of ceremonies slid into the room.

"His Majesty requests your presence." He spoke calmly enough, but I thought his eyes widened at the sight of me. He looked a little forlornly at the gift discarded on the floor, then sighed and gracefully gestured us out of the room. The gourdin fell into step behind us. I couldn't help noticing that they had acquired large, viciously topped pikes since I last saw them.

The corridors and halls of the palace were still unlit, and echoingly quiet. I realized that we had not seen a single other guest here. In my father's day this had been a cheerful, bustling place, full of people. Abheron seemed to keep it almost empty.

The little man glided before us into the entrance hall, and opened the door. Light from the lanterns outside spilled in. There was a muffled roar from somewhere below – like the noise of a large crowd. The courtyard was as quiet and empty as before, except for the open carriage that waited for us. The man at the reins nodded to us as the master of ceremonies waved us into the carriage. Two more gourdin stood on a sturdy ledge built into the back of the vehicle, directly behind the passenger seats. They also held the long war pikes.

I climbed up and sat tensely. The quiet, the calm, the air of ceremony – it was completely unnerving. The carriage dipped with Sorin's weight as he sat beside me. I met his eyes, and saw that he was aware of my tension.

"Steady," he said.

I nodded, bracing myself as the carriage jerked and then rattled into motion. The roaring noise below grew louder – and then the lake came into view. I sucked in a stunned breath.

The royal pier was surrounded by a dozen extraordinary boats anchored in a ragged circle. Flat and square, the watercraft were almost like the rafts that the fishermen used, but much larger, and with wooden rails at the edges. Most had peaked awnings erected over them in the Sedorne royal colours of green and gold, concealing the activity beneath. The central craft was joined to the pier by a long suspended walkway, about a foot above the water, made of bamboo rods and silk rope. The other ships were all joined to one another in a similar way. The arrangement reminded me of a flower or perhaps more appropriately – a spider's web.

As the carriage travelled inexorably downwards, Sorin and I craned over the side in silence to get a better view. Coloured lanterns hung from poles at the edges of the boats, and more lights floated on the jet glitter of the water like fallen stars in a shifting sky. Happy music, played on the odd, fluting instruments beloved of the Sedorne, drifted up to us, along with the increasing noise of laughter and talking.

"It sounds like they're having a fine time," I said, striving for lightness.

"Or they've been instructed to give that impression," Sorin said. "I told you that he had style – and you must admit he's set the stage exquisitely."

I looked round to see his impassive mask firmly in

place. "Yes," I said as the lights and the music came closer. "The question is, what for?"

"We'll find out soon enough." His hand touched mine, and then fell away.

Then the carriage was on the pier, the wheels thundering hollowly across the planks. We came to a stop before the first walkway, and two Sedorne serving men sprang forward immediately and opened the door. One raised an eyebrow as he saw me, but his fellow was blank-faced as I spurned his hand and jumped down unassisted. Sorin did the same, rather more cautiously, behind me.

"If my lady would care to..." The blank-faced one trailed off as he indicated the step to the walkway. He had the same hesitant manner of speaking as the master of ceremonies, and the same slightly effeminate gestures. Were all royal servants taught to be like that? I stared at him with a faint feeling of insult. He wasn't even carrying a dress sword.

I looked back at Sorin, and saw the faint glint of amusement in his face as he read my expression.

"This is an honour," he murmured. "He's indicating that we're of high enough rank not to need overt restraint. I doubt he knows Rua tradition well enough to realize that he's offering you insult by implying that you're no threat."

"You know it's an insult," I pointed out.

"I make it my business to know the traditions of my

people," he said. "Abheron and I are not much alike."

"No," I said, feeling a little jolt of fear for him. "You're not."

"My lady, my lord, if you would…" The second servant had composed his face and was wafting his fingers elaborately at the silk-rope bridge.

"Oh, very well," I said peevishly. "Stop waving your hands, will you?"

I swept past him and up onto the bridge. Sorin followed me without comment, the glint of amusement still in his eye.

The walkway allowed us to walk comfortably abreast and I was grateful for Sorin's reassuring bulk next to me. I didn't like the sensation of having nothing but air under my feet. As the arrangement of ropes and canes swayed, I almost grabbed Sorin's arm, but I saw that he was having to use his cane to help him balance, and didn't want to distract him. I clutched at the rope rail instead, and was surprised to find it slightly tacky under my fingers. The fibres must have been soaked with something to make them waterproof.

I could see more clearly now the craft we were coming to. It was the largest one, at the middle of the arrangement. The centre of the boat was empty, obviously reserved for dancing. The edges of the area were teeming with beautifully dressed people, and both Rua and Sedorne servants offering wine and food. It was here that I saw the first signs of a respectably large armed presence. Gourdin – high ranking, to judge by the elaborate patterns of enamel on their armour – stood to attention at the corners of the vessel, each holding one of those heavy pikes. One wore the crested helmet of a captain. As I approached he shifted, switching his pike from one side to the other. I thought he favoured his right shoulder slightly, and made a mental note.

We reached the end of the wobbling walkway and stepped down onto the craft. As my feet settled on the herb-strewn deck, there was a sudden loud burst of music from the musicians. This must have been a pre-arranged signal, because everyone on board instantly turned and applauded our entrance, while they stared at us in curiosity and amazement.

In the midst of the noise and confusion, Abheron appeared.

CHAPTER
TWENTY-ONE

He stalked across the deserted area in the middle of the boat like a creature of the shadows, his black doublet shimmering with an abstract pattern worked in hundreds of tiny moonstones. His hair shone golden red, braided with more moonstones and the odd glitter of diamonds. A long tear-shaped diamond hung from his left ear. He looked magnificent. The crowd around him fell silent instantly, as did the musicians.

"Welcome!" he cried, spreading his hands wide. I saw the black glove on his left hand and shivered. That was the one thing I hadn't been able to bring myself to tell Sorin about. Somehow it made Abheron and me too alike, as if we were linked for ever by the same pain, marked by the same tragedy. I didn't like that feeling.

"Welcome, welcome!" He came to a stop before us, and looked at us expectantly. We looked back at him.

"If you're waiting for us to bow, you'll wait a long time," Sorin said quietly.

Abheron arched a brow, conveying amused patience, then laughed loudly for the benefit of the watchers.

"Zahira and Sorin, my dear niece and cousin. Now that you're here, the true entertainment can begin." He clapped his hands and the musicians struck up a new tune. It was slow and rather beautiful, and horribly familiar. I could remember my mother humming it.

"My guests of honour must open this ball with a dance. If you will consent to accompany me, my dear, I will provide a delightful partner for your husband."

As he spoke, a woman detached herself from the crowd and came forward. She was clad in a grey dress decorated with mother-of-pearl discs, her pale hair shining through a smoky gemmed veil, and elaborate jet and pearl beads dangling at her ears. The dark, exaggerated lines painted around her eyes and the bright red of her lips changed her features so much that I did not recognize her until I felt Sorin stiffen beside me.

"Hello, Anca," he said expressionlessly. "I see you've come up in the world."

Anca.

I stared at her in disbelief. The woman who had taught me my wedding vows; the woman who had giggled and argued over my dress; the woman who had served me all this time...

"And you have fallen somewhat, my lord," she said primly as she executed a flawless curtsy. "Luckily some of us still have loyalty to our own people."

"Anca is a dear friend of mine," Abheron said. "She will suit your husband admirably, I think."

In the shock of dawning comprehension I let him take my arm and lead me unresistingly out into the centre of the craft. The crowd watched us in silence, the lap of water and the low, sad music filling the air. *Anca...*

I came to myself with a start when Abheron turned to face me and placed one gloved hand on my hip, clasping my fingers with the other. I pulled back instinctively, but he tightened his grip on my hand, halting the movement.

"Stay with me, Zahira," he said. "You wouldn't want to make a scene in front of all these people, would you?"

I heard the subtle threat and reluctantly complied, allowing him to pull me into motion.

One day you'll dance, your hair all braided with pearls and jewels, and all the lords and casadors will fight to be your partner.

Oh, Indira. You didn't know what you were saying...

"No wonder you found out about our plans," I said bitterly. "You had a traitor in our inner circle."

"Traitor?" He tutted, a picture of injured innocence. "Harsh words against your faithful servant. She was only there to take care of you, which she did superbly, judging by your appearance at the wedding. I only wish I had been able to spare her this evening. What on earth have you done to your hair?"

He lifted his gloved hand from my waist to touch one of the wild curls. I jerked my head away and saw, for an instant, that pulse of darkness at the back of his eyes. Then it was gone, and he replaced his hand at my waist. I could feel the weight of the metal framework inside the glove pressing into my skin.

"You should have worn the dress I sent you," he said, as if nothing had happened. "I can't imagine what you intended with this bizarre raiment. You look like a savage."

"I look like what I am," I said. "Rua."

"Half Rua," he corrected. "Never forget that, Zahira. Like those lovely blue eyes you inherited, your Sedorne blood is dominant."

"What do you hope to achieve by all this?" I demanded, sick of his verbal fencing.

"Why, nothing. I only wish to give you a glimpse of the life you will enjoy once you become my heir."

I treated that with the contempt it deserved. "Whatever you've got planned, it won't work, Abheron. I won't give you what you want."

He tugged on my arm and guided me into a whirling

movement. "Do you like this dance?" he said inconsequentially. "I find it quite refreshing."

"You're a monster!"

"Yes. I am. But I am still your uncle, Zahira. Flesh of your flesh, blood of your blood. Your only family. And you will do what I want, in the end."

I heard feminine laughter behind me, and tore my gaze from Abheron. Sorin was dancing with the still laughing Anca, his movements completely lacking their normal grace as he allowed her to steer him across the floor. Where was his cane? How much of that jerkiness was due to his struggle with his legs, and how much to emotion? As they turned, I saw that his face was set in the blank Sedorne mask. What had Anca said?

I looked back at my uncle. "If you hurt him—" I began.

He patted my hip, intending to soothe. Instead I flinched as the sharp edge of one of his metal fingers pinched my flesh. "Nothing will be done without your knowledge," he said. "I've already told you that. You can trust me."

I looked at his earnest expression. He meant it. He really thought he was being reasonable and kind. He would keep his word – for now.

But what would happen when he realized he'd never get what he wanted from me?

The sad music ended. Abheron and I came to a stop in the moment of quiet. Then the musicians began playing again, this time a quick, lively tune. The guests on the sidelines surged forward onto the dance floor, flowing around us like a multicoloured river. Abheron released me at once, stepping back into the crowd and, with that unexpected speed that had unnerved me so much earlier, disappeared.

I made my way off the dance floor to an unoccupied corner of the flat boat and scanned the crowd for Sorin. I spotted him attempting to remove Anca's fingers from his cane as she leaned towards him, speaking persuasively. He yanked the piece of black wood away and turned his back on her without answering and, catching sight of me, began to struggle through the crowd. Behind him, Anca met my eyes. Her smug expression wavered and she gave a helpless gesture with her shoulders and turned away.

"What was she saying?" I asked as Sorin reached me.

"She was trying to persuade me to divorce you," he said rather breathlessly, leaning on his cane. "It seems Abheron told her that we're only a threat to him if we're together – and that she'd be a strong candidate for a replacement wife. She doesn't know about his plan to get rid of me completely."

"How did she manage to get into the fort?" I asked, trying to keep my voice free of reproach. "I thought you said you knew everyone there."

"Anca came with letters of recommendation from a

very old and trusted friend of mine."

"Forgeries?"

"No. The letters were real. Unfortunately they were stolen from the real Anca en route to Mesgao. The poor girl was disposed of and this one sent in her place. Apparently there's enough of a resemblance that Vittoria, who knew the real Anca when they were children, was convinced, and vouched for her too."

"So carefully planned," I whispered. "He must have been desperate to get someone into the fort."

"Yes." Sorin looked at me. "He wants you very badly, doesn't he?"

I nodded, managing a smile that felt horribly twisted on my face. "He thinks I can save his soul."

We looked at each other hopelessly, in our bubble of quiet. Then I glanced away, searching for something to distract myself.

"Is it normal to be ignored like this?" I asked. Despite the fact that this was supposed to be a ball in our honour, not one person had attempted to approach us. People weren't even looking in our direction. It was as if we weren't there.

Sorin made a sound that was half sigh, half laugh. "They can feel a storm coming, and they're taking shelter as best they can. Ten years with Abheron for a king has made people very sensitive."

I sighed, then tensed at a noise by my elbow. I turned to see a Rua servant waiting humbly at my side. The man bowed deeply and wordlessly – the bow of a subject to his reia – and then held out a tall golden goblet. I accepted it with some surprise and watched him disappear into the crowd again.

"I hope no one saw," I said. "It could get him into trouble."

"I'm surprised he didn't think of that," Sorin said thoughtfully. He took the goblet from me and stared into it, then pulled something white from the cup. "I think this is for you."

I took it from his hand. It was a white canthus blossom, freshly picked, its tiny petals just opening into their starburst pattern. White canthus was the sign of the royal house of Elfenesh, symbolizing peace.

And hope.

"A message?" I whispered. "From whom?"

"I don't know; maybe it means we're not as alone here as we thought." He took the flower from me and tucked it into the hair over my ear.

There was another loud blare of music and I jumped. The guests, obviously better informed than me, immediately began filing away from the food and the dancing area, forming orderly lines as they streamed onto the walkways away from the central vessel.

"What's happening now?" I muttered.

Before Sorin could answer, I sensed a presence behind me and turned to see the gourdin captain I had noticed earlier, and another, lower-ranking gourdin, waiting on the deck. They nodded respectfully at us.

"His Majesty is going to make his announcement now," the captain said. "He wishes you to join him."

I glanced quickly at Sorin, and saw the sudden tension that he was fighting to hide. What was Abheron going to announce? He gave both of the soldiers a long look, and then nodded.

"Very well. Lead on."

The captain, blank-faced, stepped back and indicated that we were to precede him and his silent colleague.

We went where the gourdin wanted, moving deeper into the drifting pattern of boats as we crossed walkways and smaller, empty craft. Finally we stepped onto the vessel where everyone else had gathered. It was the furthest boat in the arrangement, at the peak of the outer half-circle. Beyond it, the water, trees and mountains blended into solid darkness. The craft was rectangular in shape and almost as large as the central one where we had danced, with a double-peaked gold canopy from which dozens of lanterns hung. The guests parted for us without protest as we came to a halt in the middle, the guards still at our back.

At the far end of the craft, on a low platform, a small contingent of armed gourdin stood. I could see a dark shape on the floor behind them, but their closed ranks made it impossible to tell what it was. Abheron stood near them, hands clasped behind his back as he stared down at his feet. He looked different. It took me a moment to realize why.

For the first time, he was wearing a crown, a simple red-gold circlet. It was the same one that my father had worn all his life. I stiffened as a dreadful sense of foreboding seized me. I lifted my hand to the canthus flower in my hair, and touched the delicate petals. Hope.

I willed Abheron to look at me. Just a glance, anything, to give me some idea of what he was thinking, what he was up to. Suddenly he looked up and met my gaze. I went cold. The merciless ice of his eyes held a grim mixture of determination and … apology. Then he looked away over my head.

Holy Mother – what is he going to do?

The tense, subdued muttering that had filled the space died away the moment Abheron rested his eyes on his guests. They look and act more like cowed children than lords and ladies, I thought. He's broken them. Now he wants to do the same to me.

"My lords," he began, "you have gathered here today to help me celebrate the discovery of my niece, Zahira Elfenesh, and to bless her marriage to my loyal subject Sorin Constantin – or Sorin Mesgao, as he likes to be known. Thank you for making my little party a success."

As if this was a cue, everyone burst into enthusiastic applause. I kept my hands firmly at my waist.

"Thank you." Abheron lifted his hands, and the clapping stopped dead.

"Finding that the child of my sister is alive has caused me to think seriously about the succession to the throne of Ruan." He dropped this piece of information lightly, ignoring the worried rustle it caused among his guests. "I have not been blessed with children, and in latter years this has troubled me often. When I die, who is to lead this nation? The answer, now, seems obvious. Lady Zahira is blessed with royal blood from both her mother and father, and is my only living relation."

What is he doing? I thought wildly, glancing at Sorin and the gourdin waiting behind him. He promised he wouldn't do anything unless I agreed. *What is he doing?*

"However," he went on, now addressing me directly, "my niece is blessed with great modesty and delicacy of mind, which cause her to baulk at this idea. I cannot chide her. These very traits will make her a worthy queen. We must simply undertake to persuade her that agreeing to be my heir is the only acceptable path."

More rustling filled the space as the guests hastily nodded and made gestures of assent. I looked at them contemptuously. Sorin's face was grim.

"Other traits that Lady Elfenesh possesses are a strong sense of honour, and compassion. Commendable, I'm sure you all agree." Abheron lifted an eyebrow, his eyes resting on my face. "And thinking on these, I have devised a plan which I believe will persuade her to do as we all want."

He gestured at the men beside him. The front row of gourdin stepped back, while those behind them bent and dragged something forward into the light.

There was a gasp from the guests. I clapped my hand over my mouth to hold in a cry of horror. Sorin swiftly reached out and put his hand on my shoulder, holding me steady as I stared at the woman on the platform.

She seemed barely conscious. Her face was a swollen, pulpy mess, black and purpling bruises forcing one of her eyes completely shut. A great open gash across her nose bled sluggishly. Through rips in her clothes I could see welts and wounds all over her body. One of her arms dangled uselessly at her side, clearly broken; the other was secured behind her, forcing her to slump on the ground. She had been beaten almost to death.

The woman was Rashna.

CHAPTER
TWENTY-TWO

"Dear God," I whispered, tears welling up uncontrollably. "Dear God…"

Sorin's grip on my shoulder tightened. "Courage, love. There's worse to come."

"There is a custom," Abheron said. "An ancient custom of the Sedorne. It says that when a king chooses his heir, his people, rich and poor, noble and common alike, are given a holiday, a day of freedom to rejoice. On such days, all prisoners must be pardoned – no matter what their crimes – and let free to live."

He walked across the platform and bent to crouch beside Rashna's huddled form. She jerked convulsively as he reached out, but he only laid his gloved hand on her head as he studied her.

"This woman is a Rua traitor who infiltrated my

staff, no doubt in an attempt to harm my person. When she was found out she attempted to escape, and killed three loyal gourdin before she was arrested. As I'm sure you all know, these crimes are punishable by death."

He looked at me again, and now his voice was low so that few besides Sorin and I could hear it. "If you agree to become my heir – and to all the conditions which I have already laid out – then this woman may be pardoned under the ancient custom. If you do not..." He lifted his hand, and stood again. "Then she must be executed for what she has done. The choice is yours, Zahira."

Tears trickled down my face and I bit my lip, hard. Rashna had risked everything for me; she was lying, broken and half dead, at the feet of my enemies. Yet if I agreed I would be betraying Sorin, and all my people, condemning Ruan to suffer under Abheron's rule for as long as he lived.

I looked at Rashna's poor, battered face in anguish. Suddenly her good eye flickered open and met mine. The force of her will bored into me as if she had screamed in my head, *Don't you dare cave in! Stop snivelling and face him!*

I knuckled the tears out of my eyes and pushed away from Sorin to stand on my own. Conscious that every eye was on me, I stepped forward and slowly bowed to Rashna – the deepest bow, of a servant to her reia. She jerked her head painfully in acknowledgement.

"What is your decision, Zahira?" Abheron demanded.

I looked up into his face and saw expectant confidence. I longed to smash that face. I will smash it. God help me, one day I will.

I lifted my chin, and spoke so that everyone could hear. "No."

He raised an eyebrow. "No? No what?"

"I won't be your heir."

Disbelief crossed his face, followed by grudging respect. "You're stronger than I thought," he said softly. "You will make a magnificent queen."

"You're mistaken," I ground out. "Badly mistaken. I'll see you dead for it."

Metal gauntleted hands closed hard over my shoulders, pinching painfully at my skin. I struggled, but the gourdin captain simply lifted me off my feet and clamped his arms over mine. I heard a shout and craned my head in time to see Sorin brought down by a hard blow to the back of his legs with the other soldier's pikestaff. His cane clattered out of his hand as he staggered and fell to his knees. The gourdin twisted the pike round and pressed the blade to his throat. Sorin looked at me in mute anguish, helpless.

"Gently now," Abheron said to the captain who held me. "If I find a single bruise on her I'll reopen that hole in your shoulder." The captain's grip on me eased slightly, but he didn't put me down.

Abheron looked at me. "I am sorry, Zahira. Remember, this was your own choice." Then he turned to one of the gourdin standing over Rashna's slumped form. "Proceed."

The executioner nodded expressionlessly and unsheathed his sword, lifting the blade for a killing blow. I forced myself to watch, nails biting into my palms deep enough to draw blood, my heart booming in my ears; I wouldn't look away; I wouldn't abandon her. Rashna, I swear to God I'll get him; I'll get him for you … I swear I will.

At the last instant, cowardice overwhelmed me. My eyes snapped shut. I heard a hollow *thacking*, and gagged. One of the female guests screamed. I opened my eyes to see the executioner toppling back, an arrow protruding from the gap in his armour between neck and helmet.

In the sudden silence there came a lone voice, raised in a battle cry: "For Ruan! For Ruan!"

Other voices joined the first, echoing the words: "*For Ruan!*"

The captain's grip on me tightened and he backed away, dragging me with him. A burning arrow thudded into the platform before the group of gourdin, causing them to step back hastily. The Sedorne guests drew together in fear and confusion.

Somewhere behind me there was a resounding crash, and then, from above, a sound that was horribly familiar: the hungry gasp of fire taking hold. I looked up so quickly that I banged my head against the gourdin's armour-plated chest. A great whip of fire lashed out across the golden silk canopy above us, burning through the fine fabric with terrifying speed.

The guests saw it too. Screaming broke out, and they ran, fighting and trampling over one another to get off the pleasure craft and away from the flames. More fire arrows lanced through the air, scattering across the deck before the platform. Abheron held his ground as the gourdin hastily surrounded him in a protective formation.

"No, you idiots! Get them!" he bellowed. The gourdin hesitated, not wanting to abandon their king. He shoved through them and snatched the sword from the dead executioner's hand. "Go. Kill the traitors!"

The gourdin drew their weapons and leaped down from the platform. A group of people rushed forward through the scrambling guests to meet the soldiers. I recognized them with a gasp of shock.

Among the servants, both Rua and Sedorne, I saw familiar faces. Faces that had run away from me at Mesgao a month ago, leaving fire and bitterness in their wake. I saw fighting namoa I had once trained with, Joachim the garden master, temple people. Wielding everything from meat hooks to pitchforks to battleaxes and still screaming the Rua battle cry, they charged the gourdin. The two groups met with a hideous, grinding shriek of metal.

I heard Sorin's raised voice somewhere to my left, but couldn't see him through the struggling fighters and the billows of smoke spiralling up from the deck. The captain's grip around my torso tightened cruelly as he backed away from the fighting. I gasped for breath, thinking my ribs would crack, and struggled wildly. My boot heels banged against his armoured legs, and I scrabbled for purchase over the lacquered metal, searching for any weak points as I heaved my body forward, trying to throw him off balance. An arrow zipped past us, so close that I could feel the disturbance in the air. The captain dumped me on my feet, his grip loosening minutely as he half turned to try to catch sight of the archer.

Suddenly I remembered Abheron's remark about a pierced shoulder, and how the captain had seemed to favour his right arm. Sucking in my breath, I wrenched my arms free with a grunt of effort and twisted, slamming doubled fists into the right shoulder joint of his armour. My fingers sang with pain as they thudded into the metal – but the captain went white with agony. He let go of me, instinctively clutching at his shoulder.

Released, I skipped back and caught my balance. As he reached for me, his face twisted with rage, I dodged sideways and kicked with all my strength. My booted foot landed hard on the side of his knee and the joint made a sound like a melon hitting the floor. He yelled with pain as he crumpled. I kicked again, clipping him squarely under the jaw with the reinforced toe of my boot. He collapsed.

Gasping for breath – no ribs were broken, but they were certainly bruised – I looked up to find that the sky was on fire. The canopy had gone up, and the blaze had spread to the railings and the deck, joining with the smaller fires from the arrows. The battle between rebels and gourdin was already over. I could see bodies from both sides lying on the smouldering deck. Anyone who was still alive had abandoned the ship while I fought with the captain. Where was Sorin?

I coughed painfully as I sucked smoke and heat in, turning to see Rashna crumpled at one edge of the platform. Standing near by, motionless and still holding the sword, was Abheron.

He was watching the fire, his face shiny with sweat, pupils like tiny pinpricks in the iciness of his eyes. His expression was an uneasy combination of desire and loathing as he watched the flames creep closer and closer.

Then he saw me. Before he could move, there was another crash overhead. I looked up in time to see part of the canopy and its wooden framework cave in. The flaming debris unfolded in an eerily silent drift of sparks and ash over the back of the platform where Abheron was standing. His eyes widened in alarm.

"Get off the ship!" he bellowed at me, flinging the

sword aside. The fire seemed to drape around him for a moment, like a fiery cape. Then, in a burst of supernatural speed, he dived under the flames into the dark water, and was gone. The debris collapsed backwards, enveloping the place where Abheron had stood.

By some merciful favour of God, the collapse had left both me and Rashna untouched. But fire burned between me and the platform. I looked around in panic and realized that the flames had taken nearly the whole deck. If I didn't get us off this vessel now, we'd both be dead.

I took another deep breath, almost choking on the scents of burning and blood that I remembered so well, and backed up slowly, my muscles quivering with tension. You've really gone mad now, I told myself.

I ran towards the flames as fast as I could, my breath rasping harshly in my throat as I jumped. The fire roared angrily as I passed over it, just out of reach, and landed awkwardly on the other side, fetching up against the edge of the dais. For an instant I leaned on the platform, clinging to it in sheer relief. Then I hauled myself up and bent over Rashna. I pressed two fingers to her throat and found the quick thread of her pulse. She was alive.

I slid my arms under her and arranged her as gently as possible for the rescuer's lift. She didn't even stir, draping limply over my shoulder like an old rug. She felt horribly delicate and light. Trying not to jolt her too badly, I stepped down from the platform – and stopped, dismayed. What now?

I couldn't get back over the moat of flames, not carrying Rashna. And though I thought I could keep myself afloat in the water, I knew I couldn't prevent Rashna from drowning while she was unconscious. As I stood hesitating, there was a splash and a thud behind me. I turned so quickly that I almost dropped Rashna – but I didn't care.

"Sorin!" I cried joyfully as he heaved himself painfully up out of the water, hair plastered to his head, and crawled under the smouldering rail. "You're all right!"

"Which is more than I can say for you, idiot woman," he shouted, slumping on his hands and knees. "What the sweet goddess do you think you're doing? Do you want to burn alive? Get into the lake!"

"I can't – Rashna. What about your legs?"

"My legs are fine in the water! I'll help with Rashna; there are boats coming. For Ioana's sake, Zahira! Come on!" He beckoned urgently.

I staggered to the edge, and between us we clumsily eased Rashna into the water on her back, her head on Sorin's shoulder and his arm across her chest. I slid in beside them, trying to remember the sculling motion that I had been taught when I was tiny. The water had lost any warmth the sun gave it in the day, and after the heat on the boat the cold was almost unbearable. It made my whole body burn and tingle. I wheezed, fighting for air.

"Boats – *ack*." I choked as a wave of black water broke over my head. I surfaced spluttering. "Boats coming?" I managed to get out.

"Fishing boats," he panted, struggling to keep Rashna above the jumping water.

"Who … did all this? Fire?" I choked again, and began coughing, the combination of smoke-burned throat and water too much.

"Rua people. Shut up!"

There was a shout in the distance – a familiar voice. I tried to turn in the water and went under again. I thrashed, trying to get back up, but the weight of clothes and boots felt like lead on my limbs. I should have remembered to take them off; they'd be ruined. I didn't know if my fingers were breaking the surface any more. Am I sinking, or just floating? I wondered. It was like being blind, the darkness… My chest is going to burst.

Something closed round my wrist, biting into the numbed flesh. The lake seemed to clamp down on me, and I screamed at the pressure, inhaled water – and broke the surface.

More hands closed on my arms and shoulders, grabbing my sopping clothes, and yanked me up. I was choking and coughing, water streaming out of my mouth and nostrils as I was pulled aboard the boat.

I forced my eyes open and saw Sorin leaning over me, his face dripping with water and ghostly pale in the reflected flicker of the fire.

"Thank the elements," he said, sagging with relief.

"Reia? Can you hear me?"

"Deo?" I croaked. "What – how?"

"Time enough for that later," Deo said. "Here." He tucked a thick blanket around me. It prickled against my wet skin and smelled strongly of fish, but the warmth felt like a blessing.

"Help…" I whispered. My throat felt like the time Rashna had tried to strangle me, when I was eight. "Help me up." I reached out a hand to Sorin. He tried to clasp it, but his fingers wouldn't close tightly enough; eventually I grabbed his wrist, and he was able to pull me into a sitting position. I leaned against him with a sigh, and tucked the trailing edge of the blanket around him.

I looked about me. We were in a middle-sized Rua fishing craft, five other boats of varying sizes clustered around us in the water. They were too far away in the shadows for me to make out the faces of the occupants, but I recognized several as wearing the uniforms of Abheron's servants, and was glad.

In our boat, two Rua oarsmen whom I didn't know worked hard, taking us away from the burning pleasure vessels. Deo sat with us in the stern, a northern-style recurved bow and empty quiver of arrows beside him.

He had a nasty scratch on his forehead and a spectacular black eye, but otherwise seemed to be unharmed. Between the two rowing benches Rashna had been carefully laid out and wrapped in more blankets like mine. Stefan, Sorin's man, leaned over her, holding one of her hands, while a Sedorne woman applied salve to the cuts on her face. Judging by the look of tenderness on Stefan's bruised face, Rashna would be well taken care of.

"We're even now, you know," Sorin said quietly.

I started from my half-doze. "What?"

"You saved me. Now I've saved you."

"We were already even," I said sleepily. I knew there were lots of important things to ask and tell, but at the moment my head felt as if it were full of rocks. Thinking would make them all tumble and grind together – and I wasn't too anxious for that to happen just yet. "You kept your promise when we came to you at Mesgao."

"That didn't make us even. You saved my life. Do you know that in Sedra, if someone saves your life, then your life belongs to them? I've belonged to you since you saved me from burning to death. Now I've saved you from the same fate, we're even."

I went cold. "Does that mean you don't belong to me any more?" I asked.

"No," he said, wrapping the blanket more securely around me. "It means we belong to each other."

I relaxed. "Oh. Good." I put my head on his shoulder again.

The boat had turned in the water while we were talking. We were well away from the burning ships now and I could see the whole formation. The ropes and walkways that had anchored them together gone, they were drifting slowly away from the pier, listing in the water as their crowns of flame ate at them. Fire sent streaks of light and colour across the surface of the black lake. There were dozens of figures milling about on the pier: guests, servants who hadn't rebelled, gourdin who had escaped the blaze.

A lone figure stood at the very end of the pier, completely still amid the chaos of the scene. The light gleamed wetly on his reddish-gold hair as he stared out at the burning armada of pleasure craft. Tiredness made my vision blur; I blinked. When I looked again, the figure was gone.

Something breathed into my mind, carrying with it images of gently flickering blue flames and a sense of warmth – and warning. The Holy Mother. I clutched at the comfort She offered like a child, but an instant later Her presence had faded.

I closed my eyes in weary resignation as the loss of Her warmth left me shivering. I knew what She had been trying to tell me.

Abheron is still alive. And he still wants you...

CHAPTER TWENTY-THREE

The house where Deo took us was hidden among the trees, low on the north bank of the lake, and constructed on wooden stilts that kept it out of the water when the lake rose in the rainy season. There was a crescent-shaped mooring bay beneath the house with enough room for several small fishing boats. Someone had left a lighted lamp hanging there to guide us in.

I only noticed any of this because, after the little fleet was tied up underneath the house, I had to stumble through tree roots and up stairs before I could get into it and lie down. I was conscious of light and warmth within, and people who flapped around me and my friends briskly, but that was all. I didn't even notice that for very long.

It wasn't until the next morning that I met the

people who had helped to engineer our rescue, and asked them the many questions which, after a good night's sleep, had occurred to me.

Sunlight and shadow made dancing patterns over the floor of the living area as the leaves outside the window were tossed by the rising wind. I sat cross-legged on a threadbare but comfortable cushion, with Sorin arranged less comfortably beside me – he was used to chairs, and sitting like this gave him cramp. Across the low table where our breakfast was laid out, Deo and another man sat. The other man was in his early fifties, with that hard, polished look that old soldiers get; and this was born out by the faded tattoo of a falcon across the bridge of his left cheek. What remained of his hair was white and bobbly like lambswool, and his beautiful, bright eyes were serious as he looked at us. His name was Toril and he was the leader of the Rua resistance in Jijendra. The first thing he told me was that he had been born a month after my father, and named in his honour.

While I was still struggling to think of an answer for that, Toril's daughter came in with a tray of tea and, after placing it gravely on the table, took the final cushion to my left and sat.

"How is she?" I asked. Padmina had been helping the Sedorne herb woman look after Rashna in the other room of the house. The silence from that room had been worrying me since I woke up.

"She has a broken arm and nose, four broken fingers, several cracked ribs, and very nasty bruising all over, which I hope does not reach her internal organs. She isn't awake yet – but in her condition this is perhaps a good thing." Padmina folded her hands in her lap with an air of serenity that I envied. "Stefan is resting with her now. His healer friend is fetching more things from home to tend her with."

"Do you think she will be all right?" I asked hesitantly, dreading the answer.

"I don't think she'll die. Neither does the Sedorne healer. She will be a long time recovering from this."

"She's a fighter. She'll fight her way up again," Toril added quietly.

I sighed. "Thank you." Sorin touched my shoulder comfortingly, and I managed a smile for him. He was quiet this morning, suffering from terrible pains in his limbs following the exertions of the night before.

As Padmina poured tea and passed out the cups, I looked at Deo. "Well? What happened, Deo? To you and Rashna and Stefan?"

Deo rubbed one hand over his head, taking his tea from Padmina gratefully. "If you have the patience for it, I'll start at the beginning."

"Yes, go on." I took my tea and reached for a date and honey roll, less because of hunger than because my nervous fingers wanted something to play with.

Deo explained that when we arrived at the summer

palace, one of the gourdin opened the carriage door for Anca and helped her down, and she smiled at him. There was something in the soldier's attitude, and in Anca's expression, that made Deo suddenly suspicious. He decided to go to the kitchen and make contact with Rashna and Stefan if he could – but they weren't there, and when he asked the staff about them, they seemed terrified. Deo realized then that something was wrong. He decided he had to make an effort to find Rashna and Stefan before reporting back to us, and remembered his old friend Toril, who lived in Jijendra. Deo hid in a supply cart that was heading into the city, and made his way to his friend's house – this house – hoping to get information and help. What he found was Stefan, battered half to death, sheltering there.

Here Toril took over the tale. He explained that Stefan had turned up at dawn the day before yesterday, bruised and bleeding, and claiming to be an agent of the alliance. Luckily for Stefan, word of what Sorin and I had tried to accomplish at Mesgao had reached Toril, and he believed Stefan, and took him in.

The news of an attempt at a Rua and Sedorne alliance against Abheron had come to Toril in an unexpected form. Rebel namoa and temple people – the same ones who had leaped into battle on my behalf last night – had raced to Jijendra ahead of us, and contacted the local resistance on arrival. These men and women were angry and disillusioned enough to set fire to Sedorne property in Mesgao, and to attack Sedorne wherever they found them, but they had not been willing to see me taken prisoner by the Sedorne king without acting.

I finally had my answer about Kapila's attack. The once friends who had fled from Mesgao had not wanted me dead after all. In fact, despite everything, they had risked their lives to save me.

Someone – Anca, of course – had tipped the gourdin off about Stefan and Rashna. Fortunately some of the Rua servants at the palace worked for the resistance, and after Rashna was caught, they hid Stefan and were able to smuggle him out. That was the only reason he had survived.

Deo shook his head. "I probably escaped the same fate as Rashna because Anca was hoping to get more information from me while I still trusted her. I knew we had to get you out of there as soon as possible, so we gathered up all we knew or could guess about Abheron's plans for the ball, and Toril sent word to every resistance worker and fighter he knew to attack the boats at our signal."

"You nearly killed Zahira when she got caught in the fire." Sorin spoke for the first time, grimly. "You put her in more danger yourselves than she was facing from Abheron."

Deo bowed his head, uncharacteristically cowed. "You're right. I apologize for the risks we took with both of you. We were desperate, and we lost sight of you in the smoke and confusion."

I laid my hand on Sorin's arm when he would have spoken again. "No, it wasn't their fault. Your plan was sound, Deo. The fire got away from you because the silk and ropes used to make the walkways and canopies had been treated with something – kirth oil, I think – that made them waterproof. It was like they were soaked with pitch. The fire could never have taken hold like that otherwise. Anyway, we're all here, and still alive. So you succeeded. That's all that matters."

Sorin nodded grudgingly. I tightened my grip on his arm, and looked at Toril and Padmina again.

"The question now is what we do next. Is it safe for you, with us staying here?"

"Ah." Toril smiled for the first time, the wide white grin bringing a devilish look to his face. "There is more to tell you yet."

"We had news last night, just before we left to rescue you," Padmina said. Her unsmiling face nonetheless shone with happiness. "It changes everything."

"The alliance isn't dead," Deo said, his cowed expression melting away with suspicious speed. "After we left Mesgao your allies, both Rua and Sedorne, began gathering outside the town. The prospect of losing you both seems to have stirred everyone into action. Casador Fareed and Lord Elgun met with each other and hashed out a treaty between them. They've joined together, raised a new banner in your names, and they're marching on Jijendra."

"What?" I hastily put down my tea as it threatened to slop out, and gaped at Deo.

"Marching? That implies a force of some numbers," Sorin said.

"They're gathering followers as they come. Mostly Rua, but apparently at least three new Sedorne lords have thrown their lot in too, and brought their gourdin with them. At the last count they had a force of nearly two thousand people with them."

I raked my hands through my hair, dazed. "Two thousand? The garrison here only holds five hundred gourdin."

"Exactly." Padmina sat very straight. "They'll crush them."

"Wait – what about Abheron's army? The lords still loyal to him? Won't he call them up?"

"He doesn't have time," Toril said, his grin spreading. "The standing army is stationed at Aroha – it's an eight-day march from there to Jijendra, and the alliance army is only three days away. Even if he found out about the rebellion at the same time we did, there's no way the Sedorne army could get here before the alliance. When we take Jijendra we'll be capturing more than half of his court with it. Half of his lords prisoner! We'll have broken any defence on his side before it can even form. His only option will be to run."

"I can't believe it!" Incredulous laughter bubbled from my lips. "This is—"

"A miracle," Sorin finished. He grabbed my shoulders and kissed me hard on the lips. After a moment, he pulled back to lean his forehead against mine. "He's finished," he whispered. "By the goddess, he's finished at last. We've done it. All we have to do is lie low for three days, and then this might all be over."

A sudden frantic banging at the door made us all jump. Sorin and I separated hastily, but Toril held up his hand to stay us.

"No – it's a knock I recognize. My grandson."

Padmina frowned. "He's not due back from the market until later." The banging came again as she got up and unlatched the door.

A boy of no more than twelve tumbled through and fell against his mother, wrapping his arms around her waist. As the child hid his face in her tunic, the sound of muffled sobbing reached me. Padmina quickly shut the door behind him and shot the bolt, then laid her hands on his shoulders and pulled him back to look into his face.

"What is it, Jai? Come now, calm down. Tell me what's happened."

"The Pig! The Pig got Zaffi, and Ajeet. He got them all."

CHAPTER
TWENTY-FOUR

Padmina's gentle expression froze into one of shock and she kneeled before him, taking his face in her hands. "Tell me from the beginning," she said seriously. "This is important. What did the Pig do? How did he get your friends?"

The little boy seemed to steady under his mother's calm gaze. He took a deep breath, gulped back a sob, and then began. "I was playing stones with Ajeet and Zaffi and some of the other boys in the market place. It was all like normal! There wasn't any of the things you warned about. The Sedorne stallkeepers were all there, and they weren't nervous. Then suddenly there was shouting and screaming – and the gourdin came. More than I've ever seen. They came straight through the market. They were beating everyone, not just Rua, but Sedorne too. I saw a little girl, younger than me, get hit right on the head, and the gourdin hit her mother too, when she tried to stop them. They were Sedorne."

He stopped, sniffing hard. "Ajeet and Zaffi panicked. They ran. The gourdin caught them. I did what you said, Mama. I curled into a ball and stayed really still. When they'd gone past I ran."

I looked at Jai's tear-stained face, feeling ill. Such senseless violence – why?

"Retaliation," Sorin said quietly.

"For last night?" Padmina looked up from her son's face.

"Probably. Or he might have heard that the alliance army is on its way."

I thought about Abheron's behaviour towards me; that flash of dark emotion in his eyes, reined back each time with a speed that spoke of iron control – and of fear. "No," I said.

"What else could it be?" Toril asked. "He's hitting back at us while he can."

"No," I repeated. "He's too clever for that. Now is not the time to take random revenge on the people – especially his own. He needs them and their loyalty."

"He obviously doesn't care," Deo said.

"Or he has something more important to play for," I said. "We've underestimated him. Again."

Sorin looked at me with concern. Where Abheron's

motivation was in question, I hadn't been wrong so far. "How?"

"I don't know. But he's not finished yet, Sorin. Not yet."

Padmina stood again, and drew her son to the breakfast table with an air of determination. "Sit and eat," she said firmly. "You'll feel better. We can't do anything about what is happening in the marketplace until we have more information. One of our people is sure to come soon and tell us what the Pig is up to."

She was right. A bare five minutes later, there was another knock at the door, and Padmina opened it to let in the Sedorne healer who had been caring for Rashna. The woman was chalk white and trembling, but her voice was matter-of-fact as she sat and told us what she had seen.

"Abheron's gone mad," she said. "The gourdin have raided every house, both Rua and Sedorne, on the west bank. Merchants, lords, stallkeepers, net weavers, fishermen. The whole right flank of the city."

"Raided? Were they searching for us?" I asked.

"No. Not you." Her gaze strayed to Jai, who was watching her with rapt attention. When she looked back at me, there were tears in her eyes. "They were looking for children over two years old. They took them. Every one."

There was silence. In my lap, my fingers curled slowly into fists.

"Hostages," I whispered finally. "He's holding them as hostages."

"The people will never dare fight against him if he has their children. And he must know that if the children are hurt, people will blame us for it – turn against the resistance. That's why he's doing this." Deo had gone the colour of ash.

"That isn't all," the woman said. "A royal proclamation went out just as I was about to come back here. He's saying that unless Zahira Elfenesh and Sorin Mesgao give themselves up by dawn tomorrow, he'll start killing the little ones." She brushed a tear from her face impatiently. "My sister and her family live on the west bank. I don't know ... I'll see to your wounded, but..."

"Then you must go to your family. Of course," I said, realizing as I spoke how pitifully little it was to offer her. "Go with our blessing."

She nodded at me gratefully, then got up and went into the other room.

"Abheron's not a man any more," Sorin said evenly into the silence. "I don't know what he is."

"What can we do?" Toril said, his face despairing. "Those poor little ones ... their poor mothers and fathers. There's no way to help them."

I closed my eyes. No way to help them... I remembered the refugee children whom I had taught at the House of God: so used to fear, their bony, defiant little faces just waiting for the next blow to fall. My brothers, Kiran and Pallav – boys who never had the chance to be men. My sister, Indira, who never danced at a ball or saw the casadors fight over her hand.

I remembered my own face, as I had seen it in Indira's mirror. A child's face, unscarred, innocent and full of laughter. Before everything I loved had been taken from me, including my own name and memory. Children shouldn't have to be wary and afraid. My brothers and sister shouldn't be dead. My face should still be beautiful and innocent. It was too late for them, and for me. No way to help them.

Who am I? For the first time in weeks, that question echoed in my head. I knew the answer.

I am the reia. It is up to me...

I opened my eyes and looked at Toril. "I won't let those children die because of me," I said. "I won't."

They stared at me in shock. Then the room exploded with protests.

"You can't mean—" Deo broke out.

"You can't give in to him," Padmina said, putting her arm round Jai's shoulders. "I say this as a mother, and I would say it still, even if my boy was up there with Abheron. If these children are saved by your death, how many others will die before we have another such chance to be rid of him? He will never stop. The only way to be free is to fight him."

"Please, Reia." Toril gazed at me pleadingly. "Think again."

Sorin gave me a measuring look, and held up his hands. "Quiet! For the elements' sake, give her a chance to talk."

"Thank you." I drew in a deep breath. "I don't particularly want to die. In fact, I have no intention of dying. So please stop staring at me like that." I addressed Sorin. "Abheron told me that one of the reasons he had to get rid of you was that he was sure you would challenge him to a duel of kingship. You never considered that option, never mentioned it, even before Kapila poisoned you. Why?"

Sorin looked a little taken aback. "Before I met you, Abheron took extreme care to keep me away from him. I couldn't get within a hundred yards, and you need to be face to face to issue the challenge. After I met you, it would have been completely inappropriate. A declaration that I intended to take his place as king – Sedorne king – of Ruan, bypassing you and your claim to the throne: a slap in the face to the Rua people, and your rights as the true reia."

"I see." I took another deep breath. Can I do it? What choice do I have? "Listen – I have a plan."

CHAPTER
TWENTY-FIVE

Before dawn, Jijendra was swathed in shadows like ragged grey cobwebs. The rising wind harried low black clouds so that they spilled and tumbled over the paler darkness of the sky, and gales chased each other through the narrow streets, teasing shop banners and God charms until the air seemed to shriek with the noise.

My stomach jumping with tension, I pressed my back against the wall of a warehouse and peered round the corner at the deserted marketplace. The open area was carved into the centre of the west bank so that it was relatively flat, the floor paved with yellow sandstone. It seemed hugely empty without the mess of stalls, tents, carts, animals and people that normally filled it. No one would be selling their wares here today.

At the very edge of the area, overlooking the lake, a trio of tall wooden poles had been set in the stone paving. They were new – or at least, they had not been there when I was a child. I watched the royal pennants attached to their tips snap and curl in the wind, the insignia obscured by the shadows. I could easily make out the sturdy metal brackets driven into the lower portions of the thick poles. They were example arms. Executed traitors were hanged there, as a warning to anyone thinking of following their example.

They were empty now, but for how long, only Abheron could tell. This was the place where my uncle had decreed that Sorin and I must give ourselves up at dawn today. The place where he would murder the children if we did not.

Somewhere in the shadows around the square, Sorin, Deo, Toril and a handful of other resistance fighters were hidden. We had agreed that it was safer to split up – that way if any one of us was caught, the others would be free to come to their aid. But right now I longed for someone to talk to – or at least someone to hide behind. I felt ridiculously conspicuous.

A group of men came out of a nearby shop. None of them glanced in my direction, but I tensed as they brushed by, and nervously pulled the hood of my cloak further down over my face. I couldn't afford to be seen, not until the last minute, when it would be too late for Abheron to do anything about it. I relaxed as the men crossed the path and went into a house closer to the market square.

Normally at this early hour I would have been alone in the city. Everyone should have been asleep, save the fishermen at their business on the lake below. This morning, there were no boats on the water, and it seemed that all the residents of Jijendra had left their beds early. In the half-hour since our small group had split up, a host of eerily silent townspeople had flooded the dim streets – some driving in carriages or carts, others on foot. Moving with grim purpose, they had disappeared into the houses, warehouses, shops and shadows surrounding the square.

They were here to see their children.

In the east, the sky above the mountains had been gradually growing paler and brighter. Now the glowing rim of the sun lifted onto the jagged peaks, and the first light of day unfolded over Jijendra. As I watched, there was a sudden burst of activity. As if the sun had been a clarion call, everywhere doors and windows were flung open, and people surged out to fill the road and swarm up onto the edges of the cleared market square. I was pushed forward by the press of bodies, away from my sheltered area and into the full blast of the wind. I clutched at my hood again and clapped my elbow to my side, horribly conscious of the hard points of the sword at my waist. I didn't want anyone banging into it.

I let myself be driven up to the edge of the paved sandstone, but stood firm as others pushed around me to places in the square itself. As I was buffeted by the wind and the crowd, I saw finely dressed men and women jostle against workaday net weavers, Sedorne shifting to make way for Rua, young and old squashed together. All watched the road with the same expression of fearful hope.

"Soon. Soon…" I heard a woman whisper.

The sun rose higher, flinging out great arms of gold and pink into the banks of cloud that rolled before it. The crowd grew. More and more people streamed up to join the restless, whispering ranks watching the road, until there was simply room for no more. The roofs of the surrounding buildings became packed, people jamming themselves through windows and climbing up to perch on rickety canopies to get a view of the square.

As the sun parted company with the mountains and lifted fully into the sky, a new sound reached my ears. It was the rhythmic clank and scrape of Sedorne armour: marching gourdin. Frightened cries and frantic whispering filled the air around me as a large body of soldiers – three companies at least, half of them mounted, and all armed to the teeth – came into view. The people on the road scurried back hastily to let them through, and the foot soldiers marched into the square and spread out, creating a human wall around the perimeter of the area, to keep the townsfolk back. One of them took up a position just before me. I shied away as if in fear, bowing my head to keep my face hidden.

Then Abheron came into view.

He was dressed in black. Not the fine, jewelled black of his ball costume, but the plain, slightly shabby black of a judge – or an executioner. His hair blazed in the new morning light as the splendid blood bay he was mounted on danced restively under him. As he rode past I was close enough to see his profile. It was expressionless. Nor did he look at the waiting crowd as he rode through them, along the avenue created by his men.

There was a new ripple of noise from the towns-people as the final company of gourdin passed. A Sedorne woman near by shrieked, "Ilie! Ilie! My baby!"

Everyone surged forward, displacing me and forcing me aside, but the gourdin lining the way turned on them fiercely.

"Get back!" one of the soldiers shouted. "Unless you want them to die! Go on, get back!"

Surrounded by soldiers, a little open cart bumped over the road – the kind of cheap wooden vehicle that was used to transport vegetables or wine barrels to market. In it were half a dozen girls and boys, both Rua and Sedorne, ranging in age from five to twelve or thirteen years old. Only a fraction of the children

Abheron had seized. The rest must still be under guard at the summer palace.

Cautiously I moved forward through the heaving crowd, pushing as close as I could to the line of gourdin and peering through the gaps between their shoulders. I could see no sign of blood or bruising on the children, but they sat frighteningly still, blank-faced and staring at nothing as the cart was pulled along. Looking at their glazed eyes, I realized that they had been drugged to keep them quiet, and I felt a fierce shaft of anger pierce my anxiety. Damn Abheron. Didn't he want to see his victims cry?

I turned my head to look for him. Still on his horse, he had taken up a position before the flagpoles, with the lake at his back. As the cart rumbled to a stop on his left, he lifted one of his hands from the reins. Two gourdin stepped forward at the signal and blew a long, shrill note on their pipes. The crowd immediately fell silent, waiting. I was reminded sharply of the wary Sedorne guests at Abheron's ball.

Does he really mean to do this? I wondered in bewilderment. Are fear and obedience enough for him? Why must he break everyone and everything?

"My people!" Abheron called out, his deep, melodic voice carrying easily over the crowd. "Loyal subjects of Jijendra. You all know why you are here. The night before last, traitors invaded the ball I was giving for my niece and her husband. Those rebels set fire to my pleasure craft and destroyed them, causing the deaths of many brave soldiers and innocent people."

I snorted quietly as I worked my way along the line of gourdin, searching for the best place to wait.

"They kidnapped my niece and her husband and are holding them hostage. Word has even reached me that an armed force calling itself the alliance is coming here, hoping to take the city by force. Elements only know what horrors it would perpetrate on Jijendra."

A murmur of astonishment ran through the crowd. The faces I could see didn't look too frightened, though – more incredulous. Let's hope they're not stupid enough to believe him, I thought, coming to a stop behind a gourdin almost opposite Abheron.

"I cannot and will not tolerate such random, vicious violence in my realm," he continued. "It must come to a stop, and those involved must be punished accordingly." He didn't turn his head, or gesture in any way, but I was sure that everyone's eyes strayed to the example arms behind him.

"The ringleaders of the rebels are here in this city, at this very moment. They call themselves patriots. They claim to serve you, the people of Ruan. If that is the case, then their consciences will not allow them to cause these innocent children's deaths. They will do what I have ordered: give themselves up now, and release Zahira Elfenesh and Sorin Mesgao. If they do not, your children will pay the price of that cowardice.

I hope you will know, then, who to blame for their deaths." He stopped, letting the silence hang.

Everything was still, save the wind that swept across the square. The pennants behind Abheron snapped sharply in the quiet.

"Very well." Abheron nodded to one of the gourdin next to the cart.

The soldier turned and began unlatching the back of the wooden conveyance. His movements were slow and reluctant; it was one thing to kill in the heat of battle, or to execute adults, but this was something else. Finally he pulled down the cart gate and grabbed the closest child, a pretty little Sedorne girl of about five. A horrified gasp went up from the crowd. The gourdin hesitated, and instead reached for an older boy, whose dark hair and skin identified him as Rua. There was a low hiss of anger from the Rua in the crowd, and a wail of sorrow from someone on the other side of the square. The gourdin again hesitated.

I looked at Abheron to see what he thought of this, but he wasn't watching the soldier. His eyes were scanning the crowd. For the first time, I thought I saw a hint of anxiety in his pose. He was sure we'd give in, I thought. Now he's not so confident. He underestimated us too...

A second gourdin, impatient with the first one's indecisiveness, grabbed the Rua boy, swinging him out of the cart. There was another wail. A low, angry murmur filled the air; the crowd shifted forward, pressing against the human wall of gourdin. The soldiers reached for their weapons.

Abheron called out, "Take heed of this. This is what your resistance have brought you to."

I dropped to my hands and knees and shot through the gap between the gourdin's legs. He grabbed for me a fraction too late, his gauntleted hands closing over the thick folds of my cloak. I threw myself forward, and with a wrench at my shoulders and the noise of tearing cloth, I was free. I rolled and came up on my feet inside the perimeter of guards, in front of Abheron's horse.

"No," I said. "This is what having a tyrant and a madman for a king has brought us to."

The crowd roared with surprise and relief as they realized who I was. Abheron's face relaxed and he waved the gourdin behind me back.

"You're somewhat late, my dear," he said. "I'm willing to forgive you, since you have justified my faith in your nature so admirably." He dismounted and handed the horse's reins to a guard. Facing me, he made a production of looking around. "However, I'm surprised not to see your husband with you. And what of your other little friends? I did specifically request their company. It seems rather rude of them to let you come to give yourself up alone."

"That's because I haven't come to give myself up,"

I said. I stepped back, pitching my voice to carry to the crowd. "Abheron Luminov, by the old laws of the Sedorne, I challenge you here before your people to a duel of kingship. Either accept and prove that you deserve the crown you wear, or refuse and brand yourself a coward unworthy of the throne."

This time the outburst of noise came not only from the crowd. The gourdin cried out in shock, clattering their armour – but they stayed back, adhering to the laws of the duel which I had just invoked. I felt my face splitting in a fierce grin of triumph.

Abheron was so surprised that for a moment he actually gaped at me. Then he laughed, his eyes crinkling with genuine amusement. "Ridiculous child," he said. "You can't challenge anyone."

"Oh yes, I can. By publicly declaring yourself willing to accept me as your heir, you've shown that I am equal to a man, and have all the same rights as one. That's the law."

The amusement started to fade from his face. "A king is above the law."

"Not this one," I said firmly. "Not this time."

CHAPTER TWENTY-SIX

The wind blew stray wisps of reddish hair around his forehead. "I won't fight you."

"I'm not giving you a choice." I drew my sword. The long, lethally curved blade slid from its scabbard with a quiet hiss. I prayed that it wouldn't shake in my hand as I lifted it.

"That's a big knife, my dear," he said, mocking now. "Take care you don't cut yourself with it."

The feel of the leather-wrapped hilt under my fingers calmed me. I flicked the sword through a complex pass, the blade moving with ease that spoke of long practice.

"Don't worry," I replied evenly. "I'll be careful."

The amusement was completely gone from his face now. "Stop this foolishness. Any fight between us can only end one way – with your death. I have no intention of hurting you, Zahira. You know that. Besides, how can you help your people if you're dead?"

"Better dead than forced to watch them suffer under your rule, Abheron."

"You can't provoke me into losing my temper, Zahira." He smiled suddenly. "I will not fight you."

"You don't have a choice," I repeated, keeping my eyes firmly on his. I knew that when I did manage to break through his control, the darkness there would warn me first.

I began walking, circling him – forcing him to circle too, to keep me in sight. My sash fluttered at my waist as I moved into the wind, and I tossed my head to get the hair out of my eyes. The rising sun was behind me now, and the light made Abheron's face appear as white and hard as a picked-clean skull.

"The only reason the people of Ruan tolerate your misrule is because they fear you," I said. "If you refuse this challenge, they won't fear you any more. Every Sedorne in the country will know that you were too frightened to face a woman. Even your own gourdin will no longer respect you. They'll turn on you – and probably a lot faster than you realize."

"There's a flaw in your logic, my dear," he said confidently as we circled each other. "My gourdin know that, if the desire took me, I could slice any one of them into fine strips without breaking my stride. No Sedorne man would believe for a moment that a mere girl could frighten me. They will simply think I granted you mercy, because you're a woman and a close relative."

"I doubt they'll think that," I said, suddenly realizing how I could get to him. "You're not known for showing mercy to your family."

His jaw tightened, but he said nothing. A great drift of cloud swept over the sun, and suddenly we moved in near twilight dimness, the wind wailing around us.

"No witty rejoinder?" I said lightly. "Dear me – that is a disappointment. Let's recount your mercies, shall we, and see if they loosen your tongue?"

"Zahira—"

"Oh no, this is fun, Uncle. Let's talk about your mercy to my sister, Indira. She was fifteen when you came to visit us, do you remember? She loved horses, and she liked dancing very much. She used to braid my hair and tell me stories. She's dead – because of you. My brothers. Do you remember them? Pallav took after our father. He was very kind, and good with his hands. Kiran now, he was more like Mama to look at. He could be impatient sometimes, but he was so clever. They're both dead too. Because of you."

"Stop it," he said tightly.

I was getting through. "Don't be a bore, Uncle – I'm only just starting. Remember my father? Your brother by marriage, who welcomed you into his home? He was the one you stabbed to death. And let's not forget my mother. Your beautiful, beloved Emelia. You were very merciful to her. You left her to burn to death in the wreckage of her home, crying over her murdered husband. I'm sure she'd thank you for your mercy."

His eyes blazed at me out of the shadow, like twin stars. I braced myself. Then the clouds over the sun began to shred away, and the light gradually brightened until I could see the steely control in his face.

"Well-aimed blows, my dear. But not good enough."

"There's still someone left, someone we haven't talked about, Uncle. What about me? Let's talk about your mercy to me."

He stared at me, wordless. The light flickered and shifted over his face as more cloud shreds chased across the sky, so that I couldn't quite fix his expression. He was moving in a perfect unconscious rhythm now, his shoulders tensed, one hand hovering over his sword hilt. I just had to push him over the edge. I felt a shiver of dread and forced it back.

I had to end this.

"First," I began, "I'd like to thank you for your kind gift of a scarred face, Uncle. Not to mention the revulsion and pity of strangers that come with it – I've enjoyed those over the years. What next? Well, leaving aside the fact that I lost my whole family and my home while I was still a child, there was the way you sent hired killers to the House of God and murdered Noirin Surya, the only mother I'd ever known, so that I could watch her die, choking on her own blood. Then you had the mercenaries destroy my home a second time, desecrating the centre of my people's religion."

I was panting now, emotion clogging my voice.

"You dragged me here against my will, and poured your sad little story into my ear, searching for sympathy. You threatened to kill my husband, and had my friend beaten almost to death, and now – the crowning achievement – you decide to slaughter innocent children and lay their deaths on my conscience." I made an ironic bow, sweeping my sword out. "Yes, Uncle. By this accounting, you are merciful indeed."

I lunged at him, my blade seizing the light and flinging it out as it chopped down towards Abheron's face. He jerked back just in time and I allowed the momentum to carry me past and back to face him.

"Fight, damn you!" I shouted. "Fight me!"

The sun burst through the clouds and lit his face.

"I've admitted responsibility for everything I've done. I've told you I want to redeem myself, Zahira. Why won't you let me do that?"

"For God's sake!" I screamed, despair and exasperation welling inside me. "You can't be redeemed. Don't you understand that yet? There's no hope, no salvation for you. It's too late. Every action you take only brings darkness and death, and nothing in the world can be right again until you're dead. One of us has to die here today, Uncle. One of us has to – because I won't live in a world where you exist. One of us is going to die; I intend for it to be you."

His chest was heaving now, as if he was fighting for air. A cloud shadow blew slowly across his face, and as it touched the iciness of his eyes I saw the darkness unfolding there, like black wings opening. I felt a razor-edged thrill of fear skitter down my back. I've done it now, I thought. God help and protect me; God guide my sword... Oh, God, I've really done it now.

I edged back warily. The crowd moved restlessly, but stayed silent.

His eyes seemed glazed, unfocused, as they met mine. He whispered, "So be it."

He jerked his long, straight sword from its sheath in a movement that spoke of deadly ease, and saluted me with it. Then he came at me, terrifyingly swift and graceful as a dancer. I threw myself to the side just in time and his sword point passed my stomach by a millimetre, tearing a long rent in my tunic. We both fell back, circling again.

Dear God, he's fast.

I flung my arms out and spun towards him, my curved blade slashing sideways towards his neck. He twisted like a snake to avoid the blow and went in low to thrust at my stomach again. I dodged and used the movement to flip back, kicking my legs up towards his face. I felt my foot connect with a solid thump as the knuckles of my right hand, clenched on the sword, smashed painfully into the stone, ripping the skin. I dropped, rolled and came up to see him nursing a bleeding lip.

First blood to me, I thought, giddy with the pumping of my heart. I brought my blade up in a two-handed clasp and waited.

The wind rushed at us, finding the gaping hole in my tunic and stinging against my grazed knuckles, drying the sweat on my face. He moved towards me, cloud shadows wheeling across his body so that he seemed to warp and shiver, a black flame.

Suddenly he lashed out, his sword coming up in a crescent sweep at my neck. I twisted to avoid the blow and found myself moving into his second, lightning-fast lunge at my side. I parried, but his sword glanced off mine. I gasped as a line of fiery pain flared across my upper arm, and blocked again just in time as his blade lanced towards my face. We locked, hilt to hilt. My arms trembled with the strain as he brought his superior weight and strength to bear on me. His face was only an inch from mine, his breath warm on my cheek.

"Having fun?" he asked calmly.

I wrenched away, avoiding his quick cut at my face more through luck than skill, and swung my sword up to catch his on the down sweep. I twisted my blade round his and threw my shoulder into it. I felt him falter as the hilt shifted in his fingers. Before he could readjust I pivoted round him to deliver a low kick to the back of his knee.

Our swords disengaged with a flash of sparks and he buckled, slashing at my leg as he went down. I jumped his sword and kicked again at his face. His free hand snapped up and caught my booted foot before it could land. I felt the bite of the metal fingers in his glove, then he heaved, pushing me back as he rushed upwards. Unprepared, I fell heavily and rolled sideways. His sword came down next to my face with a shriek of metal. A chip of stone hit me in the cheek, and I felt blood trickle down my face as I rolled again and came to my feet.

He lunged. I danced back, slashed two-handed at his chest – missed – twisted away from a blow to my side, and slashed again, this time at his face. He dodged just in time to avoid losing his eye, but my sword point opened a long gash down his cheek. He grunted with pain and disengaged to circle me, blood running down his face.

"That's going to leave a scar, you know," I couldn't resist taunting.

"Then we'll be more alike than ever, my dear."

"I don't think so, but come closer and I'll see what I can do."

Blood from the wound on my arm was trickling steadily down to my elbow. I shook my arm hastily to get rid of it before it reached my hands and then moved in.

I made a sideways slash at his shoulder. He parried. I twirled, bringing the blade towards his chest. He blocked just in time, and we locked again hilt to hilt, my sword point a bare inch from his chest. My shoulders screamed with the strain as I fought to break his grip. I thought I felt his arm give, ever so slightly. Then, to my horror, I realized it wasn't his arm but mine.

The blood from my arm had welled down and reached my hand. The hilt of my sword was sliding. I hung on desperately, but my grip faltered. He could feel it.

I saw his lips stretch in a terrifying grin, and then he was throwing his weight forward. The sword slipped from my blood-slick palm and flew away, landing with a clatter behind me. The metal of his gauntleted hand smashed into my face. My head snapped back and for an instant everything went black as I fell.

Then I hit the ground and cried out with pain as my skull bounced off the stone. I opened my eyes to the swirling sky and Abheron's face as he leaned over me, his sword point resting on my chest like a lead weight. My breath scraped deafeningly in my ears.

I'm going to die. Now. I'm really going to die.

I closed my eyes and lay still, waiting for him to end it. Please, Holy Mother, watch over Sorin and Deo and Mira and the baby... The excruciating weight of the sword grew heavier as he slowly pushed down. My skin opened and blood spilled out, trickling over my chest. I gritted my teeth against the pain – oh, God, forgive me for failing – and jerked as the blade grated against my breastbone. Please take care of Sorin; I love him. A tortured noise of agony burst out of my lips and I opened my eyes to meet the glazed shadows of his as he killed me.

The pressure stopped. He stood over me, utterly still, staring into my face if he had turned to stone. Something was changing behind the opaque ice of his eyes. The darkness that I had deliberately set free was slowly receding, folding back in on itself.

He shook his head. "No."

I stared at him, uncomprehending, as he carefully removed the point of his sword from my chest and stepped back.

"Pick up your sword, Zahira."

"What?" I croaked.

"Pick up your sword," he repeated.

I scrabbled to my knees, grunting with pain. For a moment, I could only clutch at the throbbing wound in my chest. Then I forced my hands away, wiped the blood off on my breeches, and reached for the fallen blade. I kept my eyes on him as I climbed awkwardly to my feet. I was dizzy, and icy cold, as if a layer of skin had fallen away.

"What's this?" I asked, my voice sounding small and scratchy to my own ears. There was no way I could win now – he must know it. Is this his way of torturing me?

"You wanted to fight me, Zahira," he said. There was something different about him. He had his control back now, but the usual air of languid mockery was gone. He was deadly serious. "Fight."

Without warning, he rushed at me. I braced, trying to ignore the pain as I lifted my blade. He feinted left. Moving on instinct alone, I blocked, then lunged, aiming for his chest.

I saw a flicker of a smile cross his face. Then – as the clouds scudded away from the sun and flooded the marketplace with light – he dropped his sword and opened his arms.

My blade went into him up to the hilt, making a soft, wet thud.

I stared at the hilt protruding from the centre of his doublet in disbelief, my fingers slipping away from it. I looked up into his face. He was the colour of chalk, his jaw clenched in pain as his hands came up and grabbed at my shoulders. He swayed, fighting to stay upright, and I found myself clutching at him, the hilt of the sword digging into my sternum. For a moment, we stood there together in a strange kind of embrace.

"Why…?" I breathed, stupid with shock.

He tried to smile, but only managed a twisted grimace, breath rasping harshly through his lips. The metal fingers tightened painfully on my shoulder as I looked into his eyes.

"Curse … broken," he ground out. His expression

changed, and I saw a flare of light, flickering like a blue flame, in his eyes. "Emelia…" he whispered.

Then he crumpled, falling away from me and sprawling on the stone at my feet.

He was dead.

CHAPTER
TWENTY-SEVEN

The sword poked out of his chest grotesquely. Some impulse made me reach down and, with a shaking hand, pull it out. Blood gushed up from the wound and pooled around the body on the golden stones, spreading with syrupy, shining thickness. My fingers clenched on the sword hilt.

I wanted to feel something. Anything. There was nothing there. No sorrow, and no happiness either. All I could call up was a distant sense of relief.

I was free. Ruan was free. And I had recognized the blue flicker that had brought Abheron ease in his final moment. The Holy Mother had embraced him. Perhaps even he was free, at last.

I heard a commotion behind me, and then footsteps thudding rapidly across the paving stones. I swung round, lifting my sword.

It was Sorin.

I dropped the sword and threw myself at him. He wrapped his arms around me and we held on to each other, wordlessly.

"That was the worst – *the worst* – thing I've ever had to do in my life. Stand and watch you. Just stand by and watch..." he said, the words muffled in my hair. I could feel him shuddering.

"I know." I sighed. I was so tired, and my head was spinning wildly. "I know. Wait a moment." With an effort I pushed away from him and turned to look at the marketplace. The human wall of gourdin had gone. I couldn't see any sign of Abheron's personal guards. They had fled, probably fearing that they would be mobbed now that Abheron was dead.

Without the barrier, the crowd had come in until they were barely a foot away from us. They formed their own wall, and they showed no signs of moving. Eerily silent and still, they stared at the scene before them.

"What's wrong with them?" Sorin said quietly.

"Shock. Fear. Anger. We've seen people like this before." I shook my head. "They've just watched me kill their king. They don't know me; they barely know who I am. Everything's changing. They don't know what to do." I had great sympathy for them. I felt much the same.

I turned away and limped towards the abandoned cart. The children were slumped against each other, seemingly half asleep now. I hoped the drugs would wear off with no ill effects. Someone had put the back of the vehicle up again, so I undid it, and then turned to face the crowd.

"Come and fetch your children," I called out.

For a moment, everything remained still, except for the wind that teased and ruffled my hair. Then, slowly, hesitantly, in twos and threes and fours, people emerged to collect their little ones. They nodded or bowed to me nervously as they came, and I tried to smile reassuringly.

Finally the cart was empty.

"What about the others?" someone shouted.

I turned to look for them, but they were hidden. There was a low murmur of agreement, and the people stirred, like the banners rippling in the wind over my head.

"What about the ones at the palace?" the same voice cried.

I sighed, then winced as the wounds in my chest and arm throbbed. My cheek stung like fire, my whole body ached, and all I really wanted was to curl into a ball and cry. But I couldn't.

These people had no reason to trust me. I had to give them one.

Sorin groaned as I turned to scramble painfully onto

the deserted cart, but he obligingly followed me up, steadying himself on the side of the vehicle.

I looked out at the crowd and saw a few familiar faces tilted up to watch me – Toril and Padmina, and some of the resistance people I knew. I saw Joachim, his head bandaged and his face grim. And there, at the very front, Deo, beaming, urging me on. I took a moment to gather myself, calling on the skills I'd once used to inspire refugee children in the House of God. *If they have pride, I can teach them strength...* My father had said that. My father, the rei.

From somewhere, the words came.

"People of Jijendra," I began, speaking as loudly as I could. "People of Jijendra, Ruan and Sedorne. My name is Zahira Elfenesh; I am the youngest daughter of rei Toril and reia Emelia, who once governed Ruan. This is my husband, Lord Sorin of Mesgao. Your children will be returned to you as soon as we can get to the palace and find them. That is my promise to you."

There was another low rumble of noise from the crowd, but I couldn't tell if it was approving or threatening.

"Before we go to the palace, I ask for a few moments of your attention." I gulped, then continued. "I would ask you to look at me and my husband. Because we are the face of your future. I ask you to listen to us, because we are the voice of the days to come.

"For many years you have lived under the rule of an

insane, broken man – this pitiful dead creature." I gestured at Abheron's body, though I kept my eyes away from it. "He tried to break you. He oppressed and hurt you in every way he knew how. Some of you may have fought back, as much as you were able. Others had too much at stake, or were too frightened. Still others" – I allowed my tone to grow steely for a moment – "may have taken advantage of the situation. Whatever you have suffered or gained under Abheron's rule, I am telling you now: that time has come to an end."

I paused, letting my words sink in. I glanced at Sorin. He gave me an apprehensive look, but nodded encouragingly. *This is your moment, so get on with it.*

The wind was dying down, and my words echoed across the market square.

"Ruan is a great land. A beautiful land. There is enough here for all of us to share – enough for everyone. There is no room for fear, or cruelty and hatred. They have no place in this land, and you don't have to put up with them. There should be justice and equality between all the people of this country, both Rua and Sedorne. Most of all there should be compassion – from us to you, and from you towards each other."

I lifted my hands up. "I am your reia. I do not know what sort of reia I will be. I don't know if I can be great. I do know that you are my family now, and I will take care of each of you – man and woman, young and old, Rua and Sedorne – as long as I live. There will be difficulties, and hard times, I know that. Whatever happens, we all have to remember one thing. You deserve better than this." I pointed again at the grisly remains of their former king. This time I forced myself to look too, at the man I had killed. "We can do better than this. If you will trust me."

I stopped, and waited. There was utter silence.

Then, at the front of the crowd, Deo lifted his fist and shook it in the air. In a clear, loud voice, he called out, "Long live Queen Zahira! Long live the reia!"

One by one, other voices took up the cry. "Long live the reia! Long live the queen!"

People began to cheer, stamping their feet, whooping and whistling. The noise rose up like a joyous wave. I saw a puff of colour fly into the wind, and then another, and for a moment didn't realize what it was – then I saw the crowd raiding the climbing flowers that grew along the edges of the marketplace and up the houses on the waterfront. Suddenly everyone was flinging handfuls of white and yellow and red petals into the air. The wild breeze rose again, caught at the flowers and sent them spiralling up. They swirled around us, catching in our hair and clothes and scattering over the sad remains of what had once been the king of Ruan.

I turned to look at Sorin and saw the emotion in his face, shining from his summer-blue eyes. He reached for my hand and held on to it tightly, tightly, until my fingers ached, and it was the most welcome pain in the world.

There was a bright, singing note in the wind, like laughter. I looked up at the gale-scrubbed sky, where a trick of light gave the flickering cloud shreds the blue and gold hue of peacock feathers. Joy bubbled under my skin. She was with me – She had always been with me.

I was a daughter of the flames.

I knew it in the warmth of blood trickling down my arm and chest, in the ache of my bones, in the clasp of my hand with Sorin's and in the sound of my own laughter, torn away by the wind and carried out over the cheering people.

My people.

ACKNOWLEDGEMENTS

Despite taking only six months to write in first draft form, *Daughter of the Flames* was a very tough book. It went through several transformations before it was finished, and there were times when I wasn't sure I would finish it at all. Thanks are owed to:

Diana Wynne Jones for writing *The Tough Guide to Fantasyland* because it made me want to find out what went on in fantasy nunneries – before they got ransacked – and how fantasy religions really worked, and got me angry about fantasy colour-coding.

Emil Fortune for looking at the synopsis and pointing his finger straight at the problem which was holding the story back and Yasmin Standen for acting as a one-woman cheering squad while I worked out how to fix it.

The Furtive Scribblers' Club – Tina, Susan, Rachel, Barbara, Holly, Brian and all the rest – who were always there to haul me out of the Pit of Despond and tell me that no, I wasn't completely mad, I was just a *writer*.

All the friends and co-workers who turned out to support me during the madness of 2007, especially Nicola Robinson, who practically set up a bookshop in her office, and Helen Mearns, who bought the last three copies of *The Swan Kingdom* so I could finally leave the bookshop and go home.

Steve Rawlings and Jim Bunker for astounding me with the most beautiful cover art and design yet again. The staff of Waterstone's Grimsby, who got behind *The Swan Kingdom* and pushed until it was in the top fifty of the Children's List.

And as always, Mum and Dad – the sun and moon of my internal landscape.

Darkness has fallen across a kingdom far, far away. The queen is dead – killed in the forest by a terrifying beast – and her daughter, Alexandra, suspects that the new woman in her father's life is not all that she seems. Exiled and betrayed, Alexandra must face magic, murder and the loss of all she holds dear in a desperate struggle against evil.

BY ZOË MARRIOTT